I hope.

Nelda Ellen Carter Sourianne

October, 2022

Love
Is
Forever

ELLEN CARTER

LOVE IS FOREVER

iUniverse books may be ordered through booksellers or by contacting:

iUniverse
1663 Liberty Drive
Bloomington, IN 47403
www.iuniverse.com
1-800-Authors (1-800-288-4677)

ISBN: 978-1-6632-0000-6 (sc)
ISBN: 978-1-6632-0001-3 (e)

Print information available on the last page.

iUniverse rev. date: 04/29/2020

Chapter 1

Julia was late. She was driving a little faster than the speed limit, but she was still going to be late. The weather was calm and clear with just a small amount of crispness in the air. There was not a cloud in the deep blue October sky, so bad weather was not an excuse.

Her car seemed to have a mind of his own when it came to starting, and today, when she really needed to be somewhere on time, he refused to start. She called her car "he" because she thought a female would be more cooperative. Although the Auto Club had come promptly, she was still running behind.

She really needed a new car, but she could not afford car payments at this time. She was beginning her second year as instructor of music at Chapman State University, a small liberal arts college in Northern Kentucky. With a student loan payment each month and the expenses of a single person living alone, she was finding it very hard to stay within her budget. A raise would be nice, but that wouldn't come until she earned a good evaluation and tenure.

She did not plan to stay at Chapman for the rest of her life. She was only here to gain a couple of years of teaching experience at the university level. With some published articles about violin teaching and a good recommendation, she should be able to secure a teaching position at a university with a more prestigious music school in a year or two. Her mother had encouraged her to continue with her education until she earned a doctorate, even if it meant incurring a huge student loan debt.

She hadn't wanted to do this gig, but Dr. Salerno, the head of the Music Department, had given her no choice. He had called her into his office a week after the fall semester began. "Dr. Crane," he had said, "the Athletic Department will be hosting a gala to dedicate their new administrative complex the first weekend in October. They would like for us to provide music while people are gathering and during dinner. Do you think the Corelli String Quartet could play for them?"

"Thank you for asking us," she had said. "But I'm not sure we can get a program together in three weeks."

"Come now, Dr. Crane," he replied with an amused smile. He was a slightly built man with olive skin and graying brown hair. His dark eyes sparkled as he peered over the top of his spectacles. "You are all excellent musicians. When you were hired last year, one of the goals I had for you was to organize a string quartet of faculty members to play at community functions. It would show everyone that we did more at Chapman State than play basketball."

Dr. Salerno had continued, "It is important that the Music Department maintains a good rapport with the Athletic Department. They support us financially in many ways. This is one way we can return the favor." Julia listened intently, knowing that things were not going to go her way. "Dr. Jennings, the president of the university, is my very good friend, and he wants this to be an elegant affair. They are expecting some very important guests."

"Very well," she said. "Perhaps we can plan an entertaining program." She wasn't going to jeopardize her future, even if it meant playing Mozart while a bunch of jocks drank beer and ate nachos.

"Excellent," Dr. Salerno said, his thin face widening into a happy smile. "I knew I could count on you." As if he could read her mind, he said, "You know, the invitation says black tie, and the menu will include prime rib and lobster. At least you will get a good meal for your efforts."

Dr. Salerno had said, "Six in the auxiliary gym." It was already a quarter after. It wasn't dark yet, but dusk was closing in as she reached the east side of campus. The setting sun was casting long shadows through the trees along the street.

Julia turned into the driveway. The new building was a beautiful three-story affair with a front facade of gray and beige stone. Tall windows stretched from the floor to the ceiling of each story. It was surrounded by what seemed like acres of parking lots. Every parking space within a mile of the building was filled. She drove through the parking lots and circled around to the front of the building.

She couldn't believe they spent $60 million on a building to benefit students whose sole ambition in life was to bounce, throw, or hit a ball. She thought of all the scholarships for average students that money could fund.

Julia didn't dislike athletes. She just thought it terribly unfair that they had so much handed to them—tuition, books, room and board. And even with all that, many of them refused to do their required schoolwork. It irked her that athletes seemed to think everyone owed them something just because they could play a game.

She couldn't believe her eyes. There was an empty space right in front of the building. There was some writing on the curb, but she didn't take time to read it. She felt sure that the owner of the space was not coming, or they would have already been there, so she pulled in. She grabbed her music bag and her violin and hurried to the door.

As she approached the front door, Julia saw her reflection in it. She had wondered what to wear. She didn't have a formal or even a nice cocktail dress, so she settled for her symphony dress. It was black velvet in a princess style with lace yoke and sleeves. It was supposed to be ankle length, but on her tall, slender frame, it was more midcalf. She wore black velvet pumps with black hose. She was pleased with what she saw, but she knew she would look like someone's frumpy grandmother when compared to the formal attire the other women would be wearing.

She went through the door into a wide lobby. The walls were painted a lovely shade of soft gray. Colorful Leroy Neiman sports prints hung on the walls amid pictures of athletic teams with a green and gold banner that proclaimed, "Midwestern Conference Basketball Champs—2015."

Glass cases filled with trophies stood along the walls. Gray slate tile covered the floors, accented with attractive floor mats that looked like fine rugs. Brightly colored chairs of imitation leather were arranged in small groups. The entire area gave the appearance of a nice hotel lobby instead of a sports complex.

Julia saw that she was right about what people were wearing. Ladies in gorgeous outfits and men in tuxes were standing around chatting in small groups. Waiters dressed in black pants, white shirts, and gold vests carried glasses of champagne and passed silver trays of small canapés.

She wasn't sure where to go. As she looked around the lobby, she saw a small sign that read "Auxiliary Gym, West Wing." She saw a few people heading down the west hall, so she followed.

When she walked in the door of the gym, she saw that no expense had been spared to change its appearance from a gym to an attractive banquet room. The moveable bleachers had been pushed against the wall, and heavy dark green felt paper covered the floor. The basketball goals had been raised up to the rafters, and drapes covered the gymnastics equipment near a side wall. Tall pots of gold chrysanthemums and other fall flowers lined the walls.

Twenty-five or thirty round tables, each set for ten guests, covered the floor. A long head table was set on a dais along one end of the room. Each table held an arrangement of golden mums and green ferns, Chapman's team colors. Waiters were filling water glasses and placing baskets of rolls on each table. Julia saw her group seated at the right of the head table. "I'm sorry I'm late. My car wouldn't start."

"You're okay," Molly said. "Everyone is still touring the building. Not many have been in yet, except the waiters. We're all tuned and ready to go."

Molly Corbin, a plump, dark-haired lady with a sweet face and hazel eyes, played second violin in the quartet. She had been on the faculty of the Music Department for about ten years. Molly's husband, Dr. Clark Corbin, was on the faculty of the History Department. Molly had been a great help to Julia last year when she was a beginning teacher. They had become fast friends.

Jonathan Carter, violist, and Peter Johnson, cellist, were the other two members. Jonathan was a short, portly man with sparse, wispy hair and light blue eyes. His tux appeared to be at least one size too small, while Peter was of average build with sandy hair, green eyes, and a thin face. His long legs were slightly bowed from having played the cello for many years.

"Is it true that they're serving prime rib tonight?" Jonathan asked.

"That's what I've been told," Julia said. "It may be a while before we get to eat. We have to serenade first."

"Prime rib will be worth the wait," he said as a smile came over his round face.

"Shall we start with a Mozart first?" Julia said, "I think no. 15 would be good. I love the first movement."

A large, black, barrel-chested man walked up to Julia. "Dr. Crane," he said in a deep, melodious voice. He was wearing an elegantly cut black tuxedo with a gold cummerbund and gold-rimmed glasses. "I am Ralph Jennings, the president of Chapman State."

Julia stood and extended her hand. "How do you do, Dr. Jennings," she said. "I'm happy to meet you."

"Yes," he said. "I'm anxious to hear your quartet. Carlo Salerno has been very complimentary of your work."

"I'm sure you know Mrs. Corbin, Mr. Johnson, and Dr. Carter."

"Oh yes, thank you for playing for us." He turned to Julia. "I would like for you to play while people are gathering and finding their places. Then I will make some opening remarks. After that, I would like for you to play again until the dessert is served. Then you may stop and have your dinner. Your table is right there." He indicated a table to the right of the head table.

"Thank you. We appreciate the opportunity to play for you," Julia said, hoping her nose didn't start to grow after such a fib. That was something her father had said when he suspected she had told a lie. If she felt her nose, then he was sure.

They had played for about fifteen minutes when Dr. Jennings gave the signal to stop. "Good evening, ladies and gentlemen. I want to welcome you to the dedication of the Frank D. Marshall Athletic Complex." He proceeded to thank everyone for coming and introduced the head table.

Julia thought Dr. Jennings was about to give the signal for the waitstaff to begin serving when she heard him say, "Come on in. This is the place." She looked at the door and saw an extremely tall man standing there looking rather lost. He seemed a little embarrassed by the attention he was getting. She heard Molly gasp. "Do you know who that is?" she asked Julia.

"I haven't a clue," Julia said. He was way over six feet tall, she estimated. He had closely trimmed black hair, a handsome face, and a wide, friendly smile that revealed gleaming white teeth. His smooth skin was the color of fine maple furniture.

"That's D. J. Cooper. He's Dr. Jennings's nephew," Molly said. Although the name was not familiar, Julia thought he was the most handsome, elegant man she had ever seen. She figured he must be an entertainer or perhaps a very important government official.

He wore a beautifully styled black tuxedo with a satin shawl collar and slim cut pants that had a satin stripe down the outside. It fit his well-proportioned body like a glove. His tucked shirt was closed with black onyx studs and matching cuff links. A maroon cummerbund and black bow tie completed the outfit.

"Come on in, D. J.," Dr. Jennings said to the man. "I was going to introduce you later, but since you have chosen to make an appearance, I will do it now. Ladies and gentlemen, I would like to introduce David J. Cooper. D. J. has been a member of the Indianapolis Pacers, professional basketball team, for the past eight years, leading them to two NBA titles." Julia couldn't believe what she had heard. This handsome, stylish man was an athlete.

"Come on up here," Dr. Jennings said, motioning to him. David headed to the podium with confident, graceful strides. "Due to an ACL injury, D. J. has retired from the Pacers, but I am pleased to report that the Pacers' loss is our gain. D. J. has successfully rehabbed his knee and has now taken a job on the coaching staff of your Chapman State Cougars." Everyone stood and clapped.

"I'm sorry I'm late," David said. "Someone parked a bucket of bolts in my parking space, and I had to hike in from the back forty." Everyone laughed. Julia gulped and felt her mouth widen in an O. Now she knew whose parking space she had taken.

Dr. Jennings stammered, "Well, well, I don't know who ..."

"That's okay," David said, smiling. "I really needed to walk. I drove from Indianapolis today, moving my things here. Thank you for the welcome, and thanks to Coach McDaniel for giving me the opportunity to coach. I look forward to helping lead the Cougars to a successful year." Everyone clapped again, and David found his place at the coaches' table.

Her heart sank. Who but an athlete could get a job at the university level with no previous experience? *Does he even have a college degree?* Julia remembered all the teacher education and violin pedagogy courses she had been required to take in order to qualify for her job.

Molly interrupted Julia's thoughts. "Clark will be so disappointed that he didn't come tonight. He loved to watch D. J. when the Pacers played. He was so good. I can't believe our university hired him."

"I guess we know how he got hired," Julia replied, "and probably at a huge salary too."

Dr. Jennings sat, and dinner was served. The quartet played more Mozart, some Brahms and Schubert, and finished with a medley from *My Fair Lady*. Everyone seemed to be enjoying themselves.

Dr. Jennings gave the signal for them to stop. He said, "I want to thank Dr. Julia Crane and the Corelli String Quartet for playing for us. All these fine musicians are members of the Chapman State Music Department faculty." They stood and took a bow, then moved to their table for dinner. After comments by several distinguished guests, Dr. Jennings thanked everyone for coming, and the dinner was over.

Julia looked over at the coaches' table. The tall, new coach kept looking in their direction. Julia thought he might be coming over. She wanted to get out of there before he discovered that it was she who had parked in his space. Even a beginning teacher knew that designated parking spaces were sacred. She thought she should go over, confess, and apologize, but she was intimidated by his confident manner. And she was afraid he might not be as gracious as he appeared. *He's probably just as arrogant, egotistical, and self-centered as most other athletes I've known.*

Chapter 2

The rain descended in a steady downpour as Julia pulled into her parking space at the music building. Saturday and Sunday had been beautiful fall days. Why did Monday have to be so dreary? She looked up just as an ambulance pulled away from the curb. She pulled up the hood of her raincoat, adjusted her umbrella, and raced into the building. Students were milling around in the lobby. "What happened?" she asked.

"It's Mrs. Corbin," a girl said. "She slipped on the wet stairs. They think she may have broken her arm."

Julia hurried into the Music Department office just as Dr. Salerno was coming out. "Dr. Crane, would you come into my office please?" Julia followed him into his office, where he sat down at his desk. He had a look of concern on his serious face. "It appears that Mrs. Corbin has broken her arm," he said. "I know you have office hours from eleven to twelve. Would you be able to take Mrs. Corbin's section of Music 101 at that time?"

"Certainly," she said. "Anything to help Molly."

"If she's out longer than this week, we'll hire a substitute. Dr. Carter will take her string classes on Tuesday and Thursday."

Julia headed for her classroom, a typical lecture room. Thirty chairs with pull-up arms to serve as desks stood in the center of the room. A teacher's desk with a computer and an overhead screen stood at the front. "Good morning, class," she said. "I hope you had a restful and productive weekend." She looked out at their eager faces.

"Today, we will begin our study of instrumental music of the Baroque era. What are the dates of the Baroque era in music and art?'

Several students said, "Sixteen hundred to 1750."

"Yes, thank you. During that time, we saw an improvement in the primitive violins of the Renaissance period. Many luthiers, or violin makers, began to produce violins that were of such excellent quality that they still exist today." She punched some keys on the computer, and pictures of stringed instruments appeared on the screen. "As a result of better instruments, there was an increase in the music written for stringed instruments." She continued the lesson, discussing styles of music and composers.

She concluded with, "Your writing assignment for Friday will be to discuss the instruments and characteristics of the early Baroque orchestra. Don't forget to name specific works and composers. If you take good notes on Wednesday, you should have no trouble writing an interesting and accurate essay."

She took a stack of papers from her briefcase. "I have your written assignments to return. I was generally pleased with your work on these assignments. Taking information from different sources and writing a coherent essay is a skill that will help you in other classes. Don't forget to use information gained from your textbook readings, classroom notes, and listening to answer your questions."

Julia began to return the papers. As she came to the last row, she said, "Mr. Bell, once again, I did not get a paper from you." A tall young man sat up straight in his chair. His frizzy blond hair was longish and held back with a headband that proclaimed a popular shoe company. Clear blue eyes peered out of a thin, pale face. He was almost as tall sitting as Julia was standing. "I take it you're on the basketball team," she said.

"Yes, ma'am," he said. "Just call me Cruiser."

"And why would I want to call you Cruiser? I thought your name was Calvin."

"Yeah, but they call me Cruiser 'cause I cruise down the court so fast that nobody can catch me." Several of the guys snickered.

Julia said, "Mr. Bell, the writing assignments will count for 35 percent of your grade. If you choose not to do any written assignments and you make 100 percent on all your tests, the highest grade you may earn in this class is sixty-five, which, according to our grading scale, is not passing. Therefore, you will fail this class, and I believe you would be in danger of losing your scholarship."

"I don't have time to do all that listening," he said, "and besides, that stuff don't turn me on."

"Mr. Bell," she said calmly, "you are not taking this class to be entertained. You are taking this class because the State Board of Regents has determined that you must have six semester hours of fine arts electives to graduate."

"That's just it," Cruiser said, "I'm not gonna graduate. I don't like all this readin' and writin' stuff. I'm just here to play basketball. I'm going to the pros just as soon as I can. Besides, Coach wants me to shoot a hundred foul shots every day. I've got to get my average up to 80 percent before the season starts."

Several students laughed, as if it were a big joke that Cruiser would shoot a hundred foul shots every day. Julia walked to the front of the room and punched two words into her computer. They flashed on the screen at the front of the room. "Mr. Bell, can you read these words?"

He peered at the screen. "Student athlete," he read.

"Which word comes first?"

"Student."

"I rest my case, Mr. Bell. I would suggest that you examine your schedule and find time to do your schoolwork, or you will be neither a student nor an athlete."

She turned to a student sitting next to Cruiser. "Mr. Wilson," she said, "I see that you have not done any work either. You too are in danger of failing and possibly losing your scholarship. This is our fifth week of school. Your third assignment is due Friday."

She returned to the front of the room. "Remember that I want no more than three-quarters of a page, so be thorough and concise. Be sure to read chapter 4 and listen to "Spring" from Vivaldi's *Four Seasons*." Julia looked at the clock. "Thank you for your attention. I'll see you on Wednesday."

As the students filed by her desk, she heard Jalen Wilson mumble something to Cruiser. He replied with a laugh, "Don't sweat it, kid. Coach will fix it for us." Julia couldn't believe his arrogance. She was just waiting for some coach to interfere. She would set him straight. No basketball coach was going to tell her how to run her class.

Chapter 3

David found his office on the third floor of the Marshall Building. He had spent Sunday moving his things into his room. Since he was late taking the job, most of the good apartments were gone, so he had taken a room in the athletic dorm. He wasn't sure this teaching and coaching job was going to work out, but he was armed with a BS degree in education and eight years of experience as a professional basketball player, so he was willing to give it a try.

He sat at his desk, trying to organize his day. He had a meeting with Rusty McDaniels, the head coach, at 9:00 a.m., but he couldn't stop thinking about the dedication gala and that girl. He had planned to slip into the proceedings unannounced. He felt like his hiring reeked of nepotism, which wasn't the case at all. Uncle Ralph had nothing to do with his hiring.

He remembered looking over at the musicians, just after Uncle Ralph introduced him. The girl on the end was beautiful. He saw her eyes widen in surprise when he made the crack about the car. Her long, dark hair was pulled back from her face on top and the sides and tied with a ribbon in back. She had a beautiful, oval face with smooth, creamy skin, a small, perky nose, and a lovely wide mouth. He smiled at the thought. She had beautiful blue eyes, not the lighter blue of most blue-eyed people but a dark midnight shade of blue. They were like deep blue pools of water, fringed with long black lashes.

After the dinner, he had wanted to go over and say something to her. She had played beautifully, and he wanted to tell her so, but someone else stopped him to talk. When he looked over, she was gone. At least he knew her name. He could find her with that, and he really did want to find her again. He gave a satisfying smile because he was sure of one more thing. He would bet money that she was the one who parked in his parking space. "Quit thinking about that girl and focus on your job," he told himself.

David stood and headed down the hall to Coach McDaniel's office. It was time to find out just what his role would be as assistant coach.

"Call me Rusty," Coach McDaniel said as David walked into the office.

"And I'm David. That D. J. business was the work of some sports writer."

"Okay, David," Rusty said. "Here's what I have in mind for you. I want you to coach the big men, especially the freshmen and sophomores. They're so used to being the biggest guy on the team in high school they don't know how to play with someone taller."

"Yes, that can be a problem," David agreed.

Rusty went on, "I also want you to do most of the recruiting trips and set up campus visits for prospective students. You have the name recognition that can influence prospective students to come to Chapman." Rusty paused. "And the last thing will certainly make you earn your salary. I want you to serve as academic adviser for the team. We have twelve scholarship athletes. Generally, the juniors and seniors are okay. It's the freshmen and sophomores who need help staying on track. Well, what do you think? Can you do it?"

"Absolutely," David said enthusiastically, as if trying to convince himself.

"Basketball practice is from one to three every afternoon. I would like for you to just observe today and tomorrow and give me your take on what we need to do to improve." Then he added, "Are you up for a hard scrimmage?"

"Sure. I'm a little out of shape, but my knee is okay. I think I can give you fifteen or twenty minutes without collapsing."

"Good," Rusty said. "Wednesday, we'll have a good scrimmage. These young guys need to face a challenging defense."

"Looking forward to it."

"Would you like me to show you around the athletic complex?"

"Certainly."

"The second and third floors are mostly coaches' offices," Rusty said. "The director of athletics' office is on the first floor as well as the auxiliary gyms and the training rooms." They got on an elevator and rode down to the first floor. "At the end of the center hall, we have a film theater where we can watch replays." He indicated a door.

"Here, we have our study rooms," he said. "We're trying to send the message to our athletes that studying is as important as training and playing." He opened a door to a room with a sign that read *Study Room A*. "Here we have computers with internet and word processing capabilities and audio players." They walked across the hall to Study Room B. "Here we have individual soundproof study and tutoring rooms." He indicated several small rooms with glass fronts.

"This is great," David said. "How did the university manage to fund such a building?"

"We had an athlete back in the seventies who was a math genius. He went on to make it big in computer software. He attributed it all to the athletic scholarship that made it possible for him to go to college. He donated fifty million dollars to the university for this building."

"We never know how important our scholarships are for some students," David observed.

After the meeting with the coach, David visited the academic dean's office. He came away with copies of everyone's schedule, transcripts of the previous year's work, and a list of basic requirements for freshmen.

That afternoon, after basketball practice, Coach Mc Daniel told the team to sit on the bleachers. "Good practice, guys," he said. "I hope everyone has had a chance to meet David Cooper. David played for the Pacers in the NBA, and I know he'll help you big guys improve your post skills. I hope you'll all give him your full cooperation. Coach Cooper will serve as the team's academic adviser. He'd like to say a few words."

David stood in front of the group. "I want to tell you how great it is to be on the coaching staff at Chapman State. I appreciate your hard work in becoming the best athlete you can be. I want to encourage you to also be the best student you can be. When you're an athlete, you never know when something will end your career; therefore, it's important to plan for life after basketball when you're in college.

"I'll be in Study Room B tonight and tomorrow night, from six to eight, to meet with the freshmen and sophomores. I want to check on your progress in your classes and offer any help I can. Are there any questions?"

"Yeah, Coach, I got one."

"Yes," David said, "and what is your name?"

"Cruiser Bell," he said with an air of importance. "Say, Coach, can you talk to that music teacher? She gives way too much homework."

"And what music teacher is that?"

"Dr. Crane."

David wondered what the knowing smirk he gave to another player was all about. "Okay, Cruiser. I'll look into it."

That night, David met with several students. There didn't seem to be any major problems, or at least none that anyone would admit to. He had stacked up his papers and was ready to leave when he saw another student sitting at one of the large tables in the center of the room. He was a tall black kid with black hair closely trimmed on the sides but long and curly on top, and he did not look happy. David walked over and said, "Are you waiting to see me?"

"Y-yeah, I guess," the student stammered.

"Okay," David said. "Let's go into the study room." He consulted his list. "Are you Jalen Wilson?" The boy nodded. "Sorry I didn't recognize you. I haven't had a chance to match names with faces yet." David sat at a small table. "Well, Jalen, you've been a college student for four weeks now. What do you think of college?"

Jalen sat opposite David. He had a sad, discouraged look on his face. "I ... I'm not sure I belong here," he said. "But I want to, Coach," he added eagerly. "I really want to be here. Oh, I don't know." He shook his head.

"College is a little scary for everyone at first," David told him.

"But, Coach, I'm in big trouble, and I don't know what to do."

"Okay, tell me about it. What's the problem?"

"Coach, I haven't done any of my assignments for music class."

"Oh," David said. "And why not?"

"At first, I wasn't quite sure about what to do, and I was afraid she would think I was dumb if I asked a question. Cruiser Bell said that teachers don't like you asking questions. You know Cruiser Bell?" David nodded. Jalen went on, "Well, Cruiser told me that since we're basketball players, we don't have to do all that homework." David listened in amazement. "Then Dr. Crane says that if we don't do the assignments, we'll fail music, and if we fail music, we may lose our scholarships."

"That's a possibility."

"But, Coach, my mother will kill me if I lose my scholarship. She can't afford to send me to college. I'll have to drop out of school and go to work at my uncle's construction company."

"Look, Jalen," David said, "this is only the fifth week of school. How many assignments have you missed?"

"Only two, but we have another one due Friday."

"We still have time to fix it, if you're willing to work. Tell me about the assignments."

"They're questions we have to answer."

"Okay. Do you have a list of the questions?"

"Well, I *did*. She called it a silli-something," Jalen said.

"A syllabus?"

"Yeah, that's it, but Cruiser said I didn't need it, so I don't know where it is." His face brightened. "But I do remember that we were to use information from our textbook and class notes to answer the questions. We're supposed to listen to this music too, but I didn't because Cruiser said we didn't have to do it."

"Now we're getting somewhere. I'll check with Dr. Crane and see what you can do to make up the assignments. You meet me here at six tomorrow, and we'll get to work on them." He looked at his list. "Have you declared a major yet?"

"No, I didn't know what to put down."

"If you had to go to work tomorrow, what kind of a job would you like?"

Jalen thought for a minute. "You know, I think I would like to be a teacher. I always liked helping my brother and sister with their homework. Sometimes I would even help the neighbor kids too."

"Okay, what would you like to teach?"

"Well," he said thoughtfully, "I'm really good at math. I made all As in high school. I think I would like to teach math and maybe coach basketball too."

"This is a start. I'll check on the requirements and get back to you. You're going to be okay," David said as he stood and patted Jalen on the shoulder.

"Thank you," Jalen said as he pumped David's hand. "I feel a lot better. I was ready to go home and not come back."

"You're too smart for that," David said. "But the next time you have a question, ask your teachers or me, not Cruiser Bell. I'll see you tomorrow night, right here, and we'll get to work on those assignments." Jalen left with a smile on his face.

David sat back in his chair and gathered his papers. "I think I handled that all right. I believe I can do this," David said to himself with a satisfied smile. But he wondered how he could get a better idea about what was happening in Music 101.

As he was leaving Study room B, he saw two very tall girls going into Study Room A. He watched as they went to the attendant's desk. She gave them a CD, and they sat at a table with a CD player. They were about to adjust the headphones when David walked over.

"Excuse me, ladies," he said. "I'm David Cooper, the new basketball assistant. May I ask you a question?"

"Sure," said a very pretty black girl with soft brown eyes and a beautiful smile. Her long black hair was pulled back into a ponytail. "I'm Lakeysha Thomas, and this is Carol Hanson," she said, turning to her friend, a broad-shouldered girl with pale blond hair and bright blue eyes. "As you can guess, we're on the women's team." She indicated a chair. "Won't you join us?"

David sat at the table beside them. "I'm sorry to disturb your study time," David said, "but I'm now the academic adviser for the men's team, and I'm trying to get some information about some of the classes they're taking. Have you taken Dr. Crane's Music 101 class?"

"Yes, we're taking it now. We're about to listen to music for the class," Carol said.

He knew this question was unprofessional, but he needed to get a handle on the situation as quickly as he could. "How do you like Music 101 and Dr. Crane?"

"Oh, we love Dr. Crane," Lakeysha said.

"She's such a good teacher," Carol agreed, smiling. "She explains everything so that even nonmusicians can understand it."

Lakeysha added, "The class is Music Appreciation, but it's more like a music history class. We're learning how our music has developed over the years."

"I understand she gives a lot of homework."

Lakeysha laughed. "Are you kidding? Who told you that? Cruiser Bell?"

"Why do you say that?" David asked, eyebrows raised in surprise.

"Because he's always complaining, and he seldom does any of his homework," Carol said. "I've known him since grade school, and he's made my life miserable ever since. And if he calls me 'sweet cheeks' one more time, I'm going to deck him."

David looked at this sturdy, tall girl with her long blond hair pulled back from her face and plaited into a long braid down her back. She reminded him of a Viking princess. In his mind's eye, he could see a roundhouse swing from Carol connecting with Cruiser's chin. He attempted to stifle a smile. "You know, Carol, I think you could take Cruiser in a fair fight."

But Carol was not smiling. "That's just it," she said seriously. "Cruiser doesn't play fair. He lies. He cheats, and he tries to get others to do his homework."

Lakeysha added, "And when he gets behind, he gets his father to complain to the teacher. My boyfriend, Kenny Williams, has warned Cruiser that if he doesn't do his own work, Chapman could be in trouble with the NCAA. Kenny plans to be an attorney."

"Kenny is right about that," David said. "The NCAA has strict policies about academic fraud. Could you tell me about the assignments you have?"

Carol pulled out her syllabus. "This explains about the class and all the requirements and when assignments are due."

"Do you suppose I could get a copy of this?" David asked.

"Sure, but Dr. Crane isn't doing her office hours this week. She's taking Mrs. Corbin's section of Music 101 since she broke her arm, but the music office should have a copy."

"Thanks," he said. "Are all the students in Music 101 doing well?"

"Well, all but maybe one or two," Carol said hesitantly

"Is Cruiser Bell one of the students who's having trouble?"

The girls looked at each other. Finally, Carol said, "Of course, but it's not because of Dr. Crane's teaching. She gives everyone a chance to make up missing work."

Lakeysha said, "Carol and I both have heavy class loads. I'm in premed, and Carol is a pharmacy major, so that's why we appreciate not having to spend much time on Dr. Crane's class. And she also lets us work ahead on our writing assignments. We hope to be through with them before basketball season starts."

"About how much time do you spend on Dr. Crane's class?"

"We listen to music for about thirty minutes per week and spend about two hours a week on reading and assignments," Carol said.

Not excessive for a three-hour class, David thought. "Thank you for the information, ladies," he said. "I shall use it discreetly." *I believe I just learned more than I really wanted to know about Cruiser Bell.*

After basketball practice on Tuesday, David yelled, "Don't forget. I'm tutoring Music 101 students at six o'clock tonight in Study Room B."

Teddy Baker said, "I'm caught up on all my assignments, but I'd like to come."

"Can I come?" Tyler asked.

"Sure," David said. "How about you, Cruiser?"

"Naw, I got it."

That evening, David met with Jalen, Teddy, and Tyler to work on Friday's assignment. He had picked up a Music 101 syllabus at the music office and an extra copy for Jalen. They read the question and talked about what it meant. Then they got to work, and soon each had finished a rough draft. David checked them over and suggested some corrections. After he read their efforts, David said, "Okay, I think you should type these. You're bound to get a better grade if the teacher can read your work." They laughed.

They each went to a computer, pulled up the word-processing program, and set to work.

Jalen said, "Now that I know what to do, I think I can do this."

When they finished, David said, "Good job, guys. If you're still behind, you need to work hard until you catch up."

"Okay, Coach," they said.

"Let me know if you need more help," David said.

"Sure thing, Coach."

David thought things were going well, but he still didn't trust Cruiser Bell. *I think it's time to confer with the elusive Dr. Crane.* He had been to the music building several times to talk to her, but she was always in class or symphony rehearsal. It was time to try a different approach.

Chapter 4

Julia awoke early on Saturday morning. She had had a rough week. Having to take Mollie's classes all week had taken her work period at school, so she had to grade all her papers at home. Then there was her confrontation with Cruiser Bell. She refused to let a dumb jock hijack her class, yet she didn't want to cause problems for the Music Department.

She knew she really should get started on her articles. Maybe she would check on the submission requirements for *Teachers of String* magazine and put together an outline for her first article. She would love a job where she taught only music majors.

She got up, showered, and ate her usual breakfast of corn flakes and fruit. She threw on a pair of jeans, a sweatshirt, and sneakers. She pulled her hair back into a ponytail and set to work. Her apartment needed a good cleaning, and she was just in the mood to do it.

She loved her apartment. It was in a complex geared to college students, but it was all she needed, and best of all, it was inexpensive. The layout was predictable. As she came in the front door, the living room, dining area, and kitchen were on the right side. A guest bedroom was on the left, followed by a bathroom that opened into the hall so it could also be used as a powder room. Behind that, the master suite consisted of a larger bedroom, walk-in closet, bathroom, and laundry room. She had turned her guest bedroom into a combination guest room, office, and teaching studio.

Although the apartment was furnished, she thought the living room needed a divider from the dining area, so she purchased a long sectional sofa. It was more than six feet long and turned the corner for another four feet, with a recliner on each end. It was too extravagant for her budget, but it created a homey look in the living room, and she loved to snuggle up on it in the evening.

She had just put a load of clothes in the washer when she heard her doorbell. She was surprised to see the handsome new coach. "Dr. Crane," he said, when she opened the door. "I'm David Cooper. Would it be convenient to speak to you about some of the basketball players who are in your Music 101 class?"

"I'm sorry," she said curtly. "This is not a good time. Could you see me during my office hours?"

"I've tried twice this week, but you haven't been there. This is really important," he said earnestly. "I hope you don't mind me coming to your home, but we need to get a few things straight. I found your address in the faculty directory."

"Very well, come in," she said. Somehow, she had been expecting a visit from a coach, but he was not going to tell her how to run her class, and he was not going to dictate how she treated her students. They would either do their work, or they would fail. "Please sit down. How can I help you?" He found a seat on the couch. *We may as well get things settled now.*

"Dr. Crane," he began, "I am now the academic adviser for the members of the basketball team. It is my responsibility to see that the members of the team are keeping up with their studies." She noticed that he looked at her earnestly. "I believe some have been less than honest with me about the work they've missed."

"And you want me to overlook the missed assignments or let them turn them in late?"

"Absolutely not," he said. "I've read your syllabus. I know that you don't accept late assignments; however, I would like to know more about the alternate work they can do. I assure you that in the future they will turn in their work on time, or they will not play."

"Are you serious?"

"Absolutely," he replied. "Too many schools do their student athletes a disservice by not insisting that they make the most of their college education. Coach McDaniel and I are committed to making sure our athletes will be prepared for the future when they graduate."

"I thought college was just a stepping-stone to the pros," she said.

He laughed. "A very small percentage of college athletes ever make it to the pros. Even if they do, there's always the danger of a career-ending injury. I'm living proof that there is life after basketball, so it's very important to me that these students pass your class, but only if they do the required work."

She gave him a disbelieving look. Although she was excited about what she heard, she was still a little skeptical. She found it hard to believe that a star athlete would be benched if he failed to pass a course. She reached into her briefcase and pulled out a syllabus. "On page six, it explains the written assignments."

"Yes," he said. "I got a copy at the music office. I've been working with some of your students."

"Then you know," she said sharply, "that we will have a total of ten assignments due at specified times during the semester. The students may earn ten points on each assignment. The total counts for 35 percent of their final grade."

"Then it's important that they do well on these assignments."

"Absolutely," she said as she opened her grade book. "Last week was the fifth week of the semester. We have had three assignments. Calvin Bell and Jalen Wilson have turned in nothing. Tyler Maxwell has turned in one. Teddy Baker and Colin Davis have turned in all the assignments." She returned to the syllabus. "On page seven, you will see the list of alternate assignments they may do. They may do these assignments at any time. They may even do more than ten if they choose."

She continued, "I know it sounds harsh, but I do not return the alternate assignments because I do not want to see the same assignment continually returning with a different name. I'm committed to each student doing his own work."

"I fully agree," David said. "But are you sure Cruiser has turned in nothing? He told me he's all caught up."

"Yes," she replied. "Nothing."

David said, "I've about decided that Cruiser's version of the truth is whatever is expedient at the time. Well, we'll see about that. Jalen Wilson is committed to catching up on his work. Tyler Maxwell had the flu and missed one assignment. I think when you grade Friday's assignments, you'll find that Jalen, Teddy, and Tyler each turned in a paper."

"Well, I certainly hope so," she said impatiently. "Was there anything else? I think you'll find all the information you need in the syllabus. Now, if you will excuse me, Mr. Cooper. I am in the middle of cleaning my apartment." She went to the door and opened it.

"Of course, Dr. Crane," he said politely. "I'm sorry to interrupt your day, but I felt I shouldn't let those students get any further behind."

"Yes," she said, "you were quite right to come."

"Thank you for your time. I only want what's best for our students."

As she shut the door, she asked herself, "How could you have been so rude to him?" She was surprised by his sincerity and concern for his students, and she was a little embarrassed by her actions, but she was not going to be bullied by the Athletic Department.

Chapter 5

David headed back to the campus. *Wow, she really has a chip on her shoulder.* He felt that dismissal was almost as bad as a slap in the face, but he had caught her by surprise. He imagined she was embarrassed by the way she was dressed. Women could be sensitive about that sort of thing, but he thought she was beautiful even without makeup. He refused to believe that anyone who looked so sweet could be as bad as she acted. Not once did he see that lovely smile, but he was not going to give up. He may have lost the first battle, but he had not lost the war. He wanted to know Dr. Julia Crane much better. In fact, he was already planning a campaign to win her over.

After basketball practice on Monday, David said, "Say, Cruiser, I really need to see you. Can you be in Study Room B at six o'clock this evening?"

"Can't do it, Coach. I've got a hot date tonight."

"Break it!" David said with authority. "If you aim to play on this team this year, you will be there. The NCAA is getting tougher about playing students who are only marginally eligible academically."

Coach McDaniel added, "From the looks of your grades last year, you need to take advantage of all the help Coach Cooper can give you."

That evening, David was waiting in a small study room with the materials he had taken from the academic dean. To his surprise, Cruiser Bell showed up on time. David said, "Thanks for coming, Cruiser. Looking at your transcript, I see that you made twenty-four semester hours last year, twenty-one hours of C and three hours of D. That's just a 1.8 grade point average. Coach wants his athletes to have at least a 2.2 to maintain good standing with the NCAA. You need to work harder and see if you can't get that grade point up."

"Yeah, I took some tough classes last year."

"Well, how are you doing this year?" David asked. "Any trouble with any class other than music?"

"No, just music. She gives too much homework."

"But are you doing it?" David asked, knowing the answer.

"Yeah, some."

"Dr. Crane tells me that you haven't turned in anything, so you'll now be three assignments behind."

"I'm planning to."

"How are you doing on tests?" David asked.

"Yeah, I'm doing okay." He pulled out a test that had C+ marked on it.

"Good," David said. "Be sure and let me know if I can help. The academic dean tells me that you still haven't declared a major. You need to do it by the end of the year."

"I haven't because I'm not going to be here very much longer."

"What are you planning to do?"

"I'm going to the pros and make me some big bucks."

"And you think you're ready for the pros?"

"Sure. Don't you?"

"Cruiser, you don't just go to the pros because you want to. Professional basketball is an industry. You have to be hired like you would for any job. And from what I saw of your play today, I can't say that you're ready."

"You're putting me on," he said. "I'm six feet eight inches tall. Any team would jump at the chance to get me."

"Maybe a few years ago, but now every team you face will have two or three guys taller than you. You have to learn *how* to play with the big guys. You wouldn't stand a chance now. But you have a lot of natural ability. With a couple of years of work, you might make it. But frankly, I haven't seen much of a desire to improve your basketball skills."

"I think I'm good enough now. I'm doing okay."

"Cruiser, every NBA player works every day to improve his skills. If he didn't, he wouldn't stay long, so I would suggest that you step up and play to your potential and do your schoolwork."

"Okay," he said.

"And one more thing," David said. "We're going to meet in Study Room B at six o'clock every evening until you get caught up with your music assignments. After that, I'll meet with you on Wednesdays for you to show me your assignments for the week. I have a copy of your syllabus, so I know when you have assignments scheduled. We have our home opener in less than three weeks, and if you don't have a passing grade in every class, you will not be playing." Cruiser looked a little chagrined, as if he knew what was coming next. "And if you ever lie to me again, you will certainly be off the team."

"Aw, Coach," Cruiser protested. "I just meant that I was gonna do them."

"Yes, you certainly are. Don't make any plans for six o'clock every evening until you're caught up," David said sternly.

"Okay, Coach," he said, then left.

Chapter 6

Friday morning, Julia taught her Music 101 class at nine o'clock. She went to her office, taught a violin lesson at ten, and had just started another lesson when she heard a knock at the door.

"Come in," she said.

The door opened, and Coach Cooper came in. "Oh, I'm sorry to disturb you. I thought you had office hours at this time."

"Usually, I do," she replied, "but today I'm doing a makeup lesson."

"I need to speak to you again about the basketball players' grades. When would be a good time?" he asked politely.

"I'll be busy all day today, but if you want to come by my apartment tomorrow, I could see you then."

"Certainly. What time would be convenient?"

"Would ten o'clock be okay?" She flashed a smile.

"Ten will be fine," he said. "I'll see you tomorrow."

She still regretted being so rude to him last week. He had been nothing but polite and certainly didn't deserve such treatment.

Saturday morning, she put on slacks and a sweater. She left her hair long and put on some makeup. When he didn't arrive promptly at ten, she got out her violin and began to practice. Soon, she heard the bell ring.

"I'm sorry I'm late," he said. "I got hung up in a meeting at the Athletic Department."

"You're not very late," she said, smiling. "Come in. How can I help you?"

"Midterm grades will be coming soon," he said. "I want to make sure everyone has a passing grade before the season starts. I believe all basketball players will have done their written assignments by midterm, but I don't know about test grades. Do you have that information?"

"Certainly," she said. "Come into my office." She went to her computer and pulled up the grades. "We will have one more assignment before midterm and a chapter test. If everyone does well on those, they should all have passing grades."

He looked at his syllabus and read "Discuss the Differences in the Concerto Grossi of Handel and the Brandenburg Concerti of Bach."

"That's next Friday's assignment," she said.

"That's great!" he said. "We'll have a good study session before the test. These are some of my favorite pieces."

This was too much. "You mean you've actually heard a Brandenburg Concerto?"

"Why, yes," he said. "I've even played all the Brandenburg Concerti." She noticed that he pronounced the word in the Italian style.

She looked at him incredulously. "*You* have played a Brandenburg Concerto. What instrument did you play?"

"First violin most of the time. Sometimes I played second."

"How long have you been playing the violin?" she challenged.

"Well, let's see." He stopped to think. "I was about three, and my sister was two when my mother dragged us off to Suzuki classes."

"You went to Suzuki classes?"

"Yes—you know, the Japanese method for teaching the violin to very young children."

"I am well aware of the Suzuki method," she answered impatiently.

"My mother loved music. She was determined that we would learn to play an instrument. As it happened, a Suzuki teacher was available, so we became violinists."

She looked at him incredulously.

He continued, "I'm thirty now, so that means I've been playing the violin for about twenty-seven years now, off and on."

"What did you do after Suzuki?" she asked.

"We took private lessons until I was in the sixth grade. Then we joined the Indianapolis Youth Symphony and played through high school with them. In the summers, we would go to Interlochen."

"You've been to Interlochen, the music camp in Michigan?"

"Yes, until I grew to be six foot two in the tenth grade, and then I would spend part of the summer in basketball camps."

Her mind was racing. She knew his family must be very affluent to afford summer camps for two children. The tuition to Interlochen alone was four to five thousand per student for a three-week summer camp.

He noticed her violin on the chair. "Dr. Crane, I'm very sorry to interrupt your practice session, but I felt I needed to make sure those students would have passing grades while there was still time."

"Yes," she said, "thank you for coming. And I'm afraid my practice session is not going very well. My second violinist has a broken wrist. We usually practice together, and I miss her very much."

"What are you playing?"

"The chamber orchestra will be doing Vivaldi's *Four Seasons* at their next concert."

"I know those pieces very well. If you have another violin, I would love to play with you."

She was doubtful but said, "Of course. I have a student violin here. I just finished putting on new strings." Was he just teasing her or could he really play? She set up another stand.

He took the violin and the block of resin she offered. He adjusted the bow, ran it over the resin and then over the strings. "Can you give me your A? The strings need a little tweaking." He twisted the tuning pegs. Soon he was satisfied. He ran a scale for a couple of octaves.

Julia listened in amazement. "Have you played much lately?" she said. She tried not to look so surprised at his ability.

"I played more than usual last summer. After my surgery, I had time to practice while I was rehabbing my knee. The Indianapolis Symphony has a Concert in the Park series in the summer, so I played several of those while I was recuperating."

They played through each movement of "Spring," repeating many of the trickier sections. Julia couldn't believe how good he was. *His bowing could be more exact, but his sense of pitch is spot-on.*

When she executed a tricky passage, she saw him smile at her, and he repeated it perfectly in the next phrase. Then they laughed together as they both flubbed a phrase of sixteenth notes. "That was a finger bender," he said.

"Shall we try that again? At a slower tempo," she said.

"I think we better," he said.

After an hour and a half, David looked at his watch. "This has been so much fun, Dr. Crane, but I really have to go. I have to grab some lunch before my two o'clock tutoring session."

"You're welcome to have lunch with me," she said with an encouraging smile. She wanted him to know she was not as bad as she appeared to be last week. "It will just be soup and a sandwich. And please call me Julia."

"And I'm David," he said. "That would be great. After two weeks of athletic dorm food, anything home-cooked would be a real treat."

"Are you living in the athletic dorm?" she asked as she went into the kitchen. He followed her in and took a seat at the bar.

"Yes, since I came late, most good apartments were already gone, and I really didn't have time to look for an apartment. One room of a suite in the athletic dorm was available, so I moved in there."

"Do you have just one room?"

"There are two rooms separated by a sitting room and a bathroom, so I'm okay for the time being. Kenny Williams and Tyler Maxwell of the basketball team are in the other room, so I'm getting to know some of the basketball players a little better."

"Do you like pimento cheese sandwiches? I make them with the bread toasted. Is that okay?"

"Yes, thank you," he said.

She couldn't believe his polite, good manners. "Would you like a soda or maybe a beer?" she asked.

"I guess I'd better have a soda," he said. "I'm meeting with students this afternoon. It wouldn't do to have beer on my breath. Uncle Ralph is already lecturing me about the proper decorum for a university instructor. He's so old-school it's ridiculous. He thinks the actions of the faculty reflect on the integrity of the school."

Julia laughed. "I've known some faculty members who could have used that lecture." She put the sandwiches on a plate with a slice of dill pickle and served the soup, steaming in large mugs.

"This is really good," he said, indicating the sandwich. "It tastes just like the pimento cheese sandwiches my grandma Jennings made. My sister and I stayed with her a lot when we were little."

"Did your mom work?"

"Yes, my grandpa Cooper had a lumberyard and a hardware store. Mom worked as a bookkeeper one summer when she was in college. She met my dad there. They were married, and she never left."

"What is your sister doing now? Does she still play the violin?"

"Oh yes. She's a concert violinist."

"She is? What's her name? I don't think I've heard of a Cooper who was a violinist."

"Her professional name is Alberta Jennings."

"Oh, you're kidding. I heard her when I was at Cincinnati," Julia said excitedly. She couldn't believe that wonderful violinist's brother was sitting in her kitchen. "She did a master class on the Bach Chaconne. I couldn't believe that anyone so young could be so knowledgeable."

"Yes," he said, "Al is very good at what she does. She got a BA from Indiana University in violin performance, and then she went to Eastman for her master's. The Bach Chaconne is one of her favorites."

"Well, it was wonderful," Julia said, remembering how the music had made her feel. She smiled as she looked into his eyes. They were a deep brown and reminded her of chocolate pudding. "Her interpretation was very romantic."

"You know," he said, returning her smile, "Bach wrote it right after his wife died. The double stops are meant to represent her playing along with him."

"Well, it was so beautiful and so moving that I started to work on it myself, but I will never do it as beautifully as she did. Her playing had such sensitivity; it was almost sensual. What is Alberta doing now?"

"Being a mom. She just had her first child about four months ago. Her husband is a trombone player in the Indianapolis Symphony. He also teaches brass at Indiana U. They live in Indianapolis."

She pulled out a plastic storage box. "Have a chocolate chip cookie."

He took a cookie and bit into it. "This is really good. May I have another for the road? I really must be going." He took her hand and said, "This has been so much fun, and thank you for lunch. Is there any chance we could do this again?"

"I practice every Saturday," she said. "I would welcome a practice partner."

"Okay, I'll see you next Saturday. After that, I don't know. Basketball season will be starting soon, and we will have some Saturday games. May I give you a call to check the time?"

"Sure. My number is on my syllabus."

"And I assure you, you will be getting assignments from the basketball players."

After he left, she told herself, "You are so dumb. Don't you know that once you start feeding a man, he will be underfoot forever?" She smiled at the thought. David was certainly different from most men she had known in the past.

Chapter 7

Hoover, Kentucky, was a beautiful little town just across the Ohio River from Indiana. The population was about twenty-eight thousand people—until fall when the college students swelled the number to around thirty-five thousand. David thought he would like it here. His parents lived about twenty miles from Bloomington, in a little place called Rockwell, so it would be little more than a two-hour drive to visit them. He thought Chapman State would be a good place for his first coaching job. It was not too large and had a strong academic reputation.

The only downside was his uncle Ralph. It was just his bad luck to be offered a job at a place where his mother's brother was the president. He may as well face it. Uncle Ralph was a control freak. He thought he knew what was best for everyone.

David sat at the desk in his office on the third floor of the Marshall Building. His office was small, but he had a wonderful view. He could see from the edge of the campus clear to the river on the east and all the way to downtown on the south. He had turned his desk chair around to get a better view when he heard a knock on the frame of the office door.

"Coach Cooper, do have a minute?"

"Certainly," David said as he turned his chair around. "What can I do for you?"

A large man with a broad, beefy face stood in the door. He was wearing gray slacks and a wine and gray sports coat.

"I'm Brandon Bell, Calvin's father," he said, extending his hand. "You probably just know him as Cruiser."

David shook his hand. "David Cooper. I'm glad to meet you."

"Coach," he said as he fell into a chair opposite David, "I don't know what to do with Cruiser." *Join the club. I don't know what to do with him, either.* "He wants to declare for the professional draft in the spring. What do you think, Coach? Is he ready for the pros?"

David thought for a minute. Then he said, "Mr. Bell, I know you want me to be straight with you, so I'm going to tell you the truth as I see it. If the pro draft was tomorrow, Cruiser's chances to make it would be slim to none."

"But, Coach," Mr. Bell said, "I didn't think he would have any problems, him being so tall and big."

"That's just the problem. Cruiser doesn't know how to use his size to an advantage, and he doesn't seem to want to learn. I've told Cruiser the same things I'm telling you, but he seems to think he's already Michael Jordan and LeBron James rolled into one." He saw that Mr. Bell was looking discouraged. "I'm ten years older than Cruiser," he continued, "and I have a bum knee, but I can still beat Cruiser down the court and block most of his shots."

Mr. Bell shook his head. "I had always hoped Cruiser would make it to the pros. And now you don't think he has a chance?"

"I didn't say that. I think he has a very good chance. He has good size and a natural ability. He's just not ready now, but I can teach him."

"That's great, Coach. Would you?"

"Sure, that's the reason I'm here. But there's just one catch. Cruiser doesn't seem to want to work at it."

Mr. Bell sighed. "Well, Cruiser has never liked to work at anything. If Cruiser declares for the draft and doesn't make it, can he still come back to school and play?"

"Sure, if he hasn't hired a sports agent to represent him and if he's eligible to return to school. When a student accepts a scholarship, it's like a contract. The school promises to give him an education and teach him to improve in his sport. In return, the student must do his schoolwork and play for the team to the best of his ability. And he needs to get his body ready to perform. Cruiser needs to spend some time in the weight room working on his upper-body strength, and he needs to work on his conditioning."

"Yeah, I get that," Mr. Bell said.

"Cruiser needs to do his schoolwork and make better grades," David said. "He lied to me about doing his music homework."

Mr. Bell grinned. "Well, Cruiser has never liked to do schoolwork. I had to get several tutors for him just to get him through high school."

David was concerned that Mr. Bell did not seem to be taking Cruiser's situation seriously, so he asked, "Are you in business, Mr. Bell?"

"Yes, I have the Ford dealership right here in Hoover."

"If Cruiser needed a job, would you hire him to work for your company? Even if Cruiser makes it to the pros, he'll still need a job sometime in the future. He needs to be preparing for that now."

"Yeah, I see what you mean, Coach."

"If I were you," David said, "I would impress upon Cruiser the importance of doing his schoolwork and working on his basketball skills for a couple of years before he declares for the pros."

"I think it's time I had a good talk with Cruiser. Thank you for your time," Mr. Bell said as he stood to leave.

"Anytime," David said. "We both want what's best for Cruiser."

Chapter 8

Julia had just returned home from school on Wednesday when her phone rang. "Hello, Julia," David said. "I want to thank you for feeding me lunch. It was wonderful."

"I'm glad you enjoyed it."

"I'm in the mood for lasagna. Would you like to go to dinner with me tomorrow night? Leonardo's has great lasagna."

Her first thought was to refuse. She had promised herself that she wouldn't get involved with anyone until she had established her career and paid off her student loans. She hadn't had many dates since she had been at Chapman. Molly had fixed her up with some of Clark's single friends, but no one was interesting enough for her to accept a second date. And one of the bad things about dating university professors was that they all had a narrow range of interests. They seemed to think everyone else was interested in their disciplines, like the zoology professor who spent their entire dinner date informing her about the sexual habits of the eastern salamander.

Don't get involved, she told herself, but she found herself saying, "Why, yes, David, thank you. That sounds very nice." What could be wrong with dinner between two friends? She could certainly have dinner with him without having a romantic relationship, and if David spent the entire evening talking about basketball, she could still enjoy dinner and not become ill, as she had with the salamander guy.

"Great. I'll pick you up about five thirty. Or is that too early?"

"No, David. That would be fine." She had only been to Leonardo's once. It was a fine dining establishment out on the bank of the river. The Music Department had held their Christmas party there last year. The food and ambiance were terrific.

When she returned home on Thursday, she pulled out an elegant new pant suit that she had bought last year but seldom worn. She had been saving it for a special occasion. Did this qualify? She added a fussy, scooped-neck blouse and some nicer shoes. She felt it would be dressy even for Leonardo's on a weeknight.

David arrived promptly at 5:30. When she opened the door, he said warmly, "You look very nice. Blue is definitely your color."

She thought David looked handsome in a lovely beige sports jacket, brown and blue plaid, open-collar shirt, and dark brown slacks. *That jacket has got to be cashmere.*

He helped her into his little silver four-by-four. She said, "I like your truck very much. I thought a famous basketball star would have a sports car of some kind."

"I do," he said, "but it's more of an investment. I seldom drive it." He backed out of the parking space and headed down the street.

"Do you go to Leonardo's often?" she asked.

"Not really. Phil Gardner, the athletic director, took some of the other coaches and me out for a welcome dinner right after I came. That's how I learned that Thursday night was lasagna night."

"Thank you for asking me. I love lasagna."

"They have a vegetable lasagna with an Alfredo sauce that's reported to be very good, but their bolognese is terrific. That's my favorite."

"That would be my choice too," she said. "I love bolognese."

It was almost dark by the time they arrived at the restaurant, which was on a hill overlooking the river. Several boats with twinkling running lights were visible on the river below.

David got out of the truck, handed the keys to the parking valet, and hurried to Julia's side. He opened the door and offered his hand to help her out of the truck. He continued to hold her hand as they walked to the door. She felt a little tingle of excitement. It had been a while since a handsome man had held her hand.

A doorman opened the door for them. "Welcome to Leonardo's," he said. As they walked into the restaurant, soft classical music was playing in the background. The lighting was subdued, and there were candles on every table. Julia loved this place. Everything was so calm and peaceful.

The maître d' met them. "Good evening, sir, madam."

"Good evening," David said. "We have reservations for six o'clock. The name is Cooper."

The maître d' consulted his book. "Of course. Come this way."

Julia followed him as he led them to their table.

"Will this be satisfactory?"

"Certainly," David said.

"Emilio will be your server. Is there anything else?"

David looked at Julia. "Would you like some wine?"

"Only if you would."

"May we see your sommelier?" David said.

"Yes, sir. Very good, sir."

Soon, a small man with a thin moustache and goatee, wearing a gold chain and medallion around his neck, came to their table.

David said, "Do you have a nice Pinot Noir or a Merlot that would pair well with the bolognese? Or perhaps you could suggest something?"

The little man smiled. "We have a magnificent 2007 Pinot Noir that would pair beautifully with the bolognese. It is the best in the house. We have other wines that are, are …" He searched for an appropriate word.

"Less expensive," David said as he consulted the wine list.

"Exactly."

"The 2007 will be perfect," David said. "Please bring a bottle."

"Excellent choice, sir. Right away." He left with a flourish, and a smile on his face.

Soon, Emilio appeared and told them about the specials.

"Are you sticking with the bolognese?" David asked.

"Yes, I think so."

"What about a salad? What's your favorite dressing?"

"I love bleu cheese."

David turned to Emilio. "We will have house salads with bleu cheese dressing and your lasagna bolognese."

Emilio was writing furiously. "Two house salads with bleu cheese and two orders of lasagna bolognese."

"That's correct," David said.

The sommelier appeared with their wine. He went through the ceremony of opening the wine and giving David a taste.

"This is excellent," David said. The little man beamed.

"And for you, Madam?"

"Yes, please," she said.

David raised his glass. "To good friends and good music."

"Yes," she said as their glasses clinked. "To good friends and good music." She took a sip. "This is wonderful," she said. She felt it would be. She had no idea what that bottle of wine cost, but she was certain she had never tasted wine so expensive before. She was blown away by the smooth way that David had ordered the wine and dinner. At first, she thought he was just trying to impress her, but she then realized that he must have done it many times before to be so casual and knowledgeable.

Emilio brought their salads and a basket of hot garlic bread. "This salad is very good," Julia said, "and the bleu cheese is wonderful."

"I believe all their salad dressings are made in-house."

Emilio brought plates of lasagna bolognese. The rich, meaty sauce was hot and spicy and filled the air with a delicious aroma. "I love the oregano and other herbs they put into the sauce," Julia said. "I always make a bolognese sauce when I make lasagna."

"You make lasagna?" he asked in disbelief. "Of course you do," he said, answering his own question. "You're a great cook. Where did you learn?"

"At home," she said. "My mom was a high school teacher, so I did a lot of the cooking to help her out. Then my dad became ill with leukemia when I was in the eighth grade. I helped Mother care for him until he died," she said as her eyes became watery.

She felt David's hand on hers. "I'm so sorry," he said gently.

"Thank you. He was ill a long time."

Emilio came to remove their plates. "May I bring a dessert menu?" he asked.

"That won't be necessary," David said. "We'll share a tiramisu, and I'd like coffee. "Would you like coffee?" he asked Julia.

"No, but I would like some herb tea. Chamomile, if you have it."

"Of course," Emilio said. "Tiramisu, coffee, and chamomile tea." He took the plates and soon returned with the dessert and drinks.

"David, I don't think I can eat another bite," Julia said. "Everything was so good."

"Would you like a taste of the tiramisu?"

She took a small bite. "This is really good. You're an expert on Italian food."

"Not really. I just know what I like. The Pacers did several preseason tours of Italy when I was playing. That's where I learned to really love Italian food."

She sipped her tea as David polished off the tiramisu.

"Have you ever made this?" he asked.

"No," she said, "but it doesn't look too difficult, if I had a recipe. I'm sure I could find one online."

"I'll volunteer to be a taste tester if you ever do."

She smiled at the implication. "I'll keep that in mind. This has been such a lovely evening," she said.

After parking at her apartment, he offered his hand to help her out of the truck. Once again, he held her hand as they walked to the door. When she turned to hand him her key, he took both her hands in his. "Thank you very much for going to dinner with me," he said. "Good food is always better when shared with someone special."

She looked up into his earnest brown eyes. "Thank you for asking me," she said. "I enjoyed it very much."

"Then we should do it again sometime."

"Yes, I'd like that very much."

He took her key and opened her door. He leaned over and kissed her on the forehead. "Good night," he said.

"Good night."

"Are we still on for music on Saturday?"

"Certainly."

"May I call you about the time?"

"Of course."

She went inside, closed the door, and leaned against it. She was a little taken aback that he had given her such a perfunctory kiss. "This just proves that he doesn't want a romantic relationship either," she said. She had to admit that this was one of the nicest dates she had ever had in her life. David was rapidly destroying the image she had of athletes being dumb jocks. He was urbane and intelligent, and she had never been out with a man who could order wine so effortlessly.

Chapter 9

Saturday, Julia got up, dressed, had breakfast, and put the dishes in the dishwasher. Midterm grades were due Monday, and she still had papers and tests to be graded. She hoped the basketball players had turned in their assignments. She knew David had been working with them.

Julia had told Molly about Cruiser Bell turning in his assignments, adding, "David said he's working harder on the basketball court. Maybe he finally got the message that he's going to have to work."

Molly had said, "I don't trust Cruiser Bell. Clark and I have known him for many years. He's a spoiled brat who's always managed to get his way. He's been known to pay other students to do his papers and assignments."

"I hope you're wrong," Julia said. "David thinks he has the talent to be a first-rate basketball player."

David was coming over later to her practice with her. She looked forward to seeing him again. She couldn't believe that she had only known him for three weeks. It seemed as if she had known him forever.

She was a little disturbed by this giddy, nervous feeling that came over her when she thought about David. She had never met anyone like him. It was not often that she found a handsome man, particularly an athlete, who liked to discuss music and teaching instead of themselves. It was such a help to have him play with her, and he seemed to enjoy it immensely.

She had finished with her papers and was about finished entering the scores into the computer when David called. "Julia," he said, "when would you like for me to come?"

"I made a pot of ham and bean soup. Come about eleven thirty. We'll eat first and then play."

"That sounds like a plan," he replied. "I'll see you in a few."

She went into her bedroom and pulled out a bright blue sweater and some gray slacks. Should she put on some makeup? Maybe a little. What about some pale blue eye shadow? She didn't want to appear to be dressing up for him. But wasn't she? Maybe he wouldn't notice.

When she opened the door for him, he just stood there and looked at her for a moment. "Gosh, you look great," he said.

"Oh, this? I just got tired of wearing jeans and a sweatshirt on Saturday." She felt her nose, but it wasn't growing.

"I brought my fiddle," he said.

"Just put it in the studio," she said as she set out two steaming bowls of soup and a plate of ham and cheese sandwiches. She got sodas from the fridge.

When he returned to the kitchen, she said, "I have good news for you. It looks as if everyone in Music 101 will have a passing grade at midterm."

"Thank goodness," he said. "My body is worn out from all those scrimmages this week and study sessions at night. I've been trying to show the basketball team what a real pro defense would be like, and it's about to kill me. Thank goodness I don't have to keep it up for sixty games."

"Is that why you retired?"

"Yes, that and my knee. Another severe injury to my knee, and I might be a cripple for life. And I don't want that. I want to be able to play basketball with my children and dance with my wife."

"Do you have a wife?" she asked as she glanced to see if he was wearing a wedding ring.

"No, but I hope to someday. It takes a special lady to be happily married to a pro basketball player or even a coach. I haven't found her yet."

Julia wondered, *Just what does it take to be happily married to a basketball coach?* Then an inner voice asked, "What do you care? You're not planning on marrying him." But she wondered anyway.

"Gosh, this is really great soup," he said, "and I love the mustard on the sandwiches."

"Would you like another soda?" she asked, noticing that he had finished his first one. "And how about a brownie?"

"Yes, please. I never refuse chocolate."

"What about ice cream and chocolate sauce on top?"

"Even better," he said. "I'm going to have to keep up the scrimmages, or I'll be gaining weight with what you've been feeding me."

She said, "The university orchestra and chorus will be doing the Christmas part of Handel's *Messiah* for our Christmas concert this year. We'll have an authentic Baroque orchestra. Dr. Rubinsky will conduct from the harpsichord, just as the Baroque conductors did."

"Really?" he said as he finished his brownie and ice cream. "Then you might want to use my violin."

"What's special about your violin?" she asked as she went into the study to set up the stands.

He came in and picked up his case. He took out his violin and tested the strings. "A little flat," he announced.

"David," she said, glancing at him. "What is that?"

"A violin," he said casually.

"Is that a Strad?" She came over for a closer look. "No," she said in disbelief. "It's an Amati. David! *You* have an Amati! Where did you get an Amati?"

"It's a long story."

"I want to hear every word. Sit down and tell me," she said as she pulled him into a chair beside her.

"Well," he said, even more casually, "I have a Guarneri also."

"David," she said, looking into his amused face, "what did you do? Rob a bank? Ordinary people don't own old instruments like that."

"They do if they've just signed a rookie contract with a pro basketball team who outbid three other teams for his services, and the young man had more money than brains."

"Start at the beginning," she said.

"When Alberta went to Indiana, she was moaning about needing a good violin. I, being the loving brother that I am, promised to get her a good violin if I ever got a pro contract. Well, I did, and she remembered what I had said."

Julia looked amazed. "But two violins?" she questioned.

David went on. "I contacted an instrument broker in New York. He told me that a Guarneri was going to be auctioned. I gave him my top price, and several days later, he called and said that he had purchased the violin. He added that he knew where I could get an Amati, too, for a bargain if I was interested.

"And of course, I was interested. I couldn't let Al have all the fun. The violin had belonged to a family in Cremona for over two hundred years. They decided they needed the money more than they needed the violin."

Julia was gasping for breath. "So you got both instruments?"

"Yes," he said. "I got them both for three point two million euros. Fortunately, the dollar was about equal to the euro then."

"Oh my gosh!" she exclaimed. "You paid three million, two hundred thousand dollars for two violins!"

"I told you, I had more money than brains then. A lot of guys buy fancy clothes and cars and gold chains when they get a pro contract. I bought violins."

"I can't believe it," she said, shaking her head.

He tweaked the strings, ran the bow over the resin, and then ran it over the strings. The clear, beautiful tone of the old violin filled the room. "Those old boys, Stradivarius, Amati, and Guarneri, really knew how to make violins. I've heard that it was the wood they used that made the tone so beautiful," David said. He turned the violin over to show her the lovely pattern on the back.

"It's the most beautiful thing I've ever heard," she said.

"Here. You play it."

"Oh, I couldn't," she said, backing away. "I might drop it or something."

"You won't."

She ran her bow over the strings, and sounds came forth that she never thought possible. She played the first movement of "Spring," and they heard the sounds of a spring rainstorm portrayed in the music.

She looked at David. There was a wide, knowing smile on his face. They began playing together. Julia lost all track of time. She could think of nothing but that wonderful violin in her hands and the sounds she was able to create.

A feeling of regret came over her when David said he had to go. She was so thankful to David for allowing her to play this wonderful instrument, and sad that the time was coming to an end.

He reached for the Amati and packed it back into its case. As he loosened the bow and put it away, he said thoughtfully, "Why don't you just keep the Amati here? We'll be going on our first preseason game next week, and I really don't want to leave it in the dorm. A violin such as this needs to be played—and often."

"Oh, David," she said, "I couldn't do that. What if something happened to it? I could never forgive myself."

"It's just a violin. There are other violins in the world."

"But this is such a special violin," she argued.

"Really, you would be doing me a favor if you just kept it here. Please play it during your performances."

"Oh, David," she said as tears came to her eyes. "Thank you so much." She wrapped her arms around him and hugged him tightly. "You're such a good friend."

He put his arms around her and pulled her close. "I'd really like to be more than a friend."

She looked up to say, "What do you mean?" When his lips came down on hers, gently and tenderly, she knew what he meant. His kiss was soft and undemanding. She felt tears running down her cheeks.

"I'm sorry. Did I offend you?" he asked shyly.

"Oh no," she whispered. She started to pull back, but her knees were weak, and she slumped against him. He pulled her closer and kissed her again, more ardently, more passionately than before. She found herself eagerly returning his kisses. Her heart was pounding, and she wondered if she could speak. A shiver of excitement ran down her spine.

He continued to hold her tightly. "That was something I've wanted to do since the first time I saw you," he said softly.

"Why?" she asked breathlessly as she wiped her eyes on her sleeve.

"Because I like to kiss lovely violinists who play beautiful music."

"How many violinists have you kissed?"

"Just one. You're the first—and I hope the last."

"You mean no more kisses?"

"I have hundreds, maybe thousands of kisses saved up for you."

"But what if I don't want your kisses?" she asked, pulling back with a flirty smile.

"From what just happened a few minutes ago, I think you do." He had an innocent, little boy grin on his face, and his luscious chocolate pudding eyes twinkled. "Call it rent on the Amati," he said, smiling. Then he added, "There *is* one more thing we need to do."

"What?"

"We need to work on your basketball education. The Lady Cougars play Appy State on Thursday night. Why don't you go with me? There are several girls in your class who are on the team."

"You mean like a date?"

"Why not?"

After he had gone, she thought about what had just happened. How could she have let him kiss her like that? And she had even agreed to go out with him again. What was she thinking? She should have told him she didn't want a romantic relationship at this time. *Perhaps I will ... in a week or two.*

Chapter 10

Thursday, David called. "May I pick you up about five thirty, and we'll go somewhere for dinner? What about Hamburger Heaven for a burger and fries? The game starts at seven."

"That's great!"

David was there promptly, at 5:30 p.m. As she climbed into the truck, she said, "I've never been to a sporting event before. I'm not sure what to do."

"Really?"

"In high school, none of my friends played sports, and then after my dad became ill, I stayed at home with him a lot. And in college, I was too busy practicing or studying or doing some kind of a gig to earn money to go to basketball or football games. My dad was more into camping and fishing, so he never went to sporting events much. He watched a little baseball on TV, but that was about it. I know very little about sports."

"Well, it's simple," he said. "You cheer for your team when they do something well and win, and you applaud their effort when they lose."

After dinner, they arrived at the field house. Fans were streaming into the arena. Both teams were on the court, shooting baskets and doing warm-up drills. The pep band was playing the Chapman State fight song. Cheerleaders were lined up in front of the home crowd, wearing stylish, new green and gold uniforms. "Look," Julia said, indicating a feisty blonde who was bouncing around, shaking her pom-poms. "There's Pat Castle. She's in my 101 class. I didn't know she was a cheerleader."

"I knew you would see a lot of your students. Everyone turns out for the home opener," he said. They saw Molly and Clark sitting behind the home bench and found seats beside them.

"I see Lakeysha and Carol. Oh, and there's Susan Howard and Becky Barnes. They were in my class last year."

David explained the scoring and a few basic rules. Then it was time for the game to start. The ball went up, and Carol got the tip. The Lady Cougars ran down the court and scored. Julia saw that everyone clapped and cheered, so she did too.

"This is great!" Julia said. "Do the Lady Cougars have a really good team?"

Clark said, "They do. They have a good chance to win the conference championship."

The ref blew his whistle, and David explained about fouls. The action was very fast as both teams ran up and down the court. Julia was really enjoying herself. She found herself cheering at every basket their team made. The Lady Cougars stretched their lead to ten points at the half.

"How about something to drink and some popcorn?" David asked.

"Sure," everyone said.

In the third quarter, the opposing team, Appalachian State, made some long baskets, and the score was growing closer. "Come on, team!" Julia yelled. "Defense!"

"You're learning fast," David said as he patted her knee. Just then, a heavyset girl with a blond ponytail whacked Lakeysha across the arm.

"Did you see that, David?" she asked as she pulled on his arm. "Wasn't that a foul? I think it was a foul!" She stood up. "That was a foul!" she yelled. "Why didn't that lady ref blow her whistle?" she said to David. "Tell her it was a foul."

"I think you're doing a fairly good job of it," he said with an amused smile. "I think she heard you, but you might want to calm down. You don't want to get tossed."

"What?" she asked. "What's tossed?"

"You know. Thrown out of the game. Asked to leave the arena."

"You're kidding," she said. "Would they really do that?"

"In a heartbeat, if you're too obnoxious. A fan has to be pretty bad to get tossed, but it's easier for a player or a coach. But it's okay. I've been tossed a few times."

"Oh no, David. Really? What did you do?"

"Officials don't take kindly to coaches, or players, or even fans questioning their judgment—or even worse, their eyesight. I told a ref he was blind as a bat."

"What did your coach say?"

"Nothing. It happens all the time. However, in the pros, it costs you a fine or even a suspension, depending on how bad your language is. In college, you get a technical foul as a warning. After the second technical foul, they make you leave the court."

In the fourth quarter, the Lady Cougars played hard and hung on to win by five points. Julia cheered and cheered. "I think you've created a new fan," Molly said to David.

"It would appear so," he said as he put his arm around her shoulder and squeezed it. She looked up at him and flashed that lovely smile.

As he drove her home, he said, "Are you up for another game, or did that one do you in?"

"Oh, David, that was so much fun. If you'll take me again, I promise I won't yell at the refs. I just got carried away in the excitement of it all."

"Okay," he said. "The men's team plays Tuesday. I'll be busy before the game, but I'll ask Clark to pick you up, and I'll bring you home."

At her door, he took her into his arms, held her tightly, and gave her a long, lingering kiss. "Did you really enjoy yourself tonight?" he asked.

"Oh, I did." Then she added, "What happens if you have to leave the arena?"

He said solemnly, "You have to walk home. But if you're lucky, your date might agree to leave a good basketball game just to take you home."

"David, would you leave a good basketball game just to take me home so I didn't have to walk?"

"In a heartbeat," he said.

After he left, she wondered how she could have wasted an entire evening going to a basketball game. She could have worked on her articles. "But don't I deserve a little fun?" she asked herself. "Certainly," that little inner voice said. "You've worked hard all your life." She had to admit that being with David was more fun than she had ever had in her entire life.

Chapter 11

The next few weeks sped by magically. David and Julia went to basketball games. They played music together, and they enjoyed each other's company. She loved cooking for him, and she felt very special when he took her out to eat at a nice restaurant. Although David kissed and hugged her every time they were together, his kisses were mostly chaste and gentle. She got the feeling that he did not want a romantic relationship either, or perhaps he was just allowing her time to get used to the idea.

The Sunday before Thanksgiving, Julia got a telephone call. "Hello, Julia dear. It's Mother."

"Hello, Mother," she said excitedly. "How are you?"

"I'm doing very well. And how are things going?"

"Very well. I'm having a good year."

"And how are your articles coming along? Have you finished any?"

"Well … no, not yet. It's taken a while to get the semester organized. Perhaps I can get started after Christmas."

"You really should, dear," her mother said. "You know we discussed how some published articles would really help your résumé when you leave Chapman."

"I know, Mother, but I'm really quite happy at Chapman."

"Yes, dear, but you could get twice your salary at a university with a more prestigious music program. After you get two or three years of teaching experience at the university level, you really should move on."

"I know, Mother," she agreed.

Her mother continued, "You know, I want you to be financially independent before you marry. That way, you won't have to rely on your husband to support you. If it's okay, I would like to come for a visit. Will you be out of school next week?"

"Of course. I have classes Monday morning and violin students Tuesday morning. Then we are out until the next Monday."

"Good, my plane arrives a little after two on Monday afternoon. Can you meet me at the airport?"

"Certainly. I look forward to seeing you, and, Mother, I have something else to tell you."

"What, dear?"

"I've been dating this very nice guy. I would love for you to meet him. Would you mind if I invited him to dinner on Tuesday evening? I know he'll be leaving on Wednesday to go to his parents' for Thanksgiving."

"No, dear, that would be fine. I would love to meet him," her mother said. Then came the question Julia knew was coming. "And what does he do?"

"He works at the university."

"How nice," she said. "Is he a teacher?"

"No, Mother. He's a basketball coach."

"A basketball coach." She heard the disappointment in her mother's voice. "Oh, Julia, I always thought that with your education, you could marry a PhD or an MD, but a basketball coach? Does he even have a BS?"

"Yes, Mother. He graduated from the University of Indiana, and he's been a professional basketball player. We're just dating. Nothing serious."

"Yes, but a basketball coach?"

"He's a very nice man, and I enjoy his company. He's also a very fine violinist."

"Well, that's something," she said. "I look forward to meeting him."

Sunday evening, when they went out to dinner, Julia told David about her mother. "She went back to teaching and taught for five more years after my dad died. Then she retired and moved to Florida. She met this woman, Murial Anderson, at her bridge club. Murial's late husband, a Texas oilman, left her more money than she can spend in two lifetimes. She asked Mother to be her traveling companion and pays most of the travel expenses."

"That's nice for your mother," David said.

"Yes," she said. "Mother deserves some fun. My dad was sick for so long, and she was completely devoted to caring for him. At least she's getting to travel some now." She looked at him. "I think you should know that my mother is not too happy with my dating you."

"Is it the race thing?" he asked quietly.

She smiled and patted his hand, as if she understood his feelings. "No, it's the academic thing."

"What?" he said incredulously.

"I guess you could say that my mother is an academic snob. She thinks anyone who doesn't have a PhD isn't good enough to date her daughter. And on her list of appropriate occupations, basketball coach is only slightly ahead of sewer worker and ditch digger."

"I have some graduate hours in sports administration. I guess I could finish that if it were a prerequisite to my seeing you."

She laughed. "No, that's not necessary. It's just that my mother knows nothing about sports. I would say you could put her sports knowledge in a teaspoon. No, make that a quarter teaspoon. Where she was teaching, the high school coaches only got a small stipend for coaching and were usually those who weren't very good teachers. I'm sure she's never heard of someone who was hired only to coach basketball."

He said, laughing, "Did you tell her I have a million-dollar fiddle?"

"No, and I'm not going to. Let her think that you're a struggling basketball coach."

He agreed. "Struggling is right. But my Music 101 students are doing better, aren't they? At least they're turning in homework."

"Yes, they are, and I appreciate your help," she said, smiling.

Tuesday, Julia prepared a pre-Thanksgiving feast, roasted Cornish game hens with wild rice stuffing, green beans almandine, homemade yeast rolls, and pumpkin cheese cake. Her mother had made a delicious strawberry spinach salad.

"You must really like this guy a lot to go to all this trouble," her mother said.

"David always has a good appetite, and you know how I love to cook. Mother, there's one more thing I've failed to mention."

"Yes, dear, and what is that?"

"He's African American. I know it's okay. I just didn't want you to be surprised."

"Certainly," she said. "Some of my best friends in the bridge club are black."

David arrived on Tuesday evening with two bottles of wine and a dozen yellow roses. When Julia opened the door, he kissed her and handed her the wine and roses.

"For you," he said. David was dressed in a luscious brown leather jacket, a brick-red cashmere sweater that set off his handsome face and brown eyes, and carefully tailored slacks.

"Come in," she said. "Mother, this is my friend David Cooper."

David took her mother's hand, leaned over, kissed it gently, and said, "Julia, this lovely young lady cannot be your mother."

"Call me Cynthia," she said with a radiant smile.

Julia was very proud of her mother. Julia's dark hair and tall frame had come from her dad, but she had inherited her mother's deep blue eyes and oval face. Cynthia's stylish blond hair and trim figure belied the fact that she was fifty-seven years old. "David, this is my mother, Cynthia Crane."

"How do you do, David. I've heard so much about you," Cynthia said as she looked at him appraisingly. "Here, let me take your coat. Come, tell me about yourself," she said sweetly. David looked over her shoulder and winked broadly at Julia as Cynthia took his arm and led him to the couch.

Julia knew he was enjoying the attention. "Would you two like a glass of wine before dinner?"

"That would be lovely, dear," Cynthia said.

During dinner, Cynthia said, "David, Julia tells me you're a talented violinist. Have you ever given any thought to playing in a symphony?"

"Yes, I played with the Indianapolis Symphony in the summer when I played pro basketball, but you see, I really always wanted to be a teacher. One of my main roles is that of an academic adviser to the scholarship athletes. I know there are a lot of young men out there who have grown up without a father figure in their lives. I feel that if I can help just one young man find a good academic future, it will be monetary compensation enough for me."

Cynthia was mesmerized. "Oh, David," she said, "you really are a dear, sweet man. Isn't he a dear, sweet man, Julia?"

"Yes, Mother," she replied as she he looked at David. He had that innocent, little boy grin. She smiled at David and added, "He's a sweetheart." *He is making every effort to impress.*

"Cynthia," David said, "Julia tells me you were a teacher."

"Yes, I taught high school English for thirty-two years. When I couldn't take the Ohio winters anymore, I retired and moved to Florida. My friend Murial and I are planning a Christmas cruise the week of Christmas. I hope you'll be around for Julia during Christmas vacation."

"Don't worry about Julia," he said. "I will see that she's well taken care of at Christmas."

He added, "The dinner was wonderful, but I have to get up early tomorrow and leave for Rockwell. My parents are expecting me. It's been so nice to meet you," he said to Cynthia as he shook her hand. "I now see where Julia gets her beauty and charm."

He walked to the door, and Julia followed. "Thanks for everything," he said as he gave her a hug and kissed her goodbye. "I'll be back late Friday. I have a meeting with the coach and the AD Saturday morning, so let's do something Saturday evening."

"Okay, thanks. Call me when you get back in town."

After he left, Cynthia said, "I have to say your young man is extremely charming and intelligent too."

"Yes, Mother, he is."

"And he has such splendid taste in clothes. Are you sure he can afford those things on a coach's salary?"

"I'm not sure, Mother," she said.

Chapter 12

As they were driving to the airport on Friday morning, Julia said, "Thanks for coming. It was so good to see you again. I'm so glad you're traveling with Murial and enjoying yourself."

"Yes, we're very compatible traveling companions." She paused. "Julia, are you happy here?"

"Oh yes," she said. "I love my teaching job. I have many friends, and since I met David, I have a very full social life."

"That's good, dear. David is a lovely man, even if he is a basketball coach. Maybe someday he'll find another way to make a living," she said thoughtfully. "How do you really feel about David?"

"Oh, I like him very much, and I really enjoy going on dates with him. He's so such fun to be with. He's the only man I've ever met who could have a discussion without telling me how great he is or how much money he makes."

"So you're enjoying your social life with him, but could you ever be really serious about him?"

"Oh, I don't think so, Mother. We both have our careers to think of."

"I don't know if you know it or not," Cynthia said, "but David is very serious about you. I can tell by the way he looks at you and by the way he kisses you that he really wants a more serious relationship."

Julia started to deny it. Then she remembered what he said the first time he kissed her: "I'd really like to be more than a friend."

"If you don't intend to get serious about him, you need to tell him now, before he gets hurt," Cynthia said. "David doesn't deserve to be dumped when you're tired of his company."

She went on, "You have the opportunity to become a foremost authority on violin pedagogy. With your doctorate, several published articles, and more teaching experience, you could qualify for a job at any university, maybe even a conservatory." She added, thoughtfully, "That is, if you don't throw it all away by marrying a basketball coach."

Julia was a little taken aback, but she hugged her mother at the gate. "Thanks for coming, and I'll think about what you said. The last thing I would want to do is hurt David." She knew she should tell him soon that she didn't want a serious relationship. But was it true?

As soon as she got home, her phone started to ring. "Hi, babe," David said.

"Are you here?" she asked.

"No, I'm still at Rockwell. I'll be there late tonight, and I have wonderful news. Al is doing the Mendelssohn Concerto with the symphony on Saturday night. Do you want to go?"

"Of course," she said, "but isn't it a little last minute?"

"Yes," he said, "but the original soloist became ill and can't go on. Al did the Mendelssohn with them about four years ago, so they've asked her to come back and do it again. There will be a black-tie reception for her after the performance, so wear something sexy."

She gulped. Did she have anything sexy?

"And pack a bag. The reception will be late, so we'll spend the night at my parents' and come back to Hoover on Sunday. Have to run. I'll pick you up about two tomorrow. The concert is at seven."

Julia was stunned. What was the matter with her? One minute, she was thinking about telling David she didn't want a serious relationship, and the next minute, she was all excited about going to a wonderful concert with him. Was she ready to meet David's parents and sister? She wondered what David had told his parents about her. Did they know she was white? Did it matter?

Of course she wanted to go. She would walk barefoot through the snow to hear Alberta Jennings play the Mendelssohn. She just had to trust that David would not have asked her if it was not okay with his family. Now, what should she wear? She called Molly and explained her problem.

Molly said, "I wish I had such a problem. Going to a wonderful concert with a handsome man." Then she said thoughtfully, "Don't you have a beautiful black silk theater suit? I know you've worn it at the symphony. Go buy a really sexy top to wear with it. You can wear your jacket for the concert and pull it off for the reception. It will be totally appropriate."

Julia had forgotten the theater suit. The jacket was cut like a man's tuxedo, and the pants were slim with slightly flaring bottoms. A new top shouldn't be too expensive. "Thank you so much, Molly," she said. "You saved me."

"I'm glad to do it. Be sure to tell me all about it."

She was ready several minutes before two on Saturday. She had gone down to The Boutique and found a bright sapphire-blue top. It had two thin spaghetti straps on each shoulder. It was nipped in at the waist with a small flare below, like a peplum. It looked fabulous under the jacket of her suit.

She even went to a beauty salon and had her long hair swept up in the back with curls. She added dangly earrings and black, strappy, high-heeled sandals. She had to admit that she did *not* look like somebody's frumpy grandmother.

When David came to the door, she had not put on her jacket. As he came in, he stepped back and said, "Wow, you really took me at my word. That's about the sexiest outfit I've ever seen." He took her into his arms, held her close, and nuzzled her neck. "I like your hair up," he said. "It gives me more neck to kiss."

As he started to kiss her, she said, "Don't mess up my makeup."

He said, "Take extra with you. I have a feeling you may have to redo it several times before the evening is over."

Perhaps Mother was right, Julia thought. It seemed as if his kisses were becoming longer and more passionate. As if on cue, he pulled her close and gave her a long, sexy kiss. She couldn't help but get that giddy, breathless feeling when he kissed her like that, and she felt a tingle all over her body. He helped her into her jacket, and they were off.

As they left the apartment, Julia saw a beautiful silver Porsche sitting at the curb. David led her to the passenger side and opened the door. "Is this yours?" she asked.

"Yes," he said. "It's a Porsche 119 Carrera. My financial manager says it would be a good investment if I didn't wreck it. That's why I don't drive it very often." He got in, the big car roared to life, and they headed out of town.

The sun was shining brightly in a cobalt-blue sky with only a hint of fall coolness in the air. "The weather is so beautiful. It shouldn't take us much longer than three hours," he said.

"How long have you had the Porsche?" she asked.

"This was a part of my rookie extravaganza," he said. "I bought the two violins, the Porsche, and gave my parents money to remodel their house. My dad had had some health problems, and he didn't need to be climbing stairs several times a day, so we added a master suite behind the kitchen. We also redid the upstairs, enlarged the kitchen, and got Mom some state-of-the-art appliances."

"You're a good son, David."

"I try to be," he said. "I'm the man I am today because of the influence of my parents. I can never do too much for them. They gave me the love, support, and discipline I needed to be successful in anything I wanted to do. So after I bought all that, I suddenly woke up and realized that I couldn't play basketball forever. I hired a financial manager, who put me on a budget and made some good investments so my money would last."

"That seems like the smart thing to do," she said.

"Yes, that's why I don't drive the Porsche very often, but tonight, I thought I would give you a treat."

"Well, it certainly is nice," she said as she ran her hand over the buttery-smooth leather seats. She relaxed and leaned back against the seat.

"David, you look so handsome tonight. I love your tux."

"This old thing?" he said. "I wore this the last time I went formal. In fact, I wear it every time I go formal."

"And I love your cologne."

"It's called Autumn Woods. Al gave it to me for Christmas one year. She said it would counteract my usual fragrance."

"Which was?"

"Eau de dirty gym socks."

She laughed. "Well, it's nice. I smell pine, lavender, citrus, and maybe a little nutmeg. But it's all very subtle."

"I thought it smelled a little like rice pudding. Grandma Jennings used to make something that had nutmeg in it. I think it was rice pudding."

"I worked in a little restaurant once that made the most delicious rice pudding. They soaked the raisins in brandy. It was heavenly. I still have the recipe."

David said, "I love rice pudding. If you ever make it, count on me to taste test it for you."

She laughed. "It looks like I'm getting a list of things for you to taste test."

"Was that while you were in college? Did you have to work much?"

"Oh yes," she said. "You know my dad was ill almost all the time I was in high school, so my college fund went to pay my dad's medical bills."

"So how did you go to college?" he asked.

"My mom went back to teaching after my dad died, so she was able to help me some, but mostly I did student loans. I got some small academic scholarships, but I also taught violin and played all kinds of gigs—weddings, funerals, anything that needed a violinist. I even played fiddle in a country and western band one summer. There's a big country and western club across the river from Cincinnati in Kentucky.

"*No*. You played in a country and western band? Was that country style hard to learn?"

"Not really. It just took practice and concentration."

"You must have worked really hard."

"I wanted to teach in college, so I was willing to do anything to make it happen." She added, "And I stuck with it until I got my doctorate. Because I worked so much, it took me eight years."

"I wish more of our students had your ambition," David said as he patted her hand. "I'm so proud of you. You are to be commended."

She wanted to say, "Now you know why I have such resentment for people who get their college education paid by playing a game," but she decided that would be a little tactless.

The shiny car stretched out and ate up the miles like a big cat flying over the ground, chasing its prey. Soon they were on the outskirts of Indianapolis. As they came under an overhead bridge, Julia saw a huge billboard on the right. It was a picture of a basketball player in a Pacers uniform, holding a milk carton in one hand and a basketball in the other. Julia read the sign, "D. J. Cooper drinks Dairy Delight milk before every game."

"David," she said, pointing excitedly. "That's you."

"Yeah," he said calmly. "Dairy Delight is one of my endorsements."

"You mean they pay you for having your picture on that sign?"

"Yes and no," he said. "Every day my picture is on that billboard, the Dairy Delight people deliver so many gallons of milk to the downtown Indianapolis homeless shelter. At the end of the month, they send a receipt to my financial manager, and we use that as a tax write-off."

"David, that's wonderful," she said. "But don't you need the money?"

"Not really," he said. "The shelter needs the milk more than I need the money."

How it would feel to not need money. I can't imagine.

David looked at his watch. "I think we have time to go somewhere special for dinner."

"Where?"

"One of my favorite restaurants." He looked at her feet. "Can you walk in those shoes?"

"Sure, if it's not too far." She looked out the window. "There don't seem to be any parking places."

"That's okay," he said. "I always have a parking place."

Yes, she thought, remembering, *if someone doesn't get it first.*

They pulled into a parking garage. The attendant handed him a ticket, and they sped up the entrance ramp. "There're no parking spaces here," she said, but he kept going. On the top floor, she saw a space. "There's a space," she said, "but it's reserved." As they got closer, she laughed and read, "Reserved for D. J. Cooper."

"I've had this space ever since I lived in Indianapolis. I just haven't gotten around to canceling it. The symphony hall and the arena where the Pacers play are close by."

They rode the elevator down to the ground floor and headed down the street. Several people on the street said, "Hey, D. J.," or "How's it going, D. J.?"

"Does everybody in Indianapolis know you?" she asked.

"Probably not everybody. Just the Pacers fans." After several blocks, they turned into an alley.

"Where are we going?" she asked. "This seems to be a rather suspicious-looking part of town."

"It's okay," he said as they went down a flight of dark stairs. He took her arm. "Be careful. The stairs are rather narrow." At the bottom of the stairs, there was a door with a lighted sconce on both sides and a sign over it that read "Charlie's."

David opened the door, and they went into a room with a dozen nondescript tables. A young Asian girl greeted them and showed them to a table. "Welcome to Charlie's," she said. Another girl came with glasses of water.

"No menus?" Julia asked.

"You don't need menus."

Just then, a small, wizened Asian man came from a back room. He was wearing a baseball cap that read "Pacers" across the front and an apron that read "We feed the Pacers." His thin face cracked into a huge smile, and his black eyes sparkled with excitement.

"D. J.," he said, pumping David's hand. "Where you been? Haven't seen you for long time."

"Yes," David said. "I'm living in Hoover, Kentucky, now. Charlie, this is my friend Julia Crane."

Julie smiled. "I'm happy to meet you."

David said, "Charlie is the world's greatest Pacers fan."

"Ah, D. J." He sighed. "The Pacers gonna miss you."

"I know," David said. "I'm going to miss them too. What are you cooking today?"

"New special," he said. "I make it just for you."

"Okay, bring us two and a pot of your special tea."

After he left, Julia said, "David, what did you just order?"

"I have no idea, but it will be delicious. That's why there are no menus. You eat whatever Charlie cooks. It's the most eclectic place you can imagine. The food is part-Chinese, part-American, and part-Italian. And, as you can see, he really enjoys feeding sports teams."

Before long, the young girl emerged from the kitchen with two huge plates of food. Charlie followed. "Duck ravioli with orange sauce and rice noodles," he announced triumphantly. "I make it just for you. Enjoy."

As David had predicted, the food was wonderful. "I've never tasted anything so good," Julia said.

The young girl brought a plate of small fortune cookies with the bill. "Wait until you taste these," he said.

She picked one up and cracked it open. It was buttery and crumbly and delicious. "No fortune?" she asked.

"Just wait," he said. "When Charlie doesn't have time to put the fortunes in the cookies, he comes out and tells you your fortune. I think he makes it up as he goes along." Sure enough, Charlie came out again.

"D. J.," he said, "you have good luck with the lovely lady."

David said, "I've already had good luck. The day I met her was the luckiest day of my life."

And to Julia, he said, "You have good luck with D. J. Marry him and have beautiful, tall babies to play basketball."

Julia blushed. "I'll think about it," she said. "Your cookies were delicious."

"Use almond flour," he said. "Make lucky cookies."

"We had better go," David said. "We've just got time to get to the symphony hall." They paid their bill and left.

On the way out, she said, "Did he know we were coming?"

"No, but it doesn't matter. We came at the right time." Then he added, "This place will be packed in another hour. Sometimes people wait two hours just to get a table."

"Well, it would have been worth the wait."

Chapter 13

They settled into their seats in the symphony hall just minutes before the lights were dimmed. The oboist gave the A, and all the members of the orchestra tuned their instruments. The house was almost full. There were very few empty seats.

The first part of the program was orchestral works from famous operas. They started with an overture from Monteverdi, several things of Mozart, and finished with Beethoven's Leonore Overture no. 3. "This was the first background music," Julia said. "It sets the mood for the story told by the opera. It's a shame that some of these works aren't played more often. They're very good by themselves."

As soon as the first part of the concert was over, the orchestra left the stage. "Are you going to go down and say something to Alberta?" Julia asked.

"No, she's probably in a corner somewhere, meditating. She does that before a concert and doesn't want anyone to say anything to her."

Soon, the musicians came back onto the stage. The orchestra tuned. The lights were dimmed, and the audience sat in a hushed silence. Everyone was waiting anxiously for the main event, Mendelssohn's Concerto for Violin and Orchestra in E Minor.

Alberta came sweeping in from the side and shook the hand of the conductor. The audience burst into a thunderous applause. She bowed low to the audience. She stood resplendent in a slim gown of red satin. One shoulder was completely bare, but the other had a large bow. Her short, dark hair curled around her lovely face. She was tall for a woman but not as tall as David. "She would have made a hell of a basketball player," David whispered, "but fortunately for the world of music, it was not her thing."

The conductor gave the downbeat, and the first chord was struck. Almost immediately, the violin began the opening theme. The Guarneri sang as an old and rare instrument should, with a clear, mellow tone, but Alberta controlled every nuance superbly. The audience reveled in each emotion as it came from the strings of the old violin—joy, sadness, and love. The intense feeling conveyed by the music was felt throughout the concert hall. The audience sat spellbound for thirty minutes until the last chord. Then the audience rose with a thundering ovation.

Alberta bowed again to the audience, then shook hands with the conductor and the concert master. She acknowledged the orchestra. They rose as a body and took a bow.

"Bravo! Bravo!" David yelled. Several in the audience took up the chant.

Then Alberta went to the microphone. "I want to thank Dr. Carsini for asking me to play tonight. As some of you know, it has been nearly a year since I have been on the concert stage. My husband and I have been involved in another project." She indicated the wings, and a handsome, slightly portly black man with a black curly beard and gold-rimmed glasses came out carrying a large picture. "My husband, Grant Hamilton. He was in the trombone section tonight." More applause. He handed her the picture. She turned it around to reveal a full-size picture of a chubby-faced baby. "Our daughter, Anna Carol. She is nearly four months old."

The audience clapped. "Everyone loves a baby," David said. "Have you ever seen a more beautiful child?" Julia said she hadn't.

Alberta handed Grant the picture, picked up her violin, and said, "In honor of Anna Carol, I will do one small encore." She began to play the beautiful strains of Brahms's *Lullaby*. The audience sat back and listened intently. Although it only lasted a few minutes, the music was a gem filled with feeling. When it was over, the audience stood and gave her another resounding ovation. Alberta bowed low to the audience. "Thank you and good night," she said as she left the stage.

David said, "I just got a text from Mom. Dad isn't feeling well, so they're not going to the reception. We'll see them at home."

"David, are you sure it's okay if we spend the night? I don't want to inconvenience your parents."

"Mom would be offended if we didn't," he said. "She loves when we have company."

They went backstage to the rehearsal hall where the reception was held. A waiter was pouring glasses of champagne. David said, "I don't usually like to drink and drive, but maybe one small glass will be okay." They stood in line to greet Alberta. David hugged her and said, "You did great, kid. I knew if you kept practicing, you would finally learn that piece." He turned to Julia. "Al," he said, "this is my friend Dr. Julia Crane. Julia," he said, "my talented sister, Alberta Hamilton."

She took Julia's hand and hugged her. "It's so nice to meet you," she said. "It now looks like you have the unenviable task of keeping my wayward brother in line." She added, "Mom and Dad tried but were not successful." David grinned a sheepish grin.

"You did a wonderful job," Julia said. "I have always loved the Mendelssohn. It's too bad he didn't write more for the violin."

David said, "We're going to go on back home. Mom and Dad have already gone. Dad wasn't feeling well."

"Yes," Al said. "I spoke to them before the concert."

"Are you coming to Mom and Dad's tomorrow?"

"No," she said. "I know it will be late when we leave, and we still have to go to Grant's parents' and pick up Anna, so I'll look forward to seeing you Christmas."

"Okay," he said as he hugged her again. "Thanks for doing such a great job." David turned to Julia. "There's one more person I want you to meet before we leave. There—I see him." David led Julia to the conductor, a handsome man with a shock of snow-white hair and piercing blue eyes.

"Hi, David," the conductor said. "How have you been?"

"Great," he said. "Rick, I want you to meet Dr. Julia Crane. Julia is professor of violin at Chapman State. Julia, this is Dr. Enrico Carsini, the conductor of the Indianapolis Philharmonic."

Julia said, "The concert was wonderful. I enjoyed it immensely."

"Yes, thank you," he replied. "Alberta is very talented." He turned to David. "Is it true? You're now coaching basketball?"

"I'm afraid so," he said.

"You know I would always give you a job in the symphony," Rick said, "but come and play with us any time you're not busy." Then he added, "Do you still have the Amati?"

David looked at Julia. "Well, yes and no."

Rick laughed. "So that's the way it is," he said as he smiled at Julia. "She's already talked you out of your fiddle. She'll have a wedding ring on your finger before long if you don't watch it."

"I should be so lucky," David said.

Julia saw that David was smiling a teasing smile. "Only if I get to keep the Amati," she said boldly and patted David's arm.

Rick laughed. "Good luck, you two. I hope you'll come back to hear the symphony very soon."

After the reception was over, David and Julia made their way back to the parking garage. There was a line of cars attempting to exit. "I think we'll sit for a minute," David said as they got into the car. "I don't want to get a dent in the Porsche. Did you enjoy the concert?"

"Oh, David, Alberta is so talented. I've never heard the Mendelssohn done so superbly."

"Yes," he said. "She was really good, but she's worked awfully hard to get where she is today. It's gratifying to see her get the recognition she deserves." He leaned over and kissed Julia. "The concert was wonderful, but it was better because I could share it with you."

Julia said, "The whole evening was wonderful—the dinner, the concert. Thank you for asking me." She had learned a lot about David tonight. She was not surprised that everyone seemed to have such love and affection for him.

Soon, the line of cars started to move, and they were able to get in line to go to the street and then to the highway.

"How far to your parents' from here?" she asked.

"About twenty-five miles. Rockwell is about halfway between Indianapolis and Bloomington. Would you mind some music? I have a favorite oldies station."

"Not at all. I love the old love songs."

He turned on the radio, and the velvety voice of a crooner sang, "When I fall in love, it will be forever."

"I love that song," she said. David sang along and tapped the steering wheel in time with the rhythm.

"Julia," David began, then paused. "Have you ever been in love?"

"I … I thought I was once."

"What happened?" She looked at his face, but he was staring straight ahead.

"Now, I'm not sure I even knew what love is. You see, I wasn't very pretty in high school, and I didn't date much."

"I find that hard to believe," he said as he patted her arm.

"It's true. Back then, I was straight as a stick. I had a few freckles on my nose and braces on my teeth. Then, after years of braces, my teeth straightened up. My freckles left, and my body started to develop some shape. I met this clarinet player my freshmen year in college. He was the first guy that had ever paid much attention to me, and I soon found myself in his bed."

"And how was it?"

"What?"

"The sex."

"I'm not sure," she said. "It didn't seem to make much of an impression on me. I didn't feel any better about myself or any differently toward him. In fact, I was a little sorry it had happened at all. Right then, I decided that I really didn't need a man in my life if that's all there was to it. After a while, we found that we had nothing else in common."

"Not even music?" he asked.

"Not even music," she replied. "You see, he was into jazz, and there's no place for a violin in a jazz band. Besides, I'm not fond of jazz. All that improvisation. I want to play music that's been beautifully composed, not made up as you go along."

"What ever happened to the clarinet player?"

"Oh, he went off to New Orleans at spring break to play in a Mardi Gras band. I don't know if he ever came back to school or not. And I was rather relieved he was gone."

"How long were you together?"

"About a month. We only had sex a couple of times."

"And there's been no one since."

"Not really," she said. "Oh, I've dated a little, but I've never met anyone that I wanted to date more than once or twice." She hesitated. "David, there's something I have to tell you."

"Okay."

"It may change the way you feel about me."

"I doubt that."

"David," she said, "I always want to be completely honest with you. Do you remember the dedication gala when someone parked in your parking space?" Before he could answer, she said, "It was ... It was me!"

He laughed.

"Well, it was serious to me," she said in a quivering voice. "I felt so ashamed that I had parked in your space and you had to walk miles with your bad knee. I should have told you that night and apologized to you right then, but I didn't have the courage."

He laughed again and picked up her hand and kissed it. "My darling," he said, "I have known for weeks that you were the one who parked in my space."

"But how?"

"When I made the crack about the car being a bucket of bolts, I was looking at you, and when I saw the surprised look on your face, I was almost sure it was you. Then, when I saw your car parked in front of your apartment, I was sure. There isn't another car like yours in the state of Kentucky." He paused. Then he asked solemnly, "Do you think you could ever love a black man?"

She said, "Well, I'm not sure."

"Is it the race thing?" he asked quietly.

"No," she said. "You see, there's this other guy that I could be falling for. He's got beautiful brown skin, a handsome smile, and eyes that remind me of chocolate pudding. I think I could seriously love him, even if he does make fun of my car."

Just then, they pulled into the driveway of his parents' house. He drove around to the garage in back and stopped the car. He pulled her close to him. She looked up into those serious brown eyes. He was smiling.

"Are you talking about me?" he asked happily.

"Who else?" she asked.

"Good. I was afraid I was going to have to challenge some guy to a duel."

"You mean you would fight for me?"

"In a heartbeat! You know, my darling, I've never really been in love either. Why don't we learn about love together?" He looked down and saw that she was smiling agreeably, so he kissed her fervently.

What am I saying? Am I falling in love? She felt as if she was being swept along in a river of emotion. But she did know that she loved the way she felt when David kissed her and held her close, and she loved just being with him.

Everyone she had met tonight seemed to think so highly of him. He was so handsome and sophisticated, but he didn't take himself seriously at all. He was definitely someone she could love. Julia sat speechless for a minute, thinking about everything David had just said.

Were things moving too fast? Perhaps she was just caught up in the excitement of going places with this wonderful, handsome man. It was very easy to forget about everything else when she was enjoying herself so much.

"Before we go in," he said, "I need to warn you about something. There's one area of my life in which I've been a failure, at least in the eyes of my mother."

"Oh, David, how could you have ever been a failure?"

"I have failed to produce a grandchild for my mother. She will remind us of that fact, ever so lovingly," David said. "Please don't be embarrassed or offended. She's basically aiming her remarks at me because I have failed to find a wife."

"I won't be embarrassed," she said. "I have already met others today who think you should be married."

"Yes, as you start approaching thirty, all your friends think you should be married." He gave her another long, loving kiss. "Thank you for being so understanding."

Chapter 14

The outside of the house was brick, with dormers on the second story. There were dark blue shutters with cream trim around the windows. A long, low brick addition extended from the rear. Julia said, "I've never seen an old house so beautifully done."

"Yes," David said. "Wait until you see the inside. About six years ago, we gave the old girl quite a face-lift. We had a contractor and a designer come out from Indianapolis. We redid the kitchen and added a master suite for Mom and Dad on the first floor. My grandpa Cooper built this house in the fifties. When Grandma died, we moved in with him."

They went into the garage. David opened the door into a hall and yelled, "We're here." David's mom and dad were waiting for them in the family room. He hugged them both.

"Were you able to stay for the entire concert?" he asked his dad.

"Oh yes, we wouldn't have missed it. She was great, wasn't she?"

David said, "Mom, Dad, this is my friend Julia Crane. Julia, my parents, Caroline and Albert Cooper." Caroline was a large woman, slightly plump, with short, curly hair and friendly brown eyes, while Albert was tall and thin. Evidence of recent illnesses showed on his gaunt face.

"Welcome, dear," Caroline said. "We are so happy to meet you." Then she added, "Would you like something to eat or drink?"

"No, thank you. It's been such a long day. I think I'm ready to go to bed."

"Very well," Caroline said. "Come. I'll show you to your room."

"You have a lovely home, Mrs. Cooper," Julia said.

"Please, call me Caroline," she said. "We completely redid the upstairs so we would have plenty of room for the grandchildren when they come to visit." David followed them up the stairs with her bag. When Julia looked at him, he gave her a wink.

When they got to the top of the stairs, he said, "We used to have three bedrooms and one bath. We took the largest bedroom and made a bath for one bedroom and a sitting room for Mom. She has an office and her sewing machine in here."

Caroline said, "I'll put you in Alberta's old room. It now has its own bathroom."

David took Julia into his arms. "Mom, do you mind if I kiss Julia good night in front of you?"

"It's about time you found a nice girl to kiss good night," Caroline said with a happy grin.

"I'm trying, Mom. I'm trying," he said, and then he gave Julia a quick kiss.

"Thank you for today. Everything was so special." She smiled a knowing smile.

"Sleep well. I'll see you in the morning. I think I'll have a beer with Dad before I turn in," he said.

The bedroom was a typical little girl's room. A shelf of stuffed animals and dolls hung over the bed, and pictures covered the wall. One picture in particular caught her eye. It was of two small brown-skinned children dressed in their Sunday best. Their freshly scrubbed faces had big smiles, and they held quarter-size violins. The little boy had on a stylish blue suit with a bow tie. The little girl wore a fluffy pink dress with a pink bow in her curly black hair. She wore black patent leather shoes and pink socks with ruffled tops. A caption at the bottom read "*Easter Sunday, 1997.*"

As Julia got ready for bed, she thought about what David had said. If she stayed with David, just loving him, kissing him passionately, and even sharing his bed would not be enough. He would want a home, and he would want a family. She turned out the light and was soon fast asleep. The emotion of the day had taken its toll on her.

In her dreams, she saw herself sitting in a chair on a beautiful green lawn. Two brown-skinned children played at her feet. "Mommy," the little girl said, "Davie took my baby."

"Davie," she heard herself say, "would you like to bring Cindy's baby back?"

Six-year-old Davie said, "The bad guys took her. They're holding her for ransom, but I'm a Super Ranger. I'm going to rescue her."

"Please do. Cindy loves her baby very much."

Four-year-old Cindy laid her head on her mother's ample lap. "Mommy, you're getting fat."

"Yes, dear. Mommy's going to have another baby."

"Let's have a sister, Mommy. No more brothers."

"But, dear," her mother said, "if it's a brother, we'll love him too, won't we?"

"Yes, Mommy, we'll love him even if he's a brother."

David entered the dream. He took her hand and helped her to her feet. "Okay, guys, let's help Mommy by picking up all the toys and taking them into the house."

"Daddy," Cindy said, "did you know Mommy is having a baby?"

"Yes, I did. Isn't it great?"

"Only if it's a sister."

Julia awoke with a start and a smile. She remembered everything from her dream, but what did it mean? Was it her subconscious foreshadowing her future with David, or was it a warning for her that she needed to decide what she wanted out of life before things went any further? Life with David would mean a home and children. But was that what she wanted?

She had always planned on a career as a teacher and violinist. Besides, David hadn't even asked her to marry him. He hadn't even said he loved her, but he would. She knew he would, and she needed to be ready with an answer. Then, from the deep recesses of her mind, she heard her mother's voice: "You have the opportunity to be a foremost authority of violin pedagogy if you don't throw it away by marrying a basketball coach."

She dressed and went downstairs. David and Albert were sitting at a beautiful granite-topped bar, drinking coffee, while Caroline was scrambling eggs.

"Did you sleep well?" David asked.

"Very well. I didn't realize how tired I was." She looked around. "You have a lovely kitchen, and so functional. It looks as if you have everything." The kitchen was at the end of a very large family room. A large stone fireplace stood at the opposite end with comfortable chairs around a huge television screen.

"I do, and I have David to thank for it. Some of my old appliances had stopped working."

"It was either remodel the kitchen or give her fast-food gift cards," David said. "I thought it would just be cheaper to just redo the kitchen."

"Well, I love it! What would you like, dear?" Caroline asked.

"I'll just have whatever you're having."

David said, "She'll have a scrambled egg and some fruit and maybe half a biscuit. Right?"

She laughed. "You know me pretty well. Yes, that will be fine."

"And a cup of tea?" David asked.

"Yes, if it's not too much trouble."

After breakfast, David said, "We probably need to hit the road. Mom and Dad will be leaving for church before long."

Caroline said, "Julia, David tells me that your mom will be gone at Christmas. We would love for you to spend Christmas with us. In the past, David has had to work on Christmas, so it will be real treat to have him home this year."

"Thank you. I'd like that very much. I always make my grandmother's fruitcake. May I bring that?"

"She makes great chocolate chip cookies too," David said.

"Bring anything you'd like. I'm so excited that you're coming."

David said it was time to go. He hugged his mom and dad. "Thanks for having us."

"Yes," Julia said, "thank you for having me. It was so nice to meet you."

In the car, David said, "Mom loves Christmas. She always makes a big production of everything. We go to the midnight service at church. Al and I play carols before the service. Then we have brunch at around eleven on Christmas Day. We have Christmas dinner later on in the day. That usually depends on when the Pacers' game is over, if they're playing."

Julia said, "Your parents' house is so lovely. You must have spent a fortune on it."

"Yes," he said. "It was something they really needed, and what good is money if you can't use it to help the people you love?"

"You're right."

"When is the last day of the semester?" David asked.

Julia said, "I believe Christmas is on a Wednesday, and the last day will be December 20. We have the Christmas concert on Sunday, the fifteenth, and then finals the next week."

David said, "I'm supposed to do a small recruiting trip the week after next, and I still have to help the freshmen and sophomores plan their schedules for next semester. I may not get to see you much until Christmas, but we should have several days together then."

She snuggled against him. "I'm looking forward to it," she said. Then she added, "There's one little favor I would like you to do for me."

When she told him, he said, "Sure, I can do that."

Chapter 15

When the students arrived in the classroom on Wednesday, they were surprised to see David sitting there. She said, "I think most of you have met Coach Cooper. What I didn't tell you is Coach Cooper is a very talented violinist."

David showed the students the Amati and explained how violins were made in the eighteenth century. Then he and Julia played several pieces from Baroque and Classical Literature. The students stared in wide-eyed amazement as she and David played.

"Is it hard to play the violin?" someone asked.

"It's easy to play but hard to master. It's like basketball. It takes a lot of practice and concentration." He lingered after class was dismissed and said, "Thanks again for going to the concert with me."

"Thank you for taking me. I had a wonderful time."

He smiled. "The men are playing Iowa State on Thursday. If you would like to go, I'll have Clark pick you up, and I'll bring you home."

Thursday, Clark and Molly picked her up. They found their usual seats behind the home bench. David had given Julia a Chapman State shirt, and she wore it proudly. Some of her students smiled and waved.

"This will be an important game for the team if they can win it," Clark said. "Iowa State is an important Big 12 powerhouse."

The game was hotly contested. The Cougars seemed to be holding their own against a more experienced team, but a lucky shot just before halftime left the Cougars five points behind. When the team returned to the court after halftime, Julia saw David get in Cruiser's face. She could hear him all the way to their seats.

"That center is pushing you all over the court. You can't let him make those layups. Keep him away from the basket. You're two inches taller than his is. Protect the rim." He swatted Cruiser on the butt. "Now get in there and work."

"Looks like David has lit a fire under Cruiser. He's playing much better," Molly said.

"I don't think Cruiser has ever worked this hard in his whole life," Clark observed. With less than a minute to go, the score was 65 for ISU, 61 for CSU. The Cougars drove the ball down the court. Kenny hit a ten-foot jump shot: ISA, 65 to CSU 63. The Iowa State guards slowly brought the ball up the court. They passed the ball around the perimeter. Precious seconds were ticking away. A guard attempted a pass to the wing. Tyler's long arm got a piece of the ball. Cruiser pounced on the loose ball, held it up above his head, and passed the ball down the court to Jalen. He took three dribbles, then stopped behind the three-point line and fired. The ball settled into the net just as the final horn sounded. The score was ISU 65 to CSU 66. The game was over. The Cougars had won.

The crowd went wild. People were jumping up and down. Julia hugged Molly. Everyone was cheering at the top of their voices. David and Rusty and the other members of the CSU staff were pounding one another on the back. The teams lined up and congratulated one another on a well-played game.

On the way home, Julia said, "That was the most exciting game I've ever seen. I didn't think they had a chance to win."

"Yes, they played well. If we can keep up this intensity after we start the conference schedule, we should have a good year. We might even make the NCAA tournament." He added, "You're turning into a real basketball fan."

"Yes, I am," she admitted. "I didn't know anything could be so much fun, and I think it's good that I see the students out of the classroom. In fact, I guess you could say I'm becoming part of the campus scene."

He smiled. "And how are my basketball players doing?"

"Everyone has been turning in their writing assignments."

"Even Cruiser?"

"Well, Cruiser has been turning in something, though reluctantly. I think he could do much better than he does."

"The guy is so lazy, even on the basketball court," David said. "He just doesn't want to work at anything. I've been meeting with them once a week for a study session and to check their work.

"By the way," he said, "I'm going to be gone a couple of days next week, a short recruiting trip to Tennessee and Alabama."

"Why do you have to go?" she asked.

"It's part of my job. The administration seems to think that since I've been a pro player, I have a certain amount of credibility about the game of basketball. They think I can entice prospective students to the university better than the other coaches. Our basketball program depends on getting good recruits every year. We really hope to get good academic students also, who will stay in school for four years."

"No more Cruiser Bells," she said emphatically

"No more Cruiser Bells," he agreed.

He parked in front of her apartment and walked to the door with her. He held her tightly and gave her a passionate kiss. "Do you want to go out to dinner on Saturday night? I have to leave early Sunday morning."

"Sure."

"Oh, and one more thing. Phil Gardner, the director of athletics for the university, and his wife are hosting a Christmas cocktail party on Friday, December 20. Would you like to go with me?"

"Sure. What should I wear?"

"The invitation says casual chic, whatever that means."

"It means you don't have to wear your tux. Do you have a nice blazer and maybe a silk turtleneck? Something like that would be appropriate."

"And you could wear something extra sexy."

"I'm running out of sexy things," she said.

"You could always wear that blue top."

Chapter 16

December flew by. David returned from his recruiting trip, excited by the new prospects he had contacted. Julia spent the evenings he was away making cookie dough and putting it in the freezer. She made her grandmother's fruitcake and put it in the freezer as well. She had planned to take gift boxes of Christmas cookies and candy. She couldn't afford to get everyone gifts, but didn't want to go empty-handed either, so food seemed to be the solution.

The basketball team had at least one game per week out of town, so Julia usually saw David only on the weekends. Friday, Julia had finished her 10:00 a.m. violin lesson and was hard at work at her desk in her office when she heard a knock on the door. "Come in."

David stuck his head around the door. "Do you have time for a quick kiss and a hug?"

"Of course," she said as she stood and moved into his outstretched arms.

"I just had to see you once more before I left," he said and then kissed her passionately and held her close. "I've got to go by the dorm, grab a bite of lunch, and be ready to catch the bus at twelve thirty. Our plane leaves at one thirty."

"What time will you get to Mobile?"

"About three thirty or four o'clock, if the weather's not bad. The game is at two o'clock tomorrow. It should be on TV. Be sure and watch."

"I wouldn't miss it. Can you win?"

"We should. South Alabama has really improved, but so have we."

"Be safe," she said and then kissed him again. "I'll miss you while you're gone."

"And I'll miss you. We won't be back until very late on Saturday night, so I probably won't see you until after the concert on Sunday, but I'll be there."

She returned to her desk and sat for a few minutes. She marveled at how David was slowly becoming a very important part of her life. She enjoyed cooking for him, playing music with him, and just being with him. She had to admit that she had not thought about her magazine articles once since her mother left. She was having too much fun going out with David.

That afternoon as she was coming out of the music building to go home, she met Harold Hartwig, the low-brass instructor. "The orchestra is sounding great," he said. "Did you have a good rehearsal last night?"

"It was very good," she said. "The students have worked hard. We have our final dress rehearsal tomorrow and the concert on Sunday."

"It's too bad there were no tubas in the Baroque orchestra. I would have enjoyed playing with you. Say, Julia, who was that good-looking lady I saw Coach Cooper with last night?"

"A student, I guess. Sometimes he tutors on Thursday nights."

"Not last night. He was out at Leonardo's with this fabulous lady. They had their heads together all night, as if they were really talking over old times."

"I have no idea who he takes out," she said sharply.

"I guess it was an old flame who finally caught up with him. Anyway, I thought you would like to know that Coach Cooper is not sitting home alone when you're not available."

Julia raced out of the building. By the time she reached her car, she felt tears welling in her eyes. "Why should I be so upset?" she asked herself. "David is certainly free to take out whoever he wishes." Julia dried her tears and started home, but she was upset and hurt and angry.

When she reached home, she sat on the couch, and the tears returned. "How could he do this?" she asked herself. "Doesn't he know that I … I …"

That you what? her inner voice asked. *You don't love him.*

"But I told him I thought I could love him," she admitted out loud.

You just want him around because he takes you nice places and makes you feel wonderful and special when he kisses you.

"Yes," she agreed, "and I can't imagine my life without David in it."

David has every right to date someone else, the little voice said.

She tried to be calm. She knew they didn't have any kind of understanding, but if it was something innocent, why didn't he tell her this morning? Perhaps he knew that she really hadn't wanted a romantic relationship. Perhaps he was thinking of breaking up with her. Wasn't that what she wanted? She wasn't sure. That's what she had been telling herself, but was it true? The thought that she might be losing David was too much to bear.

That evening before she went to bed, she got a text from David. It read, "Plane was late. Bad weather. Got here just in time for dinner and bed. Thinking of you. D."

At least she knew he was safely on the ground. She went to bed still thinking about what Harold had said. There had to be a hundred reasons why David took a beautiful girl to Leonardo's and didn't tell her about it.

In the morning, she awoke from a fitful sleep. She had been awake several times during the night thinking about David. She had to be at a final symphony rehearsal at ten o'clock, so she showered and dressed quickly. At the rehearsal, she found it hard to concentrate. After the first number, Dr. Rubinsky came over and said, "Julia, aren't you feeling well today? You've missed two entrances."

"I know, sir. I'm sorry. I've been distracted, but I'll try harder." She had to put David out of her mind and concentrate on the music. It wasn't fair to the rest of the orchestra for her to make mistakes.

After the symphony rehearsal, she rushed back home. Was she really falling in love with David? She hadn't realized just how important he was becoming to her. What if he dropped out of her life? She was naïve if she thought David would want to continue as they had been without taking their relationship to another level. She knew David would want more than just hugs and kisses, but after her previous experience with sex, she wasn't sure she wanted that. But somehow she knew that sex with David would be different. In her heart, she trusted David. He had said he was falling in love with her. She had to believe that.

That afternoon, she turned on the TV and watched the game. Even though it was early in the season, she could see that the team was playing efficiently together. She was so proud of David. He seemed to work so smoothly with Rusty, and the team responded beautifully to his direction.

Soon the Cougars were twenty points ahead. When the game was over, Julia relaxed a little and stretched out on the couch. Soon, she was asleep. When she awoke, she was not so angry. She knew there had to be a reason he was out with someone else. She sent him a text. "The game was great. Have a safe trip home. Missing you. J."

The next morning, she got up and played over all her symphony music. She knew it frontward and backward. All she had to do was concentrate.

The concert went well. The soloists and the chorus sang beautifully, and the orchestra played every note perfectly.

After the concert was over, Julia scooped up her music and violin. She thought she would avoid seeing David and go straight home. She was very tired. But when she headed off the stage, she saw David waiting for her. "The concert was beautiful, babe. There's someone I want you to meet."

"Not tonight, David," she said. "I'm so tired. I'm going home." She looked up into his pleading brown eyes.

"Please do this for me," he said. Even if she was upset, she could never deny him anything when he looked at her like that.

"Okay, just for a few minutes." He took her violin case and book bag. She followed him into the auditorium. She saw Dr. Jennings standing beside a handsome black woman with salt and pepper hair and a beautiful girl in her late twenties.

"Aunt Ophelia, Kristin, this is my friend Julia Crane."

Ophelia took her hand. "Julia, my dear. I'm so happy to finally meet you. Caroline has told me so much about you."

"I'm happy to meet you too, Mrs. Jennings," Julia said. She turned to Dr. Jennings. "It's good to see you again, Dr. Jennings."

"Ah, yes," he said. "That was a very fine concert."

"This is our daughter, Kristin," Ophelia said.

"I'm happy to meet you, Kristin," Julia said as she looked at David. He had a knowing grin on his face. "David has told me nothing about you."

"Well, he's told me all about you," Kristin said with a friendly smile. "In fact, when he took me to dinner, you were all he talked about—how smart and talented you are and how you can cook."

Julia said, "David tends to exaggerate when it comes to chocolate chip cookies."

"Yes, but it was sweet of him to entertain Kristin for us," Ophelia said. "Her husband, Edwin, had business meetings in Nashville on Friday and Saturday, so he dropped her off for a surprise visit with us. Ralph and I had a Board of Regents meeting that we couldn't miss, so I asked David to take her out to dinner. Would you two like to join us for dinner tonight?"

"I'm afraid not," David said. "The team didn't get back from Mobile until very late last night, and I know Julia is tired. I think

I'd better see her home and get back to the dorm. Next week will be a busy time for us. Thanks anyway."

"Oh yes, I forgot how hectic that last week before vacation is. We hope to see you at Caroline's on Christmas Day," Ophelia said.

"We'll be there," David said. He hugged Kristin. "Tell Edwin I said hello, and thanks for going to dinner with me."

"It was my pleasure, and it was a pleasure to meet you, Julia," Kristin said. "The concert was beautiful. I am so impressed with the way the music at Chapman has improved. Don't you think so, Dad?"

Dr. Jennings cleared his throat. "Ahem, yes," he said. "Very fine concert, very fine. We hope to have more in the future." He turned to David. "Great win for the team on Saturday."

"Yes, thank you, sir. Goodbye," David said. He led Julia to the parking lot. "Would you like to go out for dinner, or do you just want to go home? I could always get something to eat at the athletic dorm."

"I think I have some chili in the freezer. I could make some cornbread muffins to go with it."

"Why don't I go by Hamburger Heaven and pick up some hot dogs. Chili dogs would be great."

"Okay," she said, "chili dogs it is. Make mine with everything on it. I might even find an old brownie or something sweet in the freezer too."

At home, Julia changed out of her symphony dress into some comfortable slacks and a sweater. She put the pot of chili on the stove to heat.

David arrived with the hot dogs. She was hungry, and the chili dogs tasted great. She had been too nervous to eat anything at lunch.

After dinner, David sat on the couch. She brought him a glass of wine and looked down into his earnest brown eyes.

"Thank you," he said as he took the glass. "Am I forgiven?"

"What do you mean?" she asked as she sat beside him.

"I'm so sorry you were upset about me taking Kristen out to dinner," he said regretfully. She felt her eyes getting watery. "Someone told you they saw me with Kristin, didn't they?"

She nodded.

"And you've been upset all weekend."

Once again, she nodded.

"My darling, I am so sorry you were upset. I was in such a rush when I came by your office that I didn't even think of telling you about Kristin. I would never knowingly do anything that would cause you pain."

"I know," she said as she wiped her eyes. "I guess I overreacted."

He sat his wine on the coffee table and put his arm around her. "We've never talked about an exclusive relationship," he said. She felt him lift her chin with his other hand until she was looking directly into his serious brown eyes. "But I want you to know that I consider myself in an exclusive relationship with you. If I ever want to end it, I will tell you." He hugged her close and stroked her hair. "I won't go out with someone behind your back, and if you ever want to end it, I hope you will do the same.

"I think in high school or college, they call it going steady," David said. "I may have an old fraternity pin somewhere, or maybe my IU graduation ring that I could give you if it would make you feel better." When his soft, gentle mouth came down on hers, she was amazed at how David could make her feel so loved without ever saying the words. She wanted that feeling to go on forever.

"That won't be necessary," she said breathlessly. "I'll take your word for it." She laid her head on his chest. He held her tightly and patted her back. It felt so right just being in David's arms.

He said, "Since you were so upset about me dating someone else that must mean you care for me just a little."

"That's not completely accurate," she said. "I care for you a lot."

Chapter 17

That last week before winter holidays, all departments, clubs, and dorms across the campus held informal parties as the students crammed for finals and prepared to depart for home. Study Room A of the Marshall Building was filled every evening as students put the finishing touches on assignments and term papers. The basketball team had their last game of the semester. It was as if the entire university was planning a mass exodus until January, when everyone would return for the second semester.

Friday came, and it was time for the cocktail party. David stood on Julia's front porch and rang the bell. When she opened the door, he gasped in surprise. "You know, I changed my mind," he said.

"What? You've decided not to go?"

"No," he said. "I thought what you wore to Al's concert was the sexiest thing I had ever seen, but it can't compare with this outfit." He took her into his arms and held her close. "I'm not sure I want to take you to a party looking so devastatingly beautiful, with all those other coaches there."

"I could wear my symphony dress," she said, smiling.

"No," he said, "this is fine, and I do mean *fine*."

Julia was wearing the blue top over a short, black, skinny skirt. Her long, shapely legs were encased in black hose, and she wore the black, high-heeled sandals that made her long legs look even longer. She had said she hadn't worn the sandals much in the past because she didn't want to be taller than her date, but she didn't have to worry about that with him.

David was wearing a handsome blue blazer with a white turtleneck and gray slacks. "That turtleneck and blazer go well together," she said softly. "And I love your cologne. It makes me feel so ... so ..." She groped for a word.

"Sexy," David interjected.

She smiled a flirty smile. "Maybe," she said. He loved that smile. It made him feel ten feet tall, and it let him know that perhaps she was warming up to their relationship. She handed him a beautiful silver lame jacket.

"Is this new?" he asked. "This is really beautiful. If the jacket were a little longer, you wouldn't have to wear a skirt."

"You'd like that, wouldn't you?" she said as she flashed that smile. "If I don't quit buying new clothes to wear out with you, I'll never get my student loans paid off."

"But think of all the fun we're having," he said as he helped into her jacket, and they were off.

The beautiful home of their host was lavishly decorated for Christmas. A uniformed maid opened the door and took their coats. "Mr. Gardner is in the den," she said, and pointed the way.

They went into a large den. A broad-shouldered, heavyset man with graying black hair, dark eyes, and a handsome face was standing behind a bar talking to several others. He came over and shook David's hand. "David, we're so glad you could come." He looked at Julia. "And this is the lovely Dr. Crane, I presume."

"Julia," David said, "this is our host, Phillip Gardner, the director of athletics. We just call him the AD."

"I'm so happy to meet you," she said.

I hope he keeps his hands to himself. If he lays one hand on Julia, I may have to deck him, even if he is my boss, David thought, but Julia expertly intercepted the hand that was headed around her waist and shook it firmly.

"Thank you so much for having us," she said graciously. "Your home is lovely."

"David," Phil said, "have you heard the rumor that's going

around about you and Dr. Crane?" David looked at Julia. She was wide-eyed with surprise and wonder.

"No, Phil, I haven't," he said, "What rumor is that?"

"Some of the athletes were talking about it. They said that you and Dr. Crane have been *fiddling* around together. Is that true?"

"You don't know the half of it, Phil. You don't know the half."

"What are you drinking?" Phil said as he went around behind the bar.

"What do you have?"

"We have beer for the big boys and champagne punch for the sissies."

"I'll have a beer," David said.

"How about a Corona? Want a lime wedge?"

"Sure," David said. "Thanks."

Phil said, "The punch bowl is in the dining room with all the food."

They went into the dining room, where they saw a table filled with delicious things to eat. Julia helped herself to a glass of punch, while David fixed a small plate of food. "Are you going to eat?" he asked.

"Not right now," she said. "I'm not very hungry."

They mingled with the other guests. David introduced Julia to several of the coaches and their wives. He whispered to Julia, "I hope I can keep all the names straight, since I'm the new guy in town. At least here's someone we know." His uncle Ralph and aunt Ophelia came toward them.

Dr. Jennings said, "David, it's good to see you here, and ..." He looked surprised. "Dr. Crane, I didn't recognize you at first."

David said, "Aunt Ophelia, you remember Julia Crane."

"You look lovely, Mrs. Jennings," Julia said, "and it's good to see you too, Dr. Jennings."

Ophelia took Julia's hand warmly and said, "Thank you, my dear.

I am so happy to see you again." She turned to David. "Caroline is so looking forward to having you home for Christmas."

Ophelia went on happily, "And the concert last Sunday was wonderful. We enjoyed it immensely."

"Come along, Ophelia," Dr. Jennings said brusquely. "We'll be late."

"We're off to a dinner party," Ophelia said. "There's so much going on at Christmas. It's hard to take in everything. I guess we'll see you at your parents' for Christmas brunch." And they left.

"Did you think Uncle Ralph was a little abrupt?"

"Well, maybe."

"He was probably upset because you didn't have on a top up to your chin, three petticoats, and a skirt down to your ankles," David said. "Would you like to go out for dinner?"

"No," she said. "Why don't we go back to the apartment. I'll make an omelet or something."

"That sounds like a winner." David saw Phil standing by the door. "Sorry, we have to go," David said. "Thanks for having us."

"Yes," Julia said. "Everything was wonderful."

"Say," Phil said, "how did you make out with the McKinney kid in Alabama?"

"Very well," David said. "His parents were impressed with the rate our premed students are accepted into medical schools. He's a great talent and a good student. We should be able to keep him for four years."

"Great job," he said. "Let's get together with Rusty after Christmas and talk about whom to offer scholarships."

"Fine," David said. "We should be back by Friday."

In the car, he said, "That Phil is a comedian. I hope you weren't offended by what he said."

She laughed. "Let's face it, David. We have been fiddling around a lot and for several weeks now."

Not as much as I would like.

After dinner, they sat on the couch. "Can you be ready to leave by Monday morning?" David asked. "I still have some work to do before I can leave."

She said, "I have to grade my finals, calculate my grades, and email them to the academic dean. I think I can finish all that by tomorrow. I want to finish my cookie baking on Sunday afternoon."

"What?"

"I'm taking everyone a gift box of cookies and candy. The dough is all made. All I have to do is bake them."

"You know Dad is diabetic, don't you?"

"Yes, I know. I found some heart-healthy recipes online. He's getting sugar-free chocolate chip cookies. I even found some sugar-free chocolate chips. Why don't you come over and help me on Sunday afternoon? You could box cookies."

"What about taste testing?

"You can do that too."

"I never knew how much I would miss you until I was gone a few days," he said as he put his arm around her. "You know, as a coach, I'll be going away at lot during basketball season."

"I know," she said. "And I'll be so happy when you get back home."

"I want to rephrase a question I asked you a few weeks ago," he said as he pulled her onto his lap. "Do you think you could ever love a basketball coach?"

She looked up at him and smiled as he drew her closer to him. He could feel her beating heart against his chest.

"In a heartbeat," she whispered, just before her lips met his. He kissed those beautiful lips, her chin, her neck, and those lovely white shoulders. She returned his kisses eagerly. Was that a signal that she wanted to take things further? He felt as if he had won another battle, maybe even the whole damn war.

Based on her past experience with sex, he hadn't been sure she would even want a romantic relationship. He had felt a pang of compassion when she told him about her previous lover. He must have been a selfish dolt not to have considered her feelings.

He really wanted to tell her how much he loved her, but he was afraid it might scare her off. He had thought that the difference in their races might make a difference, but evidently it didn't. He would wait until he was sure she felt the same about him. He planned to show her how much he cared for her and how special she was to him. He would show her that sex was the ultimate fulfillment of love.

She might even be receptive to his advances now. He was not sure, but this was not the time. He wanted to be able to love her all night long with no interruptions. No, as much as he wanted to stretch out on that extra-long couch with her naked in his arms, this was not the time. He could be patient. He ran his hand down her hip. God, how he loved this woman!

He held her close and ran his fingers through her long, silky hair. He smelled the sweetness of her body against him. He rubbed his hand across her bare back and felt the heat of her creamy white skin. "Thanks again for going with me tonight," he said. "I'm not much for socializing, but this was something I needed to do."

"Of course," she said. "It looks like we're now officially a couple." He kissed her again. "Okay, I'll see you Sunday," she said.

"Looking forward to it," he said. *I think I'll go home, do twenty laps around the athletic dorm, and take a cold shower.*

Chapter 18

Julia lay in bed. She should be getting up, but her bed was so warm and cozy she couldn't resist staying a little longer. She kept remembering the night before, how David had held her and kissed her so tenderly. It was wonderful. She had to admit that if David had attempted to strip her naked and have his way with her, she wouldn't have stopped him. She wondered what it would be like to be in bed, totally naked, with a man. The thought of his hands on her bare body filled her with feelings of joy and desire.

The brief encounters she had previously were in his car and had little to do with loving or making love. But things would be different with David. She just knew. "David loves me." There, she had said it. David loved her, and she loved David.

"Enough of these daydreams," she said as she got out of bed. "I have to get my grades done." She was excited about going to David's parents' again and wanted to be ready on time.

David came over on Sunday afternoon. She had made chocolate chip and oatmeal raisin cookies. She found that he was very good at scooping balls of dough and putting them on the cookie sheet. She was busy making peanut butter balls. These were her father's favorite candy. They were crunchy peanut butter, graham cracker crumbs, butter, and powdered sugar rolled together in a ball and dipped in chocolate. She had already rolled the balls and put them in the freezer for a few minutes to harden. Then she dipped them into a pot of melted chocolate, lifted them out, and put them on a rack to dry.

David walked over to where she was working. "Babe, I think there's something wrong with those chocolate balls."

"What?" she said, looking carefully at the candy. "They look okay to me."

"I think I need to try one. You wouldn't want to give my family bad chocolate, would you?"

"Of course not."

He popped one in his mouth. "I'm not sure," he said with a solemn face. "I think I should try another. There's something about them that I need to check out." He popped another in his mouth.

After he had tried two more, she said, "If you don't make up your mind soon, I'm going to have to make another batch."

"I take my job as taste tester very seriously. But that might be a good idea," he said. "Those little gems will not last long. My brother-in-law will inhale these."

They boxed all the cookies and made another batch of chocolate, peanut butter balls. David said, "Why don't I help you clean up the kitchen, and then we can go to Hamburger Heaven for a burger and fries."

"Okay," she said, "but I'm surprised you have any room for a burger after all those chocolate balls you ate."

"How about a chocolatey, peanut buttery kiss?"

"Anytime."

After dinner, David said, "Don't forget to take warm clothes and your snow boots. We usually have snow around Christmas. We need to return home on Thursday. I have a meeting with Rusty and Phil on Friday afternoon. I'll pick you up around ten o'clock tomorrow morning."

Monday, they arrived at the Cooper house in the middle of the afternoon. As they were taking their bags up the stairs, Carolyn said, "Julia, dear, do you mind sleeping in the upstairs study? There's a nice daybed there. I would put David there, but his feet would hang off the end, and I need to put Alberta and Grant in her old room because they need room for the crib."

"Certainly," Julia said, "I would be happy to sleep anywhere it's convenient for you."

"Julia can sleep with me," David said. "Then you wouldn't have to make up another bed."

"Now David," his Mom said sternly. "You know better than that."

David put his arm around Julia and whispered in her ear, 'I'll get you alone yet, my pretty."

"David, please behave. We have company."

"Yes, Mother," he said contritely, and broadly winked at Julia. "Just trying to be helpful."

His mother shook her head. "He'll never grow up."

I hope not, Julia thought.

Tuesday, after breakfast, Julia was helping Caroline in the kitchen when David came in. "Babe, I need to help Dad with some errands. Will you be okay if I leave you here with Mom?"

"Sure," she said. "I'm sure Caroline can find something for me to do."

"Okay," he said. "We'll be back in a few." He gave Julia a quick kiss. Julia looked at Caroline and saw that she was smiling.

"Caroline, how may I help you?" Julia asked.

"Do you mind chopping some vegetables? I'm going to make the slow cooker full of beef stew for dinner tonight."

"Not at all." Julia peeled and chopped, while Caroline browned meat for the stew.

"You know, when he played professional basketball, he was seldom home for Christmas Day since they almost always had a game then," Caroline said. "Would you like to chop some fruit for the fruit salad while I put together the breakfast casserole for tomorrow?"

"Sure." Julia enjoyed her time with Caroline. She was full of stories about David's childhood.

"He was a handful when he was a little tyke," Caroline said. "He was always into everything, and at times, he was a little too mischievous for his own good."

"I can understand that," Julia said, smiling.

"I sent him to violin lessons so that if he got to be too much, I could tell him to go to his room and practice the violin."

Julia laughed. "I can see David being a curious little boy."

"I had always hoped he would be a violinist, but when he grew to be so tall in high school, I knew he was destined to play basketball. I guess it's my fault for feeding him all those vitamins when he was a baby. But it doesn't matter. I just want him to be happy. I'll have to say, my children have been among my greatest joys in life."

"You have children to be proud of," Julia said. "I believe David is very happy. He seems to really enjoy teaching and coaching."

In the afternoon, Grant and Alberta arrived. Alberta came in and brought the baby.

"There's Grammy's sweet thing," Caroline said as she took the baby.

Al went out and came back with a baby swing. "You might want to take her snowsuit off," Al said as she started to set up the swing. "I think it might be a little warm for the house."

"Julia, will you hold her while I try to get this snowsuit off of her?" Caroline said. "I think it's going to be a two-person job."

"Sure," Julia said hesitantly. She had never held a baby in her entire life. She had no nieces and nephews, and her cousins lived in California. She had never been around a baby. Julia sat and held the baby while Caroline unzipped and unsnapped the jacket, then tugged on the pants. Finally, the baby was free of the warm suit.

What will I do if she cries? But Anna was a chubby, cheerful baby. She laughed and cooed and pulled Julia's hair. "You are a beautiful baby," Julia said to Anna.

David went out to help Grant unload. They brought in a stroller, a high chair, an infant seat, a portable crib, a large diaper bag, and several suitcases. David said, "Is all this stuff really necessary?"

"Al seems to think it is," Grant said, "so I bring it."

David said, "How do you put up with that woman? Why don't you tell her who's boss?"

Grant smiled good-naturedly as he put his arm around Alberta's shoulder and kissed her cheek. "That won't be necessary, David. I think she already knows."

"And it's not you," David said, laughing.

"Right," Grant said as Al made a mocking face at David.

Julia couldn't get over how David and his sister teased and bantered with each other, but she knew there was deep respect and love between them. Would this have been how it was if she had a brother?

David came over and patted Anna on the back. "You know," he said, "it's funny how the homeliest people have the most beautiful babies."

"It's love," Al said, ignoring David's remark. "Love creates beautiful babies." Julia looked at David, and he smiled. "Let's put her in the swing," Al said. "I want her to take a nap." The automatic swing gently rocked to and fro, and soon the baby was fast asleep.

Al said to David, "Let's go down to the church. I want to go over our program for tonight." She turned to Grant. "What are you going to do?"

"I think I'll take a nap. Somebody's child kept me awake last night."

"Okay," she said. "I'll put her in the crib up in the bedroom, and you can nap on the bed."

"What do I do if she wakes up?"

"Just change her and give her to Mom. I'll leave a bottle in the fridge."

As they entered the old stone church, David said, "Al has played on Christmas Eve every year since she was eight years old. I played with her most of the time, but when I was in the pros, I missed a few years."

Ladies were arranging pieces of greenery in the windows around red candles in glass globes. Red and white poinsettias covered the front of the church. The effect was beautiful.

The organist was rehearsing. "Al is going to accompany the choir anthem," David said.

The music they played was gorgeous. Julia sat and marveled at the beautiful sound of Al's old violin and the clear, fluty tones of the pipe organ. Then Al and David played the music they would play before the service started.

After supper, they sat around and talked until it was time for the midnight service. "Mrs. Johnson is going to come over and sit with Anna while we're gone," Caroline said.

"She'll probably sleep the entire time," Al said, "but I'll leave a bottle in case she wakes."

Snow was gently falling as they left for the church. "You can ride with us," David said to his parents. "There's no reason to take another car." Caroline and Albert climbed into the back seat of the truck.

Inside the church, the organ was softly playing. All the candles were lit, and people were filing into the pews. At the front of the church, Al and David came out and began to play carols. They had such perfect intonation and harmony. It was apparent that they had played together for many years. It was such a beautiful introduction to the sacred service.

Julia sat quietly, reflecting on what had transpired in her life the past few months. Was this the life she wanted? She knew it could be hers for the taking. Then the service started. Julia loved the old familiar carols. She didn't have a very good voice, but she loved to sing. David came and slipped into the pew beside her. He heard his wonderful baritone singing beside her.

She heard the readings of the Christmas story. The minister began his sermon. The subject was "Love Came Down at Christmas." He read the scripture from First Corinthians. "'Love is patient. Love is kind. It does not envy. It does not boast.'" She felt David reach for her hand. She looked at him, and he smiled at her. The minister went on, "'Love always protects, always trusts, always hopes, always perseveres.'" She couldn't believe how much those words described David and his love for her. "'Love never fails.'" And later, "'These three things remain, faith, hope and love. But the greatest of these is love.'" He concluded with, "Jesus Christ brought love into the world to show us that we should love one another as he loved us."

Then Al accompanied the choir as they sang "O Holy Night." Julia's heart was full of thanksgiving to the Savior who had come into the world to teach love, and thanks to this wonderful man who had shown her what love was all about. She need never feel alone or afraid again, as she had when her father died, if she would only accept his love.

As they walked out of the church, the snow had stopped, and the air was cool and fresh. The moon shone brightly. It reflected off the snow and illuminated the area as if it were midday. "Would you like to do something foolish?" David asked.

"What?"

"Let's walk home," he said. "It's only about ten blocks. Al and I used to walk to the church all the time when we were kids." He added, "Are you dressed warmly enough?"

"I think so," she said as she pulled out her wool hat and gloves. "I'm game if you are."

David gave his dad the keys to the truck and his violin. "We'll see you in a little while," he said to his parents. He put his arm around Julia, and they set off down the street. They felt the crunch of the snow under their boots and felt the chilly air on their faces. They marveled at the covering of snow on the trees.

Julia said, "It looks as if a giant hand spread cake frosting over the trees. Everything is so beautiful."

"Yes," he said, "the snow makes everything seem so clean and fresh, as if it's covering the problems of the world." They stopped at a street corner. Julia looked up and saw that the snow was softly coming down, again. The streetlight behind the snow made it appear as if thousands of tiny, sparkly jewels were falling from the sky.

"I love you so much," he said. "When I heard the minister describing love, I knew he was describing you."

"And I thought of how much I love you," she said.

"Merry Christmas, darling," he said and then kissed her.

"Should we be kissing on a city street?" she asked.

"Why not?" he asked. "I want the whole, wide world to know that I love you!" David put both arms around her, hugged her close, lifted her off the ground, and swung her around. Then he put her down and kissed her.

When they got back to the Coopers' house, Caroline was serving hot, mulled cider and fruitcake. It was a beautiful ending to a very special day. When Julia went to bed, she knew she had some thinking to do. She knew she loved David, but was she ready for marriage?

Chapter 19

Julia was awake. She listened. The entire house was quiet. She lay snuggled in the warm bed, thinking about the love she felt for David and his entire family. She was amazed at how they had welcomed her into their lives. Was it because they knew David loved her?

She heard the sound of a crying baby. *It looks as if someone else is awake too.* The crying continued. Julia got up, put on her robe and slippers, and walked quietly down the hall. She tapped softly on the door, then opened it a crack. Anna was still crying. Al looked as if she was trying to wake up, but Grant was dead to the world.

Julia whispered softly, "I'm awake. Do you want me to take the baby, so you can get some more sleep?"

"Oh, that would be lovely," Al said. "There are diapers and a package of wipes on the chair. There's a bottle in the fridge. Thank you so much." She fell back on the bed.

Julia walked over to the crib and picked up Anna, the diapers, and a small blanket. She took her back down the hall to the bathroom and put the blanket on the counter. She laid the baby on the counter and began to remove the diaper.

"You are one wet little girl," she said.

David stuck his head into the bathroom. "What are you doing?"

"Changing the baby. Come in and help me."

"Do you know how?"

"No," she said. "But I'll figure it out." Anna kicked and cooed happily. David talked to Anna while Julia bathed the tiny bottom with a wipe, put a diaper under the baby, and fastened the tabs.

"Looks like a professional job," he said.

"I'm going to take the baby downstairs and give her a bottle. Why don't you come too?"

"Okay. Give me a minute to get some clothes on."

Julia went down to the kitchen and removed a bottle from the refrigerator. The bottle felt cold. "I really should try to warm it a little," she said to Anna, "but how does one warm a baby bottle?" She finally decided to hold the bottle under the hot water tap for a while. Somewhere, she had seen someone put a drop of milk on their wrist to test the temperature. She tried that. The milk seemed to be warm enough.

Julia went into the family room area and sat in a rocking chair beside a huge, beautifully decorated Christmas tree. She offered the bottle to Anna. She took it hungrily and looked up at Julia with smiling brown eyes. *My babies could have beautiful brown eyes.*

David came in. "Didn't you make coffee?"

"I didn't have enough hands," she said.

"I guess I'll have to do it," he said in mock exasperation. He put water and coffee into the coffee maker, then came over and kissed her. "Is it okay if I turn on the lights of the Christmas tree? We've had these lights that twinkle for as long as I can remember." He flipped a switch, and the tree was ablaze with light.

"They're beautiful," she said, "and so calming. I love them."

"Was there any of your fruitcake or oatmeal cookies left from last night? Mom said we were having brunch at eleven, but if anyone wanted anything to eat before then, they would have to fix it themselves."

"I believe there are some left, and Al brought two pumpkin pies."

"Pumpkin pie, cookies, and fruitcake. I can survive on that."

They sat quietly, enjoying the stillness of the early morning. The twinkling lights had a mesmerizing effect. Anna finished her bottle and was sleeping. Julia looked down at the sleeping child. She felt so calm and peaceful. Could she see herself holding her and David's child? Somehow the thought did not seem so foreign as it might have a few weeks ago.

After a while, Grant came down. He looked at his daughter, sleeping on Julia's lap. "It doesn't take much to make her happy, a dry diaper and a bottle of milk. We get about two hours per eight ounces. Thanks for taking her. Al has been worn out lately with all the extra music she's been doing. She needs the rest."

Grant brought an infant seat. "Let's put her in this," he said as he set the seat in a large, overstuffed chair. He took the baby, placed her into the chair, and fastened the safety straps. "She won't nap long. She'll be awake and hungry again before you know it. Speaking of which," he said to David. "What are you eating?"

"Pumpkin pie, cookies, and fruitcake."

"That sounds good to me," Grant said.

Julia laughed. "While you two are pigging out, I'm going to go get dressed."

When she came back downstairs, everyone was up, drinking coffee and eating fruitcake and cookies. David said, "I made a cup of tea for you."

"Thank you so much," she said.

"We need to gather around and open presents," Caroline said. "It's nearly ten o'clock. Ralph and Ophelia will be here for brunch at eleven."

David passed out the boxes of cookies and candy. "I made these treats for everyone," he said. Then he added, "With a little help from Julia."

Al laughed. "And just what did you do?"

"A very important job. I taste tested, and I put the cookies in the box."

"Mr. Albert," Julia said, "your cookies are sugar-free so you can enjoy them without worrying about the sugar."

"Thank you very much," he said. "I love good cookies."

"I hope mine are not sugar-free," Grant said.

"No, darling," Al said. "Keep eating cookies, and there will be more of you to love."

Julia gave Anna two CDs of classical music designed for babies. "Those are so neat," Al said. "Now Anna will be a Mozart expert by the time she's old enough for Suzuki. Thank you."

She gave Caroline a cookbook from her favorite TV chef. The Coopers gave her a beautiful blue sweater, and Al and Grant gave her blue silk scarf to match the sweater. "David said blue was your favorite color," Caroline said.

"Yes, it's beautiful. Thank you all so very much." Julia gave David a new wallet and a beautiful sweater. "I noticed your old wallet was getting a little frayed," she said. "I thought you could use a new one."

"It looks like that's all the gifts on the tree," Albert said. "Merry Christmas, everyone."

"There's one more," David said as he pulled a small box out of his pocket. Everyone looked in anticipation. Was he giving her a ring? Julia hoped not. As much as she loved David, she was still not ready to make a decision about marriage. Her mind was racing in several different directions. She didn't want to refuse him in front of his family, and she didn't want to accept either. She looked at Caroline. Her eyes were shining, and she had a happy smile on her face. *How could David do this without talking to me first? And how will my mother take the news?*

Julia opened the box hesitantly and gasped in delight. It was earrings. Each one held a blue sapphire with two pearls and a small diamond on each side. Each had two small dangles of white gold with a pearl at the end. "I thought you needed something to wear with the blue top," he said.

"They are precious. Thank you very much," she said. "What have I done to deserve such a beautiful gift?"

"Just for being you," he said. "Just for being you." He kissed her soundly.

Just then, Ralph and Ophelia arrived. "They have been to Terre Haute to spend Christmas with Kristin and Edwin," David told Julia. "They always stop by our place so that Uncle Ralph can spend some time with us. He is Mom's only brother."

Caroline set a lovely brunch table. They had ham, a breakfast casserole of sausage and eggs, biscuits with ham gravy, fruit salad, cinnamon rolls, and pancakes. "When David, Grant, and Ralph start eating," Caroline said, "I'm never sure I will have enough. But I like to see men with healthy appetites. Thanks to Julia's fruitcake and cookies," she said as she patted Julia's arm, "I didn't have to cook breakfast." Julia couldn't help but notice how much Caroline seemed to care for her. *I hope I'm not going to disappoint her.*

After brunch, David said, "Come on, babe. Let's go for a walk. I need to get a little exercise so I can come back and have a cinnamon roll." He said to his Mom, "Can you spare Julia for a little while?"

"Certainly," Caroline said. "She cooked all day yesterday. Now, you two had better bundle up. It could be getting colder out."

David and Julia put on their snow boots, hats, and coats. David took her gloved hand in his and led her out the back door across the lawn. The sun was shining brightly, but there was a chill in the air. Their warm breaths made little clouds of frost when they spoke. They passed a huge vegetable garden, plowed and covered with snow, ready for spring planting. David said, "That garden is Dad's pride. He works in it every day in the summer."

Thick woods with tall, bare-branched trees and huge evergreens ran behind the garden. They followed a path between the trees. A thick layer of snow covering the leaves crunched beneath their feet. "Our property goes down to the creek. When Grandpa built here, this land was out of town, but the town has moved out to us," David said.

"The woods are beautiful," Julia said. "It's so quiet and peaceful. Thanks for sharing them with me."

"Dad has had several opportunities to sell them, but I hope he won't." They passed a tall tree with remnants of a tree house in the upper branches. "My friends and I used to play here." A squirrel stuck his head out of a hole in an oak tree and scolded them for invading his territory. They saw tracks of other small animals in the snow. Cardinals and blue jays perched in the smaller bushes searching for seeds and berries.

They continued down the path to the creek. The stream was flowing freely, despite an inch or so of ice along the banks. "Are you okay?" David asked. "Not too cold?"

"No, I'm fine. This is wonderful," she said, squeezing his hand. They followed the creek to a gravel road that led back to highway.

When they returned to the house, David and Julia came in through the garage door and removed their boots in the hall. Julia removed her hat, coat, and gloves. "I'm taking these upstairs. Shall I take yours too?"

"Sure," he said as he handed her his things. He walked into the kitchen and noticed that the dishes from brunch were still stacked on the counters.

Al was spooning a soft-looking goo into Anna's mouth. Anna chirruped like a little bird and opened her mouth wide. "She loves applesauce," Al said.

"What's going on?" he asked.

"Dad and Grant are watching the Pacers game. Mom is lying down."

David had a feeling that something was amiss. "Is Mom sick?"

"No," Al said. "She's upset. She and Uncle Ralph had a row."

"A row?" David asked incredulously. "Whatever about?"

"You."

"Me? What have I done now?"

"You have fallen in love with a white girl without asking Uncle Ralph's permission."

"And he's upset about that. I don't think it's any of his business," David said emphatically.

"He says you'll never get a coaching job in the South if you have a white wife."

"I can't believe that. No one thinks anything about a biracial marriage anymore."

"Well, Uncle Ralph does," Al said. "You need to realize that Uncle Ralph, as president of the university, holds your future in his hands. You wouldn't be able to get a job anywhere without his recommendation."

"Well, I don't have to stay at Chapman to have a job or even have his recommendation."

"I know," Al said, "but what about Julia? She would find it hard get another job without a good recommendation from Chapman."

David shook his head, as if he couldn't believe what he was hearing. "Did they go on home?"

"Yes. Dad asked Uncle Ralph to leave because he was getting so rude and obnoxious that he was upsetting Mom. I don't think you've heard the last of it. Aunt Ophelia was upset too. You know she and Mom are very close."

"Please don't tell Julia about this," David whispered. "I hear her coming." He said louder, "Why don't we clean up the kitchen for Mom."

"Okay," Al said. "Let me fix a bottle for Anna, and Grant can give it to her while he watches the game."

Julia came into the kitchen. David was rinsing plates and putting them in the dishwasher. "Mom isn't feeling well," he said, "so Al and I going to clean up the kitchen."

"You're a sweetheart," she said to David as she kissed his cheek and picked up a dish towel.

He looked at Al. She rolled her eyes and said, "Isn't love grand?"

"You better know it," he said cheerfully, hoping his face didn't show the concern he felt.

Chapter 20

Julia woke up early the next day. She showered, dressed, and hurried to the kitchen. She saw David and Albert, with aprons on, standing in front of the range. "What are you guys cooking?" she asked.

"Breakfast, my love," he said, coming over and kissing her.

"I could live on that," she said.

Caroline came into to the kitchen, still wearing her robe. "Why didn't you wake me?" she said.

"You did enough cooking yesterday, Mom," he said. "We thought we would give you a little extra sleep."

After breakfast, David came back into the kitchen. Julia was helping Caroline clear the breakfast dishes. "Babe, I checked the weather. It looks like we're going to have some snow. The weather channel said Indianapolis and points south would be hit by several inches. I think we really need to head to Kentucky as soon as possible. Maybe we can get home before it hits. I have a meeting with Phil tomorrow."

"Whatever you think," she said. "I can be packed in ten minutes." She turned to Caroline. "Thank you so much for having me. This has been a wonderful Christmas, the best in a long time."

Caroline said, "We were so happy to have you, my dear. Come back anytime." Then she added quietly to Julia, "It does my heart good to see David with a special friend."

The sky was overcast as they loaded their luggage into the truck. Clouds in shades of gray layered the southwestern sky, and there was a certain dampness in the air. "Sure looks like snow," David said.

They had been driving about an hour when the snow began to fall. At first, it was like large grains of sand, thin and powdery.

Suddenly, the flakes grew larger, fat and gloppy. They smacked the windshield fiercely, and many of them stuck like glue. The fierce wind swept across the highway and blew harder. It hurled blobs of snow against the laboring windshield wipers.

"Can you see?" Julia asked.

"Just barely," David said. "No more than five feet in any direction." The wind swirled the snow round and round like a miniature tornado. The air was consumed with blowing particles of whiteness. Just then, the lights of a slow-moving truck appeared in front of them. "I think I'll just stay behind the truck," David said. "At least it's something I can see." Everyone was driving very slowly. "It looks like we're making about twenty miles per hour."

Julia saw that the snow was piling up by the side of the road and realized how dangerous the roads were becoming, and she was worried. But what would David think of her if she asked him to stop? Finally, caution won out. "David, do you think we should stop?"

"It would probably be a smart thing to do. I don't think it's going to get any better," he said. "See if you can find a hotel at Exit 76. We're about twenty miles away. I think there are several large hotels at that exit."

She took out her phone and checked the internet. "There are three hotels at that exit," she said.

"Good. See if you can find one with an extra-long bed."

After the second call, she said, "I found a room that has the bed, but it's a suite, and it's quite expensive.

"That's okay," he said. "Book it."

"But, David, it's very expensive."

"Do you want to sleep in the truck tonight?" he said sternly.

"N–no," she said with a quivering voice.

"Then book the room. The way people are stopping, it may be the only room available." He reached into his jacket pocket and pulled out his wallet. "Take out the credit card in the first slot and give them the number."

She did as she was told and said, "That's taken care of. We have a room for the night."

He reached over and took her hand. He raised it to his lips and tenderly kissed it. "Thank you, my love. I would have never let you sleep in the truck."

She sat back in the seat. She loved it when he kissed her hand. It was his special way of telling her he loved her. *In all my life, what have I ever done to deserve this beautiful, special man?* She was still concerned about the weather, but she knew that David would take care of her, and she tingled at the thought. *It might be exciting to spend the night in a hotel room with David.* Was that something she was ready for? In a heartbeat.

The snow came down faster as they followed the truck to the exit. "I'm sure glad we're not driving the Porsche," he said. "The truck has four-wheel drive and heavy tires."

They found the hotel and pulled into the driveway and under the portico. There was a huge truck stop across the road and a steak house restaurant beside the hotel. "Can you take the violins? We can't leave them out in this weather."

They entered the lobby, and David headed to the front desk. The clerk, a young man in his early twenties, said, "Good afternoon, Mr. Cooper. How are you today?" Then he added, "Say, aren't you D. J. Cooper?"

"I used to be," David said.

"That's right. I heard that you retired from the Pacers. What are you doing now? Still in basketball, I hope."

"Oh yes," he said. "I'm coaching at Chapman."

"I should have known you were a basketball player when your wife asked for an extra-long bed," the clerk said as he handed David his room key. "Your room is right down the hall, room 105. The breakfast buffet is open from 6:00 a.m. until 9:00 a.m."

"Okay, thanks," David said.

The clerk continued, "You know, you're lucky. Rooms are going fast. This room was last one with an extra-long bed. Well, we're glad to have you. Please let me know if you need anything."

"You know," Julia said as she followed David down the hall, "you weren't exactly honest with that man."

"Does that bother you?"

"Not in the least," she said.

"He made a reasonable assumption, my love," said David. "I saw no need to correct him." Then he added, "Besides, everyone thinks I should have a wife."

He opened the door to a gorgeous sitting room with a couch and end tables along one wall. A TV and desk were on the opposite wall. On an adjacent wall, there was a coffee bar, microwave oven, and a refrigerator. A small, round table with chairs sat at the end of the couch, while a bed as large as a small swimming pool stood in the next room.

"Babe, I'm going to go park the truck and get our bags. I'm starved. Let's go find something to eat before we settle in for the night. I think the steak house next door is open."

When they returned from dinner, David saw a radio on the bedside table. "See if you can find a station that has local weather."

Julia turned on the radio and heard a voice say, "This is station WCLS 97.7 on your FM dial, Bloomington. Twelve inches of snow are predicted for southern Indiana tonight and tomorrow. Many of the roads south of Bloomington are already closed. We will return to our regularly scheduled programming."

The music came on with a beautiful ballad. Two singers with smooth, sexy voices sang, "Tonight I celebrate my love for you." David took her in his arms and held her close as he whirled her around the room. He twirled her under his arm, then pulled her close as they danced around the bed.

"Babe, are you okay with all this?" he asked, indicating the bed and the room. "I don't want you to feel uncomfortable."

"I'm okay with everything," she said.

"I can always sleep on the couch, you know."

"What? And waste that beautiful bed."

"I have to warn you," he said. "If I spend the night with you in that bed, I might want to do something besides sleep."

The song went on, "Tonight, we will discover how friends turn into lovers."

"Promise?" she said softly and raised her face to his kisses.

Finally, he said, "I just want everything to be perfect the first time we make love."

And it was.

Chapter 21

Julia awoke to the smell of coffee and the sound of the shower running in the bathroom. She turned onto her back and stretched like a cat in the sun, luxuriating in the soft, warm bed. She sat up and listened. The shower was still running. She lay back against the pillows and closed her eyes, remembering how great last night was. Being in bed, naked with David, was every bit as incredible as she had imagined. She was amazed at the wonderful feeling of joy and happiness that flooded over her. She could still feel David's tender touch as he caressed her naked body, and his gentle mouth as his kisses aroused her. And finally, when their bodies joined, it was as if their very souls were entwined. She wondered if waking up with David every day would be like this. She felt safe and secure in his strong arms. She felt wanted and needed, and best of all, she felt loved.

Just then, David came out of the shower with a towel wrapped around his slim waist. She couldn't believe how broad and heavily muscled his upper body was. He looked at her. "So," he said, "the wanton woman that robbed me of my sleep is awake?"

She lifted the covers. "You can always come back to bed and take a nap," she said.

"Can't, babe. I'm starving. I have to go get some food," he said as he dug in his bag for some clean clothes.

She looked at the clock. "Where are you going for food? The breakfast buffet closed at nine."

"The truck stop," he said. "They always have food." He pulled back the drapes and looked out. "My gosh. It's still snowing. I bet there's a foot out there, and the wind is blowing like crazy."

She watched as he pulled on corduroy jeans and a turtleneck tee. He put on a sweatshirt and his snow boots. Then he donned a fleece-lined anorak and a fur hat with ear flaps.

She laughed. "You look like Nannook of the North."

He flexed his muscles. "Mighty Hunter go to find food." Then he grinned. "The weather channel on my phone says the temperature is twenty-two degrees out there."

"Be careful, Mighty Hunter."

"You might want to get your beautiful body out of bed and make another pot of coffee," he said as he sat on the bed and took her in his arms. "I love you."

"I love you too," she said as he looked up into his face. "Last night was incredible," she whispered.

"Now do you know what love is?" he asked, then kissed her and left.

She smiled as she got up, showered, and dressed in wool slacks and a heavy sweater. She pulled on heavy socks and boots. Then she made a pot of coffee and turned to the weather channel on TV.

The weatherman announced, "We have blizzard conditions in Southern Indiana. Twelve to fifteen inches of snow has fallen in the last eighteen hours between Bloomington and the Kentucky line. All major roads in that area are closed until further notice."

Just then, she heard a knock on the door. She opened it, and David stood there with two large bags. He sat them on the table and removed his coat and hat. "It's bad, bad out there," he said. "There's nothing moving except the wind." He reached into a bag and pulled out two large cups. "Orange juice." Out came a disposable bowl. "Raisin bran, a banana, and skim milk," he said as he set each item on the table.

"Thank you, my love," she said. "What's in the other bag?"

He flexed his muscles again. "Mighty Lover need real food." He started removing items from the second bag. "Sausage and egg biscuits, tater tots, and cinnamon rolls," he said as he set the items on the table.

"How about some coffee?" she said. Then she giggled and shook her head at his antics. "David, you are too much."

He came around the table to where she was pouring coffee. "Come here," he said. She set down the cups as he took her in his arms and held her close. He said softly, "It's okay if I'm too much, as long I'm enough. I want to be everything that you will ever want or need for the rest of your life."

She stood quietly, overcome with emotion. When he spoke to her like that, her heart wanted to melt into a small puddle at his feet. "You do a good job of it," she whispered.

After breakfast, David said, "I need to call Mom and let her know we're okay. I also have to call Phil Gardner. I don't think I'm going to make that one o'clock meeting in Hoover."

Julia said, "Okay, I'm going to see if they have a guest laundry. I'm running out of clean clothes."

As soon as Julia left, David punched in the numbers. The phone rang. "Hi, Mom. It's David." He punched the speakerphone button.

"Oh, David, did you make it home before the snow hit? They say it's really bad south of Bloomington."

"No, Mom, that's where we are. The snow came in a little sooner than they thought. We're at a hotel beside the interstate. It was getting too dangerous to drive farther, and now the road is closed."

"I'm just glad you're okay," Caroline said.

"It may be a day or two before the roads are opened."

"You just stay there until the roads are safe."

"Yes, Mom," he said dutifully. "Say, what's this I hear about you giving Uncle Ralph a hard time?"

"Me? It was him giving me a hard time. That man makes me so mad! He thinks he can tell everybody what to do."

"I know, Mom," David said calmly. "Al told me all about it."

"Do you think there's any truth to what he's saying? Would marrying Julia really keep you from getting a good coaching job?"

"I doubt it," David said. "There will always be someone somewhere who doesn't think we belong together, but biracial marriages are accepted almost everywhere now."

"Well, I hope so," Caroline said. "You know how much we love Julia. I told him to just keep his nose out of your business. Unless what you do affects the university, I can't see where he has a say in the matter." She added, "And I can't see how who you marry will affect the university."

"I'm sorry he was rude to you, but don't worry about it, Mom. Things will work out okay, but I don't want Julia to know about this."

"I know, honey," she said. "I was too embarrassed to mention it before you left. I don't want him making things difficult for Julia."

"Don't worry, Mom. I won't let it happen. I'll call you as soon as we get home. I love you." He hung up, wondering what he could do about Uncle Ralph.

He punched in Phil's number. "Hey, David," Phil said. "Where are you?"

"Hi, Phil. I'm still in Indiana. We have over a foot of snow here."

"Don't kid me," Phil said. "I bet you're somewhere shacked up in a hotel with the lovely Dr. Crane."

"I'm serious, Phil. The roads south are all closed. I don't know when I'll be there."

"Okay, buddy," he said. "Call me when you get back in town. But I still think if you had any sense, you would be shacked up somewhere with Dr. Crane."

"You're right about that. I'll call you when I get back to Hoover." David laughed as he punched the "end call" button.

"What's funny?" Julia asked as she came back into the room.

"Phil," David said. "He said if I had any sense, I would be shacked up in a hotel somewhere with you."

"Oh, David, you didn't tell him, did you?"

"Not on your life. Phil Gardner would be the last person in the world I would want to know that I was in a hotel room with you." Then he paused. "No, that's not quite right. Uncle Ralph would be the last."

Chapter 22

Saturday, David returned from the truck stop with breakfast to find Julia still in bed. Friday had passed quickly, and the night was even more incredible than the previous one had been. "The temperature is up to thirty-eight degrees," he said. "The wind has died down, and the snowplows are starting to work on the road. They hope to have the roads open to the Kentucky line by tomorrow."

After breakfast, David found a college basketball game on the television. Julia snuggled up beside him on the couch, and he explained the strategy of the game. "That coach must go to a zone defense. His two best players have three fouls each. They can't continue to defend man-to-man."

"Are you sure you're right?" she asked.

"No." He laughed. "The coach knows the strengths of his players better than I do, but he's losing. He needs to try something different." He continued to explain the fine points of the game to her. He was thrilled that she seemed to find it interesting.

After the game was over, he said, "Let's go for a walk. The sun is shining brightly, and it doesn't seem too bad outside. It's probably still a little chilly though. You might want to dress warmly." They walked down the street that ran beside the hotel. Chunks of snow were falling from the trees, and the ice on the street was beginning to be a little slushy. After several more blocks, David pointed to a sign on a building on the next street over. "There's my favorite pizza place. How about a pizza for lunch?"

"Fine," Julia said. "I'm about to get hungry."

After lunch, they decided to return down the same street that the pizza place was on. David said, "This is a beautiful part of town, lots of tall trees and lovely old houses." Soon, they came to a park. There were picnic tables, park benches, and lots of playground equipment. Near the street, they saw a basketball court that was covered in snow. Icicles hung dripping from the goals. Three young boys, wearing warm coats, mittens, and toboggan hats, were rolling big balls of snow. David walked over. "Hi, guys," he said. "You've really got a good snowman going. Can I help?"

"Sure," they said.

He turned to Julia. "Do you want to build a snowman?"

"No, you go ahead," she said as she brushed the snow off a bench and sat. "I think I'll just watch."

"I'm David," he said to the kids, "and that's Julia."

"Hi, David. Hi, Julia," they said.

One boy in a red wool cap seemed to be the spokesman. He said, "I'm Peyton, that's Josh, and he's Hoops." He pointed to a smaller kid with curly hair and black-rimmed glasses. "His real name is Harold, but we call him Hoops because he knows so much about basketball."

David started rolling a big ball of snow. Hoops took a step back and looked appraisingly at David. "Say," he said, "you look like D. J. Cooper."

"That's right. I am D. J. Cooper."

Josh motioned to the others, and they huddled a few feet away.

Then Peyton came forward. "Sir, we don't think you're D. J. Cooper," he said politely.

"Oh," David said, "why not?'

Josh said, "Two years ago, my dad took me to the Field House in Indianapolis to see the Pacers. D. J. Cooper was a lot taller than you."

"That's because I'm wearing all these clothes. They make me look shorter." The boys huddled again. David looked at Julia. He saw her hand in front of her face. He knew that behind her hand, she was laughing her head off.

Peyton came back. "We're going to give you one more chance. Hoops is going to ask you a question."

Hoops stepped closer. "In 2015, in the Eastern Conference Championship game, D. J. Cooper made a whole bunch of foul shots in a row." Hoops set up the question as skillfully as if he were Alex Trebek asking the Final Jeopardy question. "How many foul shots did D.J. Cooper make in that game, and who did the Pacers defeat for the championship?"

David said, "I'll have to think about this." The boys gave each other knowing looks. "In that game, I made thirty-six foul shots in a row, and we defeated the New York Knicks."

"And what happened on the thirty-seventh shot?" Hoops asked.

"I missed it, but there were only two seconds left, so we hung on to win by five points."

"Right!" Hoops yelled as he jumped into the air and threw up both hands like a ref signaling for a three-point shot.

Julia and the other boys clapped. Hoops ran up to David. "D. J.," he said, "can you teach me how to make foul shots?"

"I think I can give you some pointers. How old are you, Hoops?"

"I'm eleven, but I'll be twelve next month. I'm really fast, and I can handle the ball real good, but I can't make my foul shots. I'm on the middle school team. We're all on the middle school team."

David said, "It would be better if we had a ball, but we'll make do with what we have." He reached down and scooped up a big glob of snow and packed it into an almost round ball, then handed it to Hoops. "Let me see you shoot." Hoops took the ball and let it fly with a slinging motion. David took another ball of snow. He showed the boys how to position their feet and the proper hand position. Then he let it fly. The ball of snow flew up and through the rim of the goal.

"It's tempting to try to sling the ball, but you must learn to use proper form. Ask your coach to get you a smaller ball for foul shot practice until you're strong enough to use a regular ball." The boys each picked up great globs of snow and fashioned them into balls.

"Watch me, watch me," they said.

David made suggestions and encouraged each boy as he threw shot after shot. Soon they were consistently throwing the snowball through the goal. "You must always practice each shot the proper way until it becomes a habit. Never carelessly throw the ball up."

He looked over at Julia and thought he saw a shiver. "Guys," he said to the group, "I have to go. I think Julia is getting cold. Thanks for letting me play with you."

"Thanks for helping us," Peyton said.

"Boy, our coach will never believe that D. J. Cooper showed us how to shoot foul shots," Hoops said.

"Just a minute," David said, as he walked over to Julia. "Do you have a pen?" She dug into her purse and pulled one out. David took three business cards from his wallet. He wrote a note on each and handed them to the boys.

"David J. Cooper, assistant basketball coach, Chapman State University," Hoops read. Then he turned it over and read again. "To my good friend Hoops. Keep practicing. D. J. Cooper." He saw their faces light up as they read their cards.

"Now, if your coach doesn't believe you, tell him to call that number on the card, and I'll set him straight," David said.

He took Julia's hand, and they set off down the street. "Were you laughing at me?" he asked with an amused smile.

"It's okay, darling," she said. "I know you're the real D. J. Cooper." She added, "That was fun, wasn't it?"

"Yeah, it was," he agreed. "I love kids. They're so honest and so interested. Coaching never seems like work."

When they got back to the hotel, they stopped in the lobby and made hot chocolate from a powdered mix and hot water. They sat on a couch in the lobby and watched a college basketball game on TV while they were drinking their chocolate. David said, "It looks like most of the college teams are back in action. We start our conference schedule on Tuesday with a home game. I think our team will do well. They're starting to play together like a real team." He added, "If we can keep everybody academically eligible."

She said, "I'll give you a copy of my syllabus as soon as I finish, so you can help Cruiser keep track of his assignments."

"You were reading my mind." He felt Julia snuggle closer and hug his arm. He knew he could conquer the world as long as this beautiful lady was by his side. It was time to let her know his plans for the future.

Back in the room, David said, "Come, sit beside me on the couch. I want to talk to you about our future." He took both her hands in his and looked earnestly into her eyes. "I have looked all my life for someone like you," he said. "You are the woman I want for my wife. You are the woman I want for the mother of my children," And finally, he added, "You are the woman I want for my companion for the rest of my life." He saw that tears were welling in her big blue eyes.

He went on, "But I am not going to ask you to marry me." He paused. She looked surprised. "Not for a while anyway. We have only known each other less than three months. I have seen too many of my friends and teammates rush into marriage, only to find after a year or so that their wives could not stand the long separations or the pressure of being a coach's wife, so they filed for divorce. I just want you to know what you'll be getting into before we take the big step.

"I've always wanted to coach, and I know that you've spent many years preparing for your career. I want us to get to know each other a little better and see if our careers can be compatible. I have a big recruiting trip coming up, and then there are the tournaments, so you may not see much of me for a while." He saw that she was listening intently.

"If you should decide that you don't love me anymore, or you can't stand the strain or loneliness of a coach's wife, I'll understand. But if we can make it work, in about three months' time, I will ask you to marry me, and depending on what you say, we'll go from there. If our love can survive the next three months of trips, out-of-town meetings, and the tournaments, it will stand anything."

"And if we can't make it work, would you give up coaching?" she asked.

He looked at her with sadness in his eyes. "Yes, I probably would," he said. "I love you more than anything in the world."

She looked up at him, and tears started rolling down her cheek. "David," she said, "I love you too much to ever ask you to give up coaching. What I witnessed today made me realize how much you love it. We will find a way make it work."

"Yes," he said, "if the world doesn't get in our way."

"What do you mean by that?"

"Outside influences," he said. "My family, your family; my job, your job; people who don't think we belong together. They could all come between us if we let them."

"I want to be your wife. I want to be the mother of your children, but you're right. We do need to wait a little while before we start making plans," she said.

He said, "Our time together here has been incredible, but you know it's coming to an end. We have to head home tomorrow." He gathered her into his arms. "I want you to know that even though we have not made a formal announcement, I consider you to be my fiancée, because I fully intend to marry you. Do you agree?"

"Oh yes," she said and sobbed.

"I'm sorry I made you cry," he said. She sobbed louder. "Why are you crying?"

"'Cause … 'cause I'm so happy." She had no doubt that she wanted to be David's wife, and waiting three months was a good idea. It would give her time to get used to the idea, and it would give her time to convince her mother.

Chapter 23

They slept late again the next morning. Julia packed their bags while David went to get breakfast. "I'll never forget this place," Julia said as they were leaving. "I wish we could stay here forever."

David laughed. "As much fun as I am, I know you would get bored with me before long. I guess we'd better hit the road to reality." They loaded their bags into the truck and were on their way. Beside the highway, snow was piled almost four feet high in some places where it had been pushed by the snowplows. Most of the snow was gone from the highway, but there were still icy patches here and there. The ride home was quiet and uneventful.

When they arrived at Julia's apartment, David carried in her bags. "Would you like to go out to eat tonight?" he asked.

"No," she said. "Why don't I just cook something simple? We've eaten out so much."

"Okay," he said. "I'd rather eat your cooking than anyone else's anyway, but don't tell my mom." Then he said, "I've really gotten used to having you around all the time. I may have to rethink this waiting business." He kissed her. "Okay, I'll see you around six."

Julia went into the kitchen. She thawed out meat, chopped up vegetables, and put the ingredients for a bolognese sauce in the slow cooker. Spaghetti with bolognese sauce would be perfect. She punched in the numbers of Molly's cell phone.

"Julia, is that you?' Molly asked. "I was beginning to get a little worried. Are you home?"

"Yes, we just drove in."

"Have you been at David's parents' all this time?"

Julia laughed. "You'll never guess where we've been the past three days."

When she told her about the snowstorm, Molly said, "I can't believe you actually spent three nights in a hotel room with David. Tell me something. Now, if it's too personal, and you don't want to say, I'll understand. But was David a good lover?"

"You're taking a lot for granted, Molly," she said, laughing. "But yes, he was a wonderful lover. Do you remember that beautiful Romantic tone poem we played with the symphony last year?"

"Yes, I think so," Molly said.

"It started soft and slow and tender with gentle little melodic figures. The harmony builds as more instruments come in. Then it gathers more intensity and passion and finally sweeps you to a spectacular crescendo of joy and pleasure."

"Oh my," Molly gasped. "That sounds wonderful."

"That's how I would describe David's lovemaking."

"Well, I knew that as much in love as you two are, you couldn't spend three nights in a hotel room without getting together."

"How did you know we're in love?"

"Anyone with eyes can see that you two are madly in love. How did you spend that time? Other than going to bed."

"The first day, we watched an old, romantic movie. We got so turned on we stopped the movie and went to bed, right in the middle of the afternoon."

She went on, "The hotel has a great fitness room, so we worked out every day. Then, once, we took our violins to a meeting room no one was using and played together. So many people came by to listen to us that the hotel manager asked us to move to the lobby, so we gave an impromptu concert. It was so much fun, just spending time with David. It was like I imagine a honeymoon would be."

"Julia," Molly said, "with all that sex, are you're sure you're not pregnant?

Julia laughed. "David took care of that. He didn't say anything about it, but he was so caring and considerate, I knew. And when he went to the truck stop in a blinding snowstorm, I knew he wasn't going for windshield wiper blades or sausage biscuits, as he said. He was buying condoms."

"Can you buy them at a truck stop?"

"You can buy anything at a truck stop!" Then she said, "Why don't we get together this week? I need to finish my syllabus and get it to the printer. How about Tuesday afternoon?"

"Sounds great," she said.

When David came to dinner, she told him about her conversation with Molly.

"You were right," he said. "As much as I love you, and as much as I want you to be the mother of my children, I didn't think now was a good time to give Anna a cousin."

"How many children are we talking about?" she asked.

That's negotiable," he said.

"Let's have at least two. I always wanted a brother or a sister, but my parents were never able to give me one."

"I was thinking of more in the order of a basketball team."

"I'll have to think about that," she said.

"Do you want to go out on New Year's Eve?" he asked.

"No," she said. "I'll cook a good dinner, and we can sit on the couch and snuggle until midnight." Then she whispered, "You might need to find another truck stop."

Chapter 24

David's phone rang early Monday morning. It was a call he had been expecting. "Hello, Mr. Cooper. This is Mrs. Mims, Dr. Jennings's assistant."

"Yes, Mrs. Mims, what can I do for you?"

"Mr. Cooper, Dr. Jennings would like to see you this morning. Could you come at eleven o'clock?"

"Yes, I'll be there." David was not looking forward to this meeting, but he might as well get it over with as soon as possible.

"Come in, my boy," Ralph said as David entered the spacious office. The walls were covered with pictures and diplomas. Ralph sat behind a massive mahogany desk. "Sit down, please."

David found a chair. He saw the stern look on his uncle's face. "David, something has come to my attention that disturbs me very much."

"Oh, and what is that?"

"It has come to me on good authority that you and Dr. Crane spent the night together in a hotel last week. Is that true?" Then he added, "I hope you had the good sense to get two rooms."

"That's not exactly true," David said. "Actually, we spent three nights in one room."

"Surely not?" he moaned. "Don't you realize how that hurts the reputation of the university?"

"We were in the middle of a blizzard! We were lucky to get one room, let alone two. Uncle Ralph, Julia and I are adults. We are not teenagers. What we do away from school is our own business."

"But you are representatives of the university. What if someone recognized you? It would embarrass the university if someone saw you in a hotel with someone who wasn't your wife," Ralph said insistently.

"Do you honestly think I can go anywhere in the state of Indiana that I'm not recognized? There's a thirty-foot-high billboard with my picture on it in downtown Indianapolis."

"No, I guess not," Ralph said.

"We saw several people who recognized me, and they saw Julia, and not one person seemed to care if we were married or not. And let me tell you something else. A couple of weeks ago, I visited with two families who are thinking of sending their sons to Chapman. They asked about the academic reputation of the university. They asked about the training facilities and the coaching staff. They asked about the dormitory rooms and the food service. Not once did they ask if there were unmarried teachers who were shacking up together."

"But you never know," Ralph said, "when something of this sort will discourage someone from sending their child to Chapman. We are a small, state-supported school. We have to compete with every other state-supported school in the state of Kentucky for our students. We must be above reproach in every area. Our success depends upon our getting the brightest and most talented students. We have built our success upon two things, academic excellence and winning basketball." Ralph stopped to take a breath.

David slumped in his chair. He felt as if he were a school boy listening to a lecture in the principal's office. "Then, pray tell, why did you waste a scholarship on that academic dud, Cruiser Bell? And more importantly, why was it renewed for this year? He had a 1.8 GPA last year."

"David," Ralph began, "there's something you need to understand. Brandon Bell, Cruiser's father, is the president of our alumni association. We depend on gifts from our alumni to enhance programs that are only marginally funded. Alumni giving is up 100 percent since Brandon has been president. He was instrumental in securing the additional funding for the Marshall Building, as well as a new science lab and twenty new computers. In fact, we have not had to hire a professional fundraiser since Brandon has been president of the association." Ralph took off his glasses and cleaned them on his handkerchief.

"It wouldn't be fair to Brandon if we didn't renew Cruiser's scholarship. We had to pull his older brother's scholarship after just one year."

"And why was that?"

"Marvin was not very talented, and he had several minor scrapes with the law. Brandon shipped him off to the navy before he did something that would get him sent to prison."

"I'm beginning to get the picture," David said, straightening up in his chair. "So we have to put up with Cruiser Bell and make sure he passes all his classes until we can foist him off on the NBA."

"Doesn't Cruiser have the talent to play professional basketball?"

"Sure, he does, if he would just work at it a little. But now he's too lazy to breathe."

"Well, see what you can do, my boy. See what you can do." He paused, then said, "Now what are you going to do about that girl?"

"If you mean Julia," David said, "I love her very much, and I plan to marry her."

"You can't marry her," Ralph said. "She is not the girl for you."

"And who are you to make that decision?"

"You want a home and a family. She wants a career, and besides, it would be devastating to your career."

"And why is that?"

"Because she's white," he said. "You'll never get a job coaching in the South if you have a white wife. Do you think the University of Kentucky would have hired that famous black coach if he had had a white wife?"

"Probably not, but that was twenty-five years ago. Things are a lot different now. And if I can't get a job in the South, I'll go where I can." David turned to go. "And I don't appreciate your harassing my mother about this."

"I wasn't harassing her. I just think she should know what's at stake if you marry that girl. I told her she should stop encouraging the relationship."

"Her name is Julia."

"Surely you don't want to leave this area. I had hopes of you being the head coach of a Division I powerhouse someday. All the schools in the SEC are improving their basketball programs, trying to keep up with Kentucky, and there should be plenty of Big Ten jobs available too." David sat listening quietly. He couldn't believe what he was hearing. But Uncle Ralph was not finished.

"It would break your mother's heart if you weren't close by so she could see her grandchildren grow up."

"Uncle Ralph, Julia and I will work it out. You can't tell me who I can marry and where I should work."

"Now, David, I have always thought of you as the son I didn't have. I just want what's best for you."

"Then let me live my life as I choose," David said as he walked out the door.

Chapter 25

The new semester began on the first Monday in January. Julia got the list of her students for her Music 102 class. It was a continuation of Music 101, and most of the same students had signed up. She would also be teaching an upper-division class on Romantic opera for music majors. She would be coaching the violin section of the orchestra, and she had ten private violin students. This was a lot of work, but she wanted to be busy. She knew David would be away a lot, and she wanted to prove to herself that she could survive when he was gone.

She hurried to her classroom a little before nine. Everything was the same as last semester. She loaded her notes on the PowerPoint program on her computer. It would send the information to the screen at the front of the room. Students were coming in. Carol and Lakeysha were in the class again. Cruiser Bell and the other athletes followed them in and took their usual seats on the back row.

Julia passed out the syllabuses, reminding students that the same policies as last semester were still in effect. "We have five written assignments due before midterm," she said. "I hope everyone will keep up with their assignments. I have included several optional written assignments so you will have some choice in the assignments you choose."

Julia began her lesson. "We will begin the semester with our study of opera." Several students groaned. "Yes, in today's society," she said, "opera is not very popular; however, the purpose of this class is to teach you about how music of the past has influenced the music we have today."

She punched a key on the computer, and a list of the characteristics of an opera flashed on the screen. The students began writing furiously, taking notes.

"Opera was created during the Baroque period as a source of entertainment. You will remember that during that time, we had no movies, no television, and no recording. People who wanted to hear music had to hear it live." Julia noticed that some of her students were starting to listen intently. "Has anyone ever seen a real opera?"

Kathy Smith raised her hand. "I've heard opera songs," she said, "but never a whole opera." She added, "They were singing in a foreign language, and they were singing with a big voice that was hard to understand. Why do they do that?"

"There was no amplification," Julia said, "so singers had to develop their voices to be very powerful and to carry a long way. Some of the opera houses of the time would hold two or three thousand people. Can you imagine singing loudly enough so that many people could hear you? And since operas were created in Italy, and the Italian language is very musical, many composers continued to use the Italian language."

Julia continued, "The most important part of the opera was the arias or the solo songs. In an aria, a main character sings about how they feel about whatever action has taken place. Arias became a vehicle for all kinds of human emotion—love, hate, jealousy, joy, grief, or sorrow. It was the job of the composer to portray this emotion in his music."

She continued, "During the Romantic era, the nineteenth century, patrons of the operas loved emotional stories. Subjects that were sad and heartrending were very popular. A popular subject dealt with lovers who could not be together. Usually things such as culture, religion, race, or social standings kept them apart. It has been said that almost no one ever lived happily ever after in a Romantic opera. In some stories, a person would commit suicide if their lover did not return their love, or sometimes they would choose to die together."

Julia looked around at her class. "Have any of you ever loved someone who didn't love you? Do you remember how you felt? Did you think your life was over? What emotions did you feel? Would you ever kill yourself if you couldn't be with the person you loved?"

A boy raised his hand. "I really loved this girl in high school, but she dumped me for a football player. It hurt so bad I wanted to die. I might have killed myself."

Carol raised her hand. "Not me," she said. "I would never love anyone that much."

"Me either," another girl said.

Julia put the following question on the screen: *How Do Composers Use Music to Create Emotion?* "This is your first writing assignment. Use information from your text and your listening assignments to answer this question. Be sure to give examples."

"I'm going to play a modern song for you that's very emotional. It's not from an opera, but it has been used in several movies. As you listen, look for ways that the composer created emotion."

A sultry soprano voice sang, "If I should stay, I would only be in your way. So I'll go, but I know I'll think of you every step of the way. And I-I-I will always love you." The song went on. Julia noticed that several of the girls had tears welling in their eyes.

When the song was over, Julia asked, "Any comments?"

Lakeysha said, "Kenny and I saw that movie on TV several weeks ago. It was so sad I cried all through the last part."

"So you felt the emotion in the music?" Julia asked.

Lakeysha nodded.

"What made it sad?"

Lakeysha said, "The words were sad, and the music was soft and slow. The story was heartbreaking."

Julia said, "When you watch a TV drama or movie, close your eyes and listen to the background music. Can you tell what's happening on the screen? That's the way it was in a good opera. The feelings of the words were shown in the music."

She continued, "On Wednesday and Friday, our class will meet in the film room of the Marshall Building. We will see some videos of parts of operas, so information from the videos may be included in your assignments. Be sure to read chapter 6 in your text book. Let's have fun with opera," she said as she dismissed class.

January went by swiftly and uneventfully. David was busy on the weekends, entertaining prospective recruits who had come for a campus visit, so Julia didn't see much of him.

He came to dinner on the last Sunday in the month. She served him pot roast with gravy and roasted vegetables. David brought a fine merlot. After dinner, they sat on the couch with a glass of wine.

"How are my athletes doing? David said. "I have been holding two study sessions per week with them. I don't want anyone to get behind, not with the tournaments coming up. We need everyone to be in good standing academically."

"So far, everyone has turned in all their work; however, we've only had two assignments," she said. "We'll have three more before midterm."

He took her hand. "Babe, I'm leaving Thursday for a long recruiting trip. I have to visit five recruits in Missouri, Kansas, Oklahoma, and Arkansas. I'll be gone at least ten days and maybe more. There will be a lot of hard driving and possibly bad weather, but it's part of my job."

"I know," she said wistfully. "I wish you didn't have to go."

He went on, "We want to have all our recruits signed by February 10. The success of our teams in the future will depend on how successful I am."

"I know you will do well," she said. Then she added, "How can anyone resist you? I'm sure you will sign them all."

"How about now?" he asked. "Am I irresistible now?

"Absolutely," she said as she lifted her face to be kissed. He took her in his arms and kissed her passionately. Then she said, "It looks like tonight will have to last us for a while, so let's make the most of it."

She led him to the bedroom, and they began undressing each other. She put a CD in the player. A smooth voice sang, "When I fall in love, it will be forever."

He held her close. "I love you so much," he said. She could feel his desire growing, and her heart beat faster.

She wrapped her arms around him and felt his hard-muscled back. Being in his arms felt so right. David always made her feel so special, like she was the most important person in the world. He was always so tender, so considerate, so loving, so wonderful.

After the lovemaking was over, she said, "I love you."

"I know."

"I really wanted you."

"I know, and it was great!"

"Does tonight have to end?" she asked quietly.

"I'm afraid so," he said. "But I could really get used to this. Just as soon as the tournaments are over, we have to start making plans."

They dressed. "Would you like another glass of wine?" she asked.

"Sure," he said.

When it was time to leave, he said, "I'm going to be really busy this week, but let's go out to dinner Wednesday night. I have to see you one more time before I leave."

"Okay, but I wish you didn't have to go," she whispered. But as painful as it was, there was no argument. She knew it was his job.

Chapter 26

When Julia awoke on Thursday morning, her first thought was about David. At their date last night, he had explained again the reasons he had to go, but it didn't make his leaving any easier. Before he left her last night, he promised to call or text every day. She checked her cell phone. She had a text. It read, "I love you. I will think about you every minute I am gone. D."

She started her day with her usual routine and headed to school. Her violin students were doing well. She thought the videos she was using with her Music 102 class helped. Students needed to see the costumes and scenery as they listened to the music to get the whole picture. The symphony was playing exciting music. All in all, she had nothing to complain about except that David was gone.

That evening, David called. "I'm in western Missouri. It's been a good trip so far. No bad weather," he said.

"I'm glad," she said. "I'll pray that you stay safe."

"I have an extra stop to make," he said. "Phil heard about a kid he wants me to check out. I'm a little anxious because I know nothing about this kid." They continued to chat. Finally, he said, "I'll call you tomorrow. Love you and miss you."

"Thanks for calling. I love you too."

The next day went smoothly, but by ten o'clock that night, she still had not heard from David. She tried not to worry. There were a hundred reasons why he had not called. She decided to go on to bed. At ten thirty, the phone rang. He said, "I'm sorry to call you so late, but I have news that just won't wait until tomorrow."

"That's okay," she said. "I wasn't asleep, and tomorrow is Saturday. What's your news?"

"You know that kid I was telling you about? Dennis Bradley. I visited with him and his family this afternoon, and you're not going to believe this, but he'll be a music major. He's a trumpet player. He wants to be a band director."

"You're kidding me," she said.

"No," he said. "Just wait until you hear this. His mother is a large black woman, the mother of six kids. She is very insistent that he be a music major. I think some other schools have told her that he wouldn't have time for music if he signed with them."

"Is he talented?" she said.

"I don't know. I didn't hear him play. Then I told her that I had been able to play in the symphony while I was playing basketball. Well, that did it! She pulled out this old violin for me to play. I think she thought I was just telling her something to get her son to sign with us."

"Surely not? Did you play?"

"Well, it took me probably twenty minutes to tune the thing, and I had to replace one string. Finally, I got it in playing order."

"What did you play?"

"I started with some fancy stuff, some Mozart and Brahms, but what really got her were the hymns."

"You played hymns?"

"Yes, she asked me to play 'Amazing Grace.' I could play that by ear. Then she asked me to play another hymn that I didn't know, so she pulled out a hymn book and accompanied me on the piano. We probably played for an hour. Then they invited me to stay for dinner before the game."

"That was great, David," she said.

"By then, she was ready to sign on the dotted line, and I hadn't even seen the kid play. My anxiety level was out the roof. I didn't know if this kid even knew which side of the ball went in the hoop."

"What?" she said.

"That's a basketball joke. You know. Some kids are so bad they don't know which side of the ball goes in the hoop. Shall I explain?"

"No, I'm very basketball literate now," she said, laughing. "I know the ball is round. What happened? Could he play?"

"Fortunately for me, the kid was the real deal. He's six five and has a great jump shot. He made twenty-five points tonight against a very strong defense. He'll make a great shooting guard or a small forward, and he plays great defense too. He will really fit into our program. And he's a great student. He has nearly a 3.8 point grade average after three and a half years in high school."

"Are you going to sign him?" she asked.

"I just talked to Phil. He said to use my judgment and sign him if I thought he was good enough."

"That's great, David," she said. "Your first signee."

"But what if he turns out to be a lemon?"

"He won't, David," she said encouragingly. "You know what you're doing."

"I hope so. It's kind of like my reputation is on the line. At any rate, I'm meeting with them at 10:00 a.m. tomorrow to sign him."

"David," she said, "thank you for calling to tell me. I love you."

"I need to get to bed," he said. "Thank you for your love and support. I love you too."

The next few days went by slowly. Julia filled the time by doing her schoolwork, practicing the violin, and cooking. She baked bread and made several casseroles to go in the freezer. Every morning, she had a text, and most evenings he called.

When David called on the next Friday, he said, "Great news, babe. I managed to sign two of the five kids I visited, plus the kid from Missouri, but I'm really beat. I have only slept in a bed that was long enough about two nights since I've been gone. In most places, the beds were so narrow I couldn't even sleep diagonally. It's hard to get any rest when your feet are hanging off the bed."

"When will you be home?" she asked.

"I'm at Little Rock," he said. "If things go well, I should be there by six, no later than six thirty."

"What would you like for dinner?"

"How about something Italian?"

"Sure," she said. "Anything else?'

"I would really like something chocolate. I haven't had a good chocolate pie in years. Do you do chocolate pie?"

"Absolutely," she said. "Do you want meringue or whipped cream?"

"My mom always put meringue, so I guess that's what I want. I love you, and I'll see you tomorrow."

"Love you too. Drive safely," she said. "Your little truck definitely would not look good as a hood ornament on an 18-wheeler."

He laughed. "Not if I can help it."

By six o'clock, Julia had dinner together—lasagna, homemade garlic bread, a green salad, and chocolate pie.

A little before six thirty, David arrived. When she opened the door, he took her in his long arms and held her tightly. "You don't know how much I've missed you," he said.

She thought he looked exceptionally tired. Dark circles were under his eyes, and there were lines in his face she hadn't noticed before.

"Yes, I do," she said, "because I've missed you too."

"Babe, I'm starved," he said. "I haven't had anything to eat but a fast-food burger at about noon. Everything smells great." She led him to the dining table, beautifully set with her grandmother's silver and china. She poured a glass of Merlot and fixed his plate. After the first bite, he said, "This is tremendous. I didn't realize how hungry I was." He ate several helpings of everything, and then he said, "That was great, but I need to rest a minute before dessert."

He took his glass of wine and sat on the couch. She sat beside him, and he regaled her with stories of his travels, like the time he spent the night on a lake in Arkansas at Bob's Motel and Bait Shop. "You won't believe this," he said. "But this place didn't even have a lock that worked, just a sign to put a chair under the doorknob if you didn't want anyone to come in." And another time, when the motel didn't have an extra-long bed, the owner brought in another chair and a stack of pillows to put his feet on.

"Most people I met were really helpful and did everything possible to make me comfortable. It's just all that driving that tired me out."

"Are you ready for dessert?" she asked. "I made a chocolate pie."

"I think I had better have some coffee too. I'm not sure I'll make it back to the dorm without some."

As she left to make the coffee, Julia saw David stretch out on the couch. He pulled off his shoes, got a couch pillow, and made himself comfortable on the extra-long couch.

When she returned to the living room, he was sound asleep. *I'll just let him rest a while.* She went back to the kitchen and quietly began cleaning up. After an hour, he was still sleeping. She went to her bedroom and got a blanket and covered him. She turned out the lights, leaving a night-light in the powder room.

At ten thirty, she checked again, and he was still sleeping, so she turned out the bedroom lights and went to bed. She heard no sound from him but the soft breathing of a really tired man.

The next morning, she showered and dressed. David was still asleep, so she made fresh coffee and started cooking sausage. She was sure he would want a hearty breakfast. She saw him stumble into the powder room. When he came out, he said, "I found a new toothbrush in the drawer. I hope it was okay that I used it."

"Sure, that's what it's for."

"Sorry I missed dessert last night, but I feel a lot better."

She made blueberry pancakes and sausage. "Would you like an egg too?"

"Yes," he said, "if it's not too much trouble."

"Nothing is too much trouble for you, my love."

After breakfast, he said, "I need to go home and take a shower. I have to do a report for Phil, and maybe I'll take another nap. Is it okay if I come back tonight?"

"Sure," she said. "We'll have leftover lasagna and chocolate pie."

"Great," he said. "Thanks for taking care of me last night."

"Anytime."

Chapter 27

David had barely reached his office Monday morning when his phone rang. "Mr. Cooper," Mrs. Mims said, "Dr. Jennings would like to see you as soon as possible. Could you come to the office this morning?"

"Sure," David said, "I'll be right there." He looked forward to telling his uncle about the prospective students he had signed.

When David walked into the office, Ralph was seated at his desk. "Sit down," he said sternly. "What do you have to say for yourself?"

David launched into a litany of his trip's successes. "No, no," his uncle said. "I know about your trip. What I want to talk about is your truck being in front of Dr. Crane's apartment at three o'clock on Sunday morning. That's a little late to be watching TV, isn't it?"

"Yes, but I wasn't watching TV. I was sleeping."

Ralph sputtered. "You—you can't be spending the night in that girl's apartment."

"Uncle Ralph," David said patiently, "I left home a week ago Thursday. I traveled nearly two thousand miles and visited with six families. I mostly ate at greasy spoon diners or fast-food places. I got very little sleep because most places didn't have extra-long beds. I drove over three hundred miles on Saturday to get to Julia's by dinnertime. She fed me a good meal, which included two glasses of wine, and I fell asleep on her couch."

"You could have gotten up and gone home."

"Yes, I could have," David said, "but I was dead tired. She covered me with a blanket, and I slept there all night." He stood up and looked at his uncle disgustedly. "I have spent the past ten days touting the virtues of Chapman's academic program and trying to ensure the success of our basketball program, and *you* are worried that I may discredit the university by sleeping on my fiancée's couch all night."

He continued, "I woke up at eight o'clock. Julia fed me blueberry pancakes and sausage. Then, still wearing the same clothes that had not been off my body for twenty-four hours, I went back to the dorm, took a shower, wrote my report to Phil, and took another nap. Now, if you are satisfied with my actions, I need to get back to the office."

"So are you still planning to marry that girl?"

"Absolutely!"

"But she is not right for you. Don't you want a wife who will make a home for you and take care of your children? You don't want your children to be raised by a nanny."

"Uncle Ralph," David said calmly, "I don't want a wife whose sole interest in life is me. I want someone who has her own interests that I can share but who enjoys spending time with me and sharing my interests. And most importantly, I want someone who loves me. I think I've found the perfect person with whom to spend the rest of my life, and I plan to marry her, if she will have me."

"Have you?" he questioned, with a scornful look on his face. "She took one look at your millions and said, 'Goodbye, money worries.' You know she has a huge student loan debt and lives in a cheap student apartment."

"I know," David said. "She worked hard to put herself through college with very little help from her mother."

"What if, after a couple of years, she divorces you and gets half of your money?"

"I trust Julia not to do that."

"And what will she do when her children face discrimination because their father is black?"

"Uncle Ralph," David said impatiently, "all children face many challenges when they're growing up. Our children will learn how to deal with difficulties that occur in their lives because they will have the love and support of their parents."

"You just won't listen to reason, will you?"

"When I hear a valid reason, I might listen. But so far, I haven't heard a reason that makes sense."

"But what if Julia isn't here next year? You know that I'm the one who decides if she'll be rehired."

"If Julia is not rehired, I will leave too. Is that what you want?" With that, he stalked out of the office.

When David got back to his office, he received a more pleasant phone call. "Hey, David," Clark said. "I'm taking Molly to the big Valentine dance at the country club on Friday night. Would you and Julia like to go with us?"

"I'll have to check with Julia. I'll get back to you."

After her 10:00 a.m. class, Julia ran into Molly outside her office. "Do you have a minute?" Molly asked.

"Sure, come in," Julia said. "Have a seat."

Molly said, "Clark is taking me to the big Valentine dinner-dance at the country club Friday night. Would you and David like to go with us?"

"I don't know," Julia said. "I'm not sure of David's schedule."

"Clark is going to call him. I just wanted to give you a heads-up so you would have time to think about it."

"But, Molly," she protested, "I don't know any of those modern dances that people are doing today."

"You don't have to worry about that," Molly said. "Most of the music at the country club is geared for the over-forty crowd. Oh, once in a while, they'll play something modern, but mostly they play dance music for people who really dance, not just jump around like they were in an exercise class."

"That's about my speed," she said. "I'm sure David would really love it." She paused thoughtfully. "I don't have a nice ball gown, and I'm not sure I can afford one."

"Julia," Molly said sternly, "what's more important? Making your student loan payment or knocking David's socks off when he sees how beautiful you are? Anyway, that's what credit cards are for."

As if on cue, she heard her cell phone beep. She picked it up and punched a button. It was a text from David. She read out loud. "Do you want to go to the country club dance on Friday?" She punched in "Yes."

"Great," Molly said. "Now, let's go shopping. I don't have to be back until two for string rehearsal."

"Me neither," Julia said.

They drove to The Boutique downtown. The sales clerk, a small lady with greenish eyes and brown hair drawn back in a bun, wore a stylish dress and high-heeled shoes. She said, "You're really here at the right time. We just received a new shipment of ball gowns. It will soon be time for spring formals and proms."

Julia said, "I would like to find something that will match my new earrings." They searched through the racks.

Suddenly, Molly said, "Here's your dress." She held up a beautiful sapphire-blue gown. The satin bodice had a deep V in front and back with inch-wide straps that went over the shoulder. The bodice was covered with blue sequins and small rhinestones. The full skirt was made of yards and yards of silk organza. "You have to try this on," Molly said. "It's just your size. Now don't look at the price tag until you see how great it looks on you."

When Julia came out of the dressing room, Molly said, "That dress is absolutely perfect. You really should get it."

Julia knew the dress was much too expensive, but she did want to look nice for David. "If you say so," Julia said as she pulled out her credit card. "All this shopping has made me hungry. Let's go to the Italian place for lunch."

As they were eating their salads, Julia shook her head. "I really shouldn't have bought that dress," she said.

"Nonsense. Your new earrings will be perfect with it," Molly said. "They're so beautiful. He must have paid a fortune for them."

Julia said, "I don't think they're all that expensive."

"Listen, girl," Molly said, "my dad was a jeweler. I know stones, and those stones are perfect sapphires, to say nothing of the pearls and diamonds."

"I wish he wouldn't buy me expensive gifts," Julia said. "I'm not sure he can afford them."

"What are you talking about?" Molly asked in disbelief. "David has all kinds of money."

"I know he had a lot when he signed his rookie contract, but I think he spent it all. He bought two expensive violins and a Porsche and remodeled his parents' house."

"Get real," Molly said. "His rookie contract was for $41,000,000 for the first four years. After that, he made about $40,000,000 per year for the next four years. I also know he got all kinds of endorsements and incentive pay when the Pacers won the championship." She laughed. "I don't think he could have spent all that."

Julia sat stunned. "Are you sure? How do you know?"

"Clark looked it up on Google. It tells the net worth of all professional athletes."

"Oh my," Julia said, with a surprised look on her face. "I know he has a financial manager who takes care of his money." She nodded. "Perhaps he does have money, but I don't want to know about it. I love him for who he is, not what he has."

Chapter 28

Thursday, David and Julia found their seats beside Molly and Clark in the student section. The Lady Cougars were playing Eastern Indiana. David said, "This is a big game. The other team is second in the conference."

"They really have some big girls," Julia observed.

"Lakeysha and Carol are tall," David said, "but they're quick too. That counts for a lot."

Molly whispered to Julia, "I love your new dress. It's going to look so good on you."

"What's this about a new dress?" David asked, smiling.

"You were supposed to be surprised," Julia said.

"My darling, I'm always surprised when I see how gorgeous you look," David said as he squeezed her shoulder.

Just then, Cruiser Bell and another guy came up the steps in the arena. The other guy was not nearly as tall as Cruiser, with a medium build and brown hair. "Hi, Coach, Dr. Crane," Cruiser said as they passed by and found seats behind them.

"Hi, Cruiser," David said, as he watched them go by. "Who was that with Cruiser?" David whispered.

"On my," Molly said. "That's Cruiser's brother, Marvin."

"I've heard of Marvin Bell, but I have never met him," David said.

"I thought he was in the navy," Clark said. "Perhaps he's just home on leave." He went on, "Not only was Marvin Bell a poor student, he was deceitful and dishonest. I think Brandon must have pulled some strings somewhere to keep him out of jail."

I hope his dishonesty doesn't rub off on Cruiser. He remembered what Carol and Lakeysha had said about Cruiser earlier.

The Lady Cougars were playing superbly and built a ten-point lead at the end of the first quarter. Marvin turned to Cruiser. "What's with you?" he said. "Are you going to declare for the pro draft this year?"

"I'd like to. I've about had it with school, but Coach Cooper says I'm not ready yet."

"Wasn't that him we passed?" Marvin asked. "D. J. Cooper ought to know. He was in the pros for a long time, and he was really good."

"Don't I know it?" Cruiser said. "He runs me ragged every day at practice."

"But are you getting any better?"

"Yeah, I guess."

"Then what's the problem? You finish this year of school. You get a pro contract and make a million bucks."

"The problem is all this schoolwork. I worked my butt off the first semester, and all I got for it were lousy Cs. That music class is a real bitch. We have to do all these assignments."

"Are you kidding me? When I took that class, all we did was sit around and listen to music and take a few tests. We did have a term paper, but I just copied something off the internet."

"Well, we have a lot more than that, and if I don't do it, I'll have an F at midterm," Cruisers said. "That Dr. Crane is one tough lady. I found a girl who's been doing my assignments for me, but it costs me twenty-five dollars apiece. And now she doesn't want to do them anymore. I had to show them to Coach Cooper so he'd think I did them. If I don't turn in my assignments, he won't let me play, and if I don't play in the NCAA tournament, the pro scouts won't see me."

"You think your team will make it to the NCAA tournament?"

"Sure. We're eighteen and two right now. We've got a great team. Coach thinks we can win the Midwestern Conference tournament, but I won't be there if I fail music."

"I can't believe you're letting some music teacher push you around."

"But what choice do I have?"

"Get rid of her. Get the old man to lean on Jennings and get her fired."

"I don't think that would work. I'm sure she's got some kind of contract, and the word is Coach Cooper is sleeping with her."

"You're kidding me. D. J. Cooper is sleeping with some music teacher!"

"Yeah, they say his truck is parked in front of her apartment until real late on the weekends, and you can't tell me that a stud like D. J. Cooper is spending all that time watching TV and eating brownies." He pointed. "That's her right there beside him."

"Wow," Marvin said. "I can see what he sees in her. Let me think about it. There must be something we can do to make her leave of her own accord."

"But what good would it do if she left?" Cruiser whined. "They would just hire a substitute."

"Cruiser, you're dumb as a doorknob. Don't you know anything?" Marvin demanded. "Substitute teachers aren't as gung ho as the regular teachers. They don't pay them much, so they don't like to grade papers and do anything extra."

"Really?"

"A substitute would probably never make another assignment, so you would be free for the rest of the semester."

"That would be great, Marv, if you can get rid of her," Cruiser said, "but no rough stuff. I don't want to get in trouble with the law."

"I promise I won't lay a finger on her, but …" He thought a

minute. "You know, I think she would spook real easy. I think she needs a little silent intimidation. Before I get through with her, little Miss Dr. Crane will leave this place and never look back."

"What are you going to do?" Cruiser asked.

"You don't want to know," Marvin said. "You've got a big mouth, and besides, I don't think you could pass a lie detector test. Can you get me a copy of her class schedule?"

"Sure," Cruiser said. "It's posted on the door of her office."

"Good. I want to know where she is every minute of the day, and when you get your million-dollar rookie contract, I certainly want you to remember your big brother."

Chapter 29

Friday, Julia went to the hairdresser and had her hair done up in curls in the back. She knew David liked it that way. She pulled on sheer hose and her silver pumps. She thought they would be better for dancing than sandals. She did her makeup, and last, she put on her new dress. She adjusted the back zipper and added the new earrings. She looked in the mirror. What she saw reminded her of pictures of Cinderella in her childhood picture books. But her Prince Charming would be coming in a silver Porsche instead of a pumpkin carriage.

When David arrived, he said, "Babe, you look amazing. That dress is the most beautiful thing I have ever seen, and the earrings are perfect." He handed her a box with a wrist corsage of white roses, trimmed with silver.

She smiled and whirled around so he could get the full effect. "I'll pin my corsage to my purse," she said, "until we get there." She picked up her jacket and gave it to him to hold while she put it on.

"Just a minute," he said as he pulled a small, elegantly wrapped box from his jacket pocket and handed it to her.

"What is this?" she asked.

"A little *sorry I've been neglected been neglecting you* gift."

"But, darling," she said, as she ripped off the paper, "you've been traveling for work. You couldn't help being gone." As she opened the box, she said, "Oh my." It was a sapphire surrounded by diamonds in the shape of a heart on a slender platinum chain.

"Happy Valentine's Day, babe. Thank you for understanding," he said as he fastened the beautiful necklace around her neck. "Perfect," he proclaimed. "I looked for something to match your earrings." He took her into his arms and kissed her.

As they approached the curb, she saw that he, indeed, had brought the Porsche. He opened the door and helped her in with her skirts, and she, indeed, felt like Cinderella.

As they entered the ballroom at the country club, they saw that Clark and Molly were already at their table. The room was beautifully decorated with hearts and red roses. "They have a new chef here. The food is fabulous," Molly said. "Clark ordered a bottle of Pinot Noir. I hope that's okay."

"Great," David said.

The waiter brought the wine as soon as they sat. It was superb. Dinner was wonderful—Chateaubriand for two, potatoes au gratin, fresh asparagus, and strawberry tarts in the shape of a heart.

Julia was so happy. David looked wonderfully handsome in his tux. She noticed that he had a new cummerbund. It was a deep blue with a matching handkerchief.

When she mentioned it, he said, "I called Molly to find out the color of your dress and decided to spruce up myself as well."

"You look wonderful," she said as she squeezed his arm, "and you're wearing my favorite cologne."

After dinner, the band started tuning up. "I love this band," Molly said. "They play everything from country to modern to the sentimental oldies, but everything they play has a great beat for dancing." They started playing a slow number.

"Shall we?" David said.

"I'm not a very good dancer," she said.

"But I am," he said matter-of-factly. "Don't worry. I won't let you step on my toes." And he was. He guided her around the dance floor with smooth, flowing movements. At times, he would put his long arm around her waist and sweep her completely of the floor. And sometimes, he would dip her so low that she thought she would fall, but he always managed to gather her up again.

The slow dance was over, and the band began a bouncy modern tune.

"David," she said, "I don't know what to do to this music."

"Neither does anyone else. Just do what I do." He glided from side to side and swung his arms over his head to the beat. Then he swung his arms from side to side and bent his arms and legs at crazy angles.

Julia did her best to keep up with him but finally gave up, laughing. "You are too good for me," she said, out of breath. "Where did you learn all those moves?"

"The club sent us to a modern dance class once. They thought it would help our footwork," David said.

"Did it?"

"Not really, but it was a lot of fun."

They sat out the next number, and then the band gave the intro for a waltz.

"Come on," he said. "I love to waltz."

A handsome young man stepped to the mike and began crooning in a smooth baritone, "Could I have this dance for the rest of my life?" They stepped onto the dance floor, and David took her into his arms.

"That's Scottie Duncan," she said. "He's a music major. Don't you remember? He did a baritone solo in the Christmas concert."

"And now he's singing with a dance band," David said, laughing. "You music people will do anything to make a buck."

"You're right about that. We don't get scholarships for playing games. We have to work for a living," she said.

"Point taken," he said. "The song is beautiful, and he's doing a great job." They moved smoothly around the dance floor. He twirled her under his arm and then pulled her close in a sweeping circle. Her huge skirts billowed around her.

David began singing with Scottie. "When we're together, it seems so right. Could I have this dance for the rest of my life?"

A fast, modern number came next. Julia tried her best to keep up but knew she was falling short. David seemed to be enjoying himself, and that was enough. When the number was over, she said, "I need to sit for a while."

When they went back to the table, David asked Molly to dance. She readily agreed. Clark said to Julia, "If you don't mind, let's sit this one out."

"I don't mind a bit," she said. "He's about to wear me out." She added, "This has been so much fun. Thank you for asking us."

When they returned to the table, Molly said, "Thank you, David. You are one great dancer." Scottie returned to the mike. The band struck up a familiar country ballad.

David said, "This is one of my favorites. We have to dance to this." He reached for Julia and led her to the dance floor. "Every time I heard this song while I was away, I thought of you."

Scottie began to sing in a soft, sentimental voice, "Maybe I didn't love you quite as often as I could have." She put both arms around David's neck and laid her head on his chest, and he pulled her close. "But you were always on my mind."

The smell of his wonderful cologne made her feel so relaxed. She molded her body to his and flowed with his movements. "I'm so happy that you're mine," David sang in her ear. "You were always on my mind."

"I wouldn't mind the separations so much if all the homecomings could be like this," she said.

"I know how we could make it ever better," he said.

"I would gladly spend the rest of my life dancing with you," she said. "I love you so much." She didn't want this magical moment to end. She would always remember this evening, the way David held her close and sang to her. It was the most romantic thing that had ever happened to her.

"I love you too, babe."

As they headed to the table, they met Ralph and Ophelia leaving. "Hello, Uncle Ralph," David said. He hugged Ophelia. She was wearing a beautiful gown of pink chiffon. "You're looking lovely, Aunt Ophelia," he said.

"She should be, for what she paid for that dress!" Ralph said.

"You are nothing but romantic, Uncle Ralph," David said, laughing, but Uncle Ralph did not seem to be happy.

Ophelia hugged Julia. "And you are looking particularly radiant tonight, my dear." She whispered, "Do I see something new around your neck? Do you two have an announcement for us?"

Julia smiled. "No, not yet. It's just a Valentine gift."

Ophelia said, "Great! Well, we have to go. We're both a little tired."

Ralph shook David's hand. "Good luck in the tournament next week," he said as they left.

They had danced several more dances when Julia said, "I think I'm ready to go. This has been so wonderful."

They said goodbye to Molly and Clark and left.

When he took her to the door, he said, "I may not see much of you next week. I have to leave Monday to go to St. Louis for a pretournament conference meeting, but I'll be back on Wednesday morning. Our first game in the conference tournament is Thursday evening. If we win, we'll play on Friday and then on Saturday."

"Thank you for tonight," she said. "It was lovely."

"I'll see you Sunday. May I call you?"

"Certainly. I'm looking forward to it," she said.

Chapter 30

David took Julia out to dinner on Sunday night. He apologized for being gone most of the coming week. "If I ever get a head coaching job, I'll have an assistant to do most of the traveling," he said.

"I can't wait, but I understand."

Julia woke up Tuesday morning with a scratchy throat. She didn't feel too bad, so she went on to work. She had nothing but violin students. Things were going smoothly when she received a call from Mrs. Mims. "Dr. Crane, Dr. Jennings would like to see you today. Could you come at one o'clock?"

"Yes," Julia said, "I'll be there." She was beginning to get a headache, and her stomach felt as if she had swallowed a brick. She supposed Dr. Jennings had that effect on people.

After her 11:00 a.m. student, she went to Molly's office. "I'm not feeling well. Can you take my string class at two o'clock? I have to see Dr. Jennings at one, and then I'm going home.

"Sure," Molly said. "We'll work on symphony music. The second violins will benefit from hearing the firsts." Then she added, "Are you sure you want to talk to Dr. Jennings when you're not feeling well?"

"I'd feel worse if I waited, wondering what he wanted," she replied.

"Good afternoon, Dr. Crane," Mrs. Mims said as Julia entered her office. "Please go right in. Dr. Jennings is expecting you."

Julia went into the office. Dr. Jennings sat behind his desk and indicated a chair. "Please sit down," he said. Julia wondered why he didn't stand to greet her. "There are several things we need to discuss.

I'll get right to the point. I received a very troubling telephone call from Brandon Bell, Cruiser's father."

"Oh, and what is Mr. Bell's concern?"

"He is very upset at the way you have been treating Cruiser."

"And what is that?" she asked, a little skeptical, as if she knew what was coming.

"He says that you did not tell Cruiser that an assignment was due, and he missed it because the team was away. Then you would not let him turn it in late. Is that true?"

"Hardly. Cruiser seems to bend the truth to suit his current needs," Julia said as she pulled a booklet from her briefcase. "This is a copy of my class syllabus. It was given to every member of my Music 102 class the first day of the semester. It has all the assignments for the semester and the dates they are due." She handed it to Dr. Jennings.

She went on. "Cruiser knows exactly when his assignments are due and what he can do to make them up. And you're right, I do not accept late assignments; however, I have a list of alternate assignments that student may do if they miss one."

"But isn't that a lot of written work for an elective three-hour course?" Dr. Jennings asked.

She told him about the directive from the dean of academics.

"Yes," he admitted, "we do need to work on improving our written expression."

"Most of my students tell me they spend less than three hours per week on my class. That is not excessive for a three-hour course. So wouldn't you say that Cruiser Bell misrepresented the truth somewhat?"

"Well, ah, perhaps, but, Dr. Crane, wouldn't you agree that as teachers, we sometimes have to adjust expectations for some students in some circumstances?"

He didn't hear a word I said.

"Absolutely," she said. "Last year, I allowed a student to give two of his assignments as oral reports because he had a sprained wrist and couldn't write. But Cruiser Bell has no special circumstances other than he is lazy and has chosen not to do his work. If he can run up and down a basketball court, he should be able to do his assignments." She added, "I'm sorry, but I will not give Cruiser Bell credit for work he did not do."

"You must know, Dr. Crane, that you do not have tenure. I think you should be aware that a note in your personnel file saying you do not cooperate with the administration, or that you are inconsiderate of the needs of students, and you will never work at the university level again." He continued, "And if Cruiser Bell does not play in the NCAA tournament, your contract for next year may not be renewed."

Julia knew her face showed a look of surprise, perhaps even shock. *Is he actually threatening me?*

"And another thing I want to discuss with you is your relationship with David Cooper."

"There's nothing to discuss," she said confidently. "David loves me, and I love him."

"I'm sure he has told many girls that he loved them just to get them into his bed. You are probably no different. Has he asked you to marry him?"

"Well, no." She nervously twisted a tissue in her hands. "Not in so many words, but we have talked seriously about it."

"When it comes down to it, he probably won't," Ralph said. "David has been very adept at evading fortune hunters."

"What do you mean?" she asked anxiously.

"Women who want to marry him for his money."

Julia was stunned. She knew David had money, but she preferred to not think about it. Then she remembered the expensive gifts he had given her.

Ralph continued, "Do you realize how devastating it could be to both your careers if you were to marry?"

"And why is that?"

"You have spent many years preparing for your career. Are you willing to give it up because of marriage?"

"I'm not planning to give up my career. I plan to go on teaching,"

Ralph looked at her as if he were explaining something to a child. "Dr. Crane, David will probably not stay at Chapman forever. I predict that in a year or two, many top universities will be looking to hire him as a head basketball coach. University officials are reluctant to hire both a husband and a wife at the same university."

"Why is that?"

"Because if one of the pair is not competent or successful and has to be let go, they lose both employees. Replacing a head basketball coach is a long and expensive process, so you may not be hired if David finds another job. At best, you might be hired only as an adjunct or a part-time employee. Are you willing to give up your career after all the time and money you have spent preparing for it—or worse, stand in the way of David's advancement?"

Julia's stomach was churning. She felt her anxiety growing. She hadn't considered that. All she had ever wanted to do was teach, but she could never stand in the way of David and a head coaching job. She was getting more confused. Her headache was getting worse, and she was finding it hard to think.

"And there is always the problem of David finding a coaching job in the South if he has a white wife. Dr. Crane, I think it would be in your best interest and David's if you were to leave the university at the end of the year."

Julia tried to get her emotions under control. She refused to let Dr. Jennings see her cry.

"I think I could find a position for you at a first-rate university as a full professor at probably double your salary, if you would agree to leave quietly."

Julia couldn't believe what she was hearing.

"Think about it," he said. "I don't have to know now. And please don't say anything about this to David until after the tournaments. I don't want him to be distracted by a personal problem when he should be focusing on his coaching. I know you will find a way to tell him tactfully once the tournaments are over."

Is this really happening? Dr. Jennings was sitting with his elbows on his desk and his hands clasped beneath his chin, smiling at her with a satisfied smile, as if he knew she was powerless to refuse his offer. As president of the university, he was used to getting his way. What could she do but obey his wishes? Julia couldn't stand to hear anything more. She rushed out of Dr. Jennings's office and went straight home.

Chapter 31

When she entered the apartment, she sat on the couch, and the tears flooded forth. Her mind was in a muddle. She just couldn't make sense of what she had heard. Her headache was getting worse. All her life, she had tried to work hard and play by the rules. Now that happiness was within her grasp, it seemed to be snatched away. It wasn't fair. It just wasn't fair.

She tried to replay in her mind everything Dr. Jennings had said. Would she really be fired if Cruiser Bell failed her class? It was true she had planned to leave Chapman, but she wanted it to be on her terms. She didn't want David's money. She hadn't even known about it when she fell in love with him. She had been so sure that David loved her. Could she be wrong? Was what Dr. Jennings said true? Had David been lying to her?

She made her way to the bedroom and put on some pajamas. She took two aspirins, picked up a blanket and pillow, and headed back to the couch. She couldn't stop sobbing. She wished David was there. He would make things better. No, definitely not! She couldn't face David right now, not after what Dr. Jennings had said. She was glad he was gone.

Julia dozed for a while, then woke up and sobbed some more. She made her way to the kitchen and fixed a sandwich, but after three bites, she felt it coming up. She ran to the bathroom. What was the matter? Was she pregnant? She thought women were just sick in the morning.

The next morning, she felt no better. Every bone in her body ached, and she had a temperature. She looked in the mirror. Her eyes were watery and puffy because of all the crying. Her nose was red and stuffy, and her head ached. She attempted to brush her tangled hair, but it hurt, so she decided wasn't worth the effort.

At eight o'clock, she called the music office and told them she wouldn't be in. She made a cup of tea and a piece of toast but was dismayed when it came back up. There was no doubt about it. She must have the flu. She felt so bad that she wished she could die. She was chilled, so she wrapped up in her blanket on the couch.

Julia was sound asleep when she heard the doorbell. No one knew she was at home. She would ignore it, and they would go away. The ringing continued insistently. She slowly walked to the door and opened it. It was David. He was holding a large bag, "David," she said weakly, "you can't come in. I have the flu."

"I know," he said as he brushed past her and set the bag on the bar.

"How did you know?"

"As soon as I got back in town, I stopped by your office to see you. Dr. Salerno's secretary told me you were ill. It's okay. I've had a flu shot. Just try not to breathe on me." He looked at her sympathetically, "Gosh, babe, you look awful."

"I know," she said weakly. "What's in the bag?" she asked as she followed him into the kitchen.

He started taking items out of the bag. "Chicken soup, lemon-lime soda, orange juice, and a bottle of the pink stuff," he said. He looked in a drawer, pulled out a big spoon, and poured a spoonful of the pink stuff. "Down the hatch," he said and poked it in her mouth. Then he poured another.

"Is that necessary?" she whined.

"Absolutely." He poured a glass of soda. "Now go sit on the couch and sip this slowly. I'll fix some soup. We have to get fluids down you, or you will be dehydrated." Julia sipped her soda very slowly. "Would you like to try some soup?"

"Just a little," she said.

She came to the table and ate a few spoons of soup and a cracker. "The soup is good," she said. "It seemed to be staying down. I think the pink stuff is working, but I'm so tired I can't eat anymore." She made her way to the couch and stretched out. Soon, she was breathing heavily.

David rinsed the dishes and put them in the dishwasher. He cleaned the sink and sprayed the countertop with a disinfectant spray. He went into the living room to tell her he was leaving when she sat up.

"David," she said in a weak, sleepy voice, "did you ever tell a girl you loved her so she would sleep with you?"

"I have slept with a few girls in my time, but I never had to tell them I loved them. In fact, I don't think I have ever told any girl that I loved her. You were the first, my dear," he said. Then he paused, "No, there was this girl in the first grade. She had a jelly doughnut in her lunch. She said if I loved her, she would give me her jelly doughnut. So I told her I loved her."

"That's nice," she said, and flopped back down on the couch.

"Julia," he said, "are you awake?"

"Mmm," she said.

"Julia, I have to go to the office, but I'll be back this evening to check on you. Get some rest and don't forget to drink plenty of fluids. I love you."

"Mmm," she said.

Julia slept for an hour or two. When she woke up, she felt better but very weak. She took a shower and put on a jogging suit. She got a clean blanket and pillow and stretched out on the couch again. She turned on the television and watched until she fell asleep.

At six o'clock, David rang the bell. He came in and set another bag of food on the counter. He gave Julia a long-armed hug and said,

"You're looking better, babe, and I see that you've combed your hair. Are you feeling better?"

"Yes," she said, "but I'm still so weak. I wanted to wash my hair but didn't have the energy. My headache is better, and I'm keeping food down."

He brought two plates, covered with plastic covers, out of the bag. "You need to eat," he said. "We have baked chicken and pasta."

"Where did you get the food?" she asked.

"From the cafeteria at the athletic dorm. The dietitian there fixed it specially for you. She said only bland food and lots of carbs." He laughed. "Even they can't ruin baked chicken." He fixed their plates and took a bite of the chicken. "You know, I don't think a little salt and pepper on my chicken would hurt you."

She ate a little, and after dinner, he gave her another spoonful of the pink stuff and another glass of soda. "I think you're on the road to recovery," he said. "But you still need to take it easy for another day."

"Yes, Doctor," she said.

He took her hand. "You know, my love, you are very precious to me. I can't stand to see you in pain." She looked into his serious brown eyes and believed every word he said. She felt immensely better.

When it was time to leave, he hugged her again. "I'll take a rain check for a kiss at a later date," he said. "The team is leaving at 9:00 a.m. to go to St. Louis. The game will be on television at 6:00 p.m. Be sure to watch us. I think we have a good chance to win the entire tournament if we play well."

"Good luck," she said. "I'll be watching."

After David left, she thought about what Dr. Jennings had said. She probably wouldn't have been so upset if she had felt better. She would wait until after the tournaments, and then she would talk it over with David. But she refused to give Cruiser Bell credit for work he did not do. She knew David would back her up on that. Midterm grades would be out before the NCAA tournament. Unless Cruiser came through with his assignments, he would not be playing. David didn't have to tell her he loved her. He had shown her in so many ways. She went to bed that night and slept soundly.

Chapter 32

Thursday morning, Julia felt much better, but she was still careful with what she ate—just oatmeal, toast, and tea for breakfast. She got a text from David: "We're on our way to St. Louis. Drink. Drink. Drink. Love, D." She smiled as she read his reminder for her to stay hydrated.

She rested most of the morning. In the afternoon, she chopped up the remainder of the chicken and pasta and added some vegetables to make some chicken noodle soup. She felt stronger. She should try to go to school tomorrow.

Before six o'clock that evening, she had a bowl of soup and a glass of soda and settled herself on the couch to watch the game on television. When the game came on, the announcer said, "We welcome you to the evening session of the Midwestern Conference tournament. Our first game is between the Chapman State Cougars and the Eastern Illinois Panthers. The Cougars have already earned a berth in the NCAA tournament by virtue of having won the conference."

"That's right, Chip," another voice said. "The Cougars have put together a twenty-two and three record before the tournament. It looks like the new assistant coach, former pro star D. J. Cooper, has certainly improved the play of the Cougar big men."

The game started badly for the Cougars. After taking the initial tip, Teddy Baker threw an errant pass to Tyler. The Panther player snatched it out of the air and drove in for a layup. It was apparent from the beginning that the refs were not going to call the game closely.

The opposing center was almost as tall as Cruiser and a lot bigger. He pushed and shoved Cruiser from the start. Rusty yelled at the refs, but they continued allow the rough stuff. An opposing guard, while bringing the ball up, stuck his arm out and knocked Jalen flat. Rusty ran out on the court and yelled at the ref, "Are you blind? Don't you know a foul when you see one?"

The official pointed his finger at Rusty. "Warning," he said.

David pulled Rusty back to the bench." Julia could see that Rusty was getting frustrated, both at the refs and at his team's inability to perform. The Cougar basket seemed to have a lid on it as they missed many three-point shots. Even some of the layups failed to fall.

Teddy was bringing the ball down the court. An opposing player fell as if Teddy had run into him. A foul was called on Teddy. "That was a flop," Julia yelled at the TV. "Teddy didn't touch him."

"That was a flop," she heard Rusty yell at the officials. "Don't you know a flop when you see one?"

The ref blew his whistle. "Technical foul."

With about three minutes to go in the half, Kenny attempted a three-point shot. The defender knocked him down. Still, no foul was called. Again, Rusty ran onto the court, yelling at the ref. The ref blew his whistle. "Technical foul!" he yelled, pointing at Rusty. "The coach is disqualified."

Julia saw a policeman come to escort Rusty from the building, but just before he left, the camera was on him as he looked at David. "Sorry about that, kid," he said. "It's your game now." At the half, the score was Panthers 32, Cougars 20. Julia prayed that David would keep his cool. What would happen to the team if all the coaches got tossed? She felt so sorry for David. How would he handle the situation?

The announcer came into view. "Well, Chip, it looks like things are going badly for the Cougars."

"That's right, Pete. It will take some tremendous coaching from the first-year coach, D. J. Cooper, if he can get the Cougars back on track." Julia went for another soda and returned just as the halftime break was ending.

Julia thought the team had a lot more enthusiasm when they came running onto the court after the halftime break. She saw the announcer head for David. "Coach, what does your team need to do to get back in this game?"

"Well, Pete," David said, "we're not taking care of the ball, and we're not waiting for good shots. We have twenty minutes left in the game. We need to outscore our opponents by three points every four minutes and not try to get it all back at once."

"That's good advice, Coach," Pete said.

Julia wondered if the team could actually do what David wanted.

The team seemed to be more patient and deliberate as the game went on. David paced the sidelines and managed the team magnificently. He praised the team when they succeeded and encouraged them when they failed. Slowly, the Cougars cut into the Panthers' lead.

Julia saw that David consistently was consistently changing defenses and shuffled players in and out expertly to meet the needs of the game. With ten seconds to go, the Cougars had a one-point lead. The Panther guards brought the ball up, and one fired up a three. It missed. Jalen got the rebound and was fouled.

The announcer said, "It looks like the Cougars can hang on to win this game if they can make their foul shots. If not, the Panthers have a chance." Jalen calmly made two foul shots, and time ran out before the Panthers could get off a shot. Cougars 50, Panthers 47.

Chip the announcer said, "This is a huge win for the Cougars. Pete, what did you think about the Cougars' defense?"

Pete said, "It was tremendous. You seldom see college teams use multiple defenses like that. But it really saved the game for the Cougars."

Chip said, "I predict D. J. Cooper is going to be getting some head coach offers before long."

Pete said, "That's right. D. J. Cooper is definitely head coach material."

Julia was so proud of David. He really helped the team turn the game around. She went to the bathroom. When she returned, she saw that they were interviewing David.

Chip said to David, "That was a great win for Chapman."

"Yes," David said. "The Panthers are a good team. We were lucky to beat them, but our team played hard when it counted."

Chip said, "D. J., have you given any thought to a head coaching job?"

"If the right job came along, I would sure consider it. I've always wanted to be a head coach."

"Well, congratulations on your win," Chip said. "Good luck in the next round."

Julia was going to have some thinking to do. She saw how much coaching meant to David. She remembered what Dr. Jennings had said. Could she get a good job if they left Chapman? Did she want to live in David's shadow for the rest of her life? Would she ever have the successful career that she so desperately wanted? Maybe she should just take Dr. Jennings's offer of a full professorship. She would talk to David after the tournaments. Could she convince David that she didn't love him? Did she want to?

Chapter 33

On Friday, Julia felt much improved. She would do her two classes and come home and rest until two. Then she would go back for symphony practice and maybe to the grocery, if she felt like it.

When Julia got to her office, she noticed a plain white envelope in the box on the wall beside her door. She tore open the envelope and was surprised at what she saw. She read, "It's coming soon. It's coming now. You won't know when. You won't how!"

What on earth is this? Was it a joke, or was it a threat? And who would send her such a thing? She thought of Cruiser Bell, but he was in St. Louis. She refused to take it seriously. She wadded up the paper and threw it into the trash.

When Julia came out of the music building after symphony rehearsal, she saw a man wearing a green Chapman State hoodie, leaning against the wall beside the door, with one foot pulled up against the wall. He also wore gloves and large sunglasses with bright yellow rims. She thought that was strange since it was a cloudy day. She walked past him and headed to the parking lot. The man followed her, walking perhaps twenty feet behind. When she came to her car, she stopped. The man walked on, but as he came by her, he flashed a smirky smile, as if he knew a secret and she didn't.

Julia left the parking lot and headed for the grocery. She picked up a few things, and as she came out, there was the man in green, standing against the wall by the door. As she passed, she frowned at him, but he gave her that smirky smile. She turned away and headed for her car. Once again, he followed but said nothing and walked on past. "What's going on?" she asked herself. Surely, it was not a coincidence that the same man had been in the same place as she.

Julia went home and put away her groceries. She felt much better, but she was really very tired, so dinner was just soup and a grilled cheese sandwich. She was still giving her stomach a break.

She put on her pajamas and hurried to the television. She curled up on the couch to watch the next game. Rusty was back and appeared to be a little calmer. The team was playing with more purpose. Julia thought David seemed to be in charge of the defense. She watched him giving defensive signals to Kenny, and the team responded beautifully. They were taking better shots and soon built up a big lead. "Thank goodness," Julia said. "I'm not sure my nerves could take another close game."

About thirty minutes after the game, David called. "How are you, babe?" he asked. "Did you watch the game?"

"I'm much better," she said, "and I watched every minute." She added, "Your defensive strategy was perfect. They never knew what hit them."

He laughed. "How did you know I was running the defense?"

"You forget. I'm now basketball literate." Then she confessed, "The announcer of the game mentioned what a great job you were doing with the defense."

David laughed. "It makes me happy that you're enjoying the game."

Julia slept late the next morning. At about ten o'clock, she got a call from her mother. "Julia, darling," her mother said, "how are you?"

"I'm fine now," she said, and told Cynthia about her illness.

"I'm so glad you're better. You need to take care of yourself and get plenty of rest."

"I am, Mother," she said. "I'm planning to rest all day.

"Dear, I just called to tell you that Muriel and I are going on an extended tour of Europe for the next five weeks. We leave next Friday and will spend a week in each of five cities."

"That will be wonderful, Mother."

"Just think of it. We'll spend an entire week in Amsterdam during the Tulip Festival."

"Mother," Julia said, "I may be leaving Chapman at the end of the semester. I may have the opportunity to get a full professorship and a higher salary somewhere else."

"Oh, darling, that's wonderful," Cynthia said excitedly. "That's what we've always wanted." Then she asked, "And how is David taking the news?"

"I don't know, Mother. I haven't told him yet."

"But he'll be happy for you, won't he?"

No, Mother, he will be devastated.

"I don't know," she said hesitantly. She hoped her mother couldn't hear the ambivalence in her voice. "Besides, I haven't decided for sure yet. It's just something I'm thinking about."

Cynthia said, "Julia, you sound a little depressed. Have you and David broken up?"

"I'm not sure, Mother. Maybe," she said.

"Oh dear, I'm so sorry, but you really need to do what is best for your future. You seemed so sure that you loved him the last time we spoke." Julia thought she heard a touch of compassion in her mother's voice.

"I'll be home sometime the end of March. Please think about this carefully and don't make any decisions until I get home," Cynthia said. "In spite of everything, I *do* want you to be happy."

"I know, Mother. I hope you and Muriel have a great trip."

In the evening, Julia ate a little and eagerly got ready for the game. This was the finals of the Midwestern Conference tournament. They were playing the second-best team in the conference.

The game was hotly contested throughout. Chapman would be ahead a while; then the opposing team would be ahead. The team seemed to be doing their best. At the end, a long three-point shot by the opposition went in just as the buzzer sounded, and Chapman was defeated by one point.

When David called after the game, Julia was surprised that he was not disappointed by the loss. He said, "I'm really proud of the team. It's tough to lose, but this game will be good experience for them."

"But they played so hard," she said. "They deserved to win."

He said, "Everyone deserves to win, but sometimes it just doesn't happen. But we will have another chance in the NCAA tournament."

"Can you win it all?"

"Probably not. There are many more teams that are much more experienced than we are. If we could win two games, I would count our season a huge success. Who knows? Maybe, in a few years, we might win the NCAA." He added, "We are coming home later tonight. I'll take you out to dinner tomorrow evening, if you are up to it."

"Call me tomorrow. I'll see how I feel. Thank you again for taking care of me. I love you."

"Always, my love. If I never do anything else, I will always take care of you."

Sunday, David called around one in the afternoon. "Hi, babe," he said, "How are you feeling?"

"I'm feeling okay," she said, "but I still get tired rather quickly."

"Would you like to go out for dinner, or would you like me to bring something?"

"I have a chicken casserole and homemade bread in the freezer. Why don't you go by the Italian place and get some salads. We can eat here."

"Okay, if you're up to it."

After dinner, they were sitting on the couch with a glass of wine, watching a basketball game on TV. "Babe, I'm so glad to see you looking better," David said. "I promised myself I would never lie to you, but I sure came close that morning I came by when you had the flu. You looked awful."

"I felt awful too," she said.

"I think you need a small vacation," he said. "How would you like to go to Nashville for the weekend? The women's team will be playing there in their conference tournament. I think they should win their first game on Thursday, so we could watch the Friday and Saturday games. Could you be ready to leave on Friday around three thirty?"

"I don't know," she said. "I suppose I could get away."

He went on, "We are going to have hard scrimmages on Monday through Thursday, then give the team Friday off. We will have light workouts next week. Our first game will probably be Thursday or Friday."

After David left, Julia wondered if she should go off with David for the weekend when she was still trying to decide what to do. It would be so great just to forget about everything that was happening here, but she knew it would be dishonest to go off with David as if nothing had changed.

How could she pretend to love David when she had these doubts? But there was no pretense involved; she did love David, and she loved him very much. How could she make a decision to leave him? When you love someone more than yourself, the decision is easy. She would try to do what was best for David, no matter how much it hurt.

Her options were clear. She could have David and an iffy chance of a fulfilling job. Or she could have her dream job with a full professorship, but that would mean she wouldn't have David. Maybe she would find someone else, but he wouldn't be David. She loved David very much, but sometimes love is not enough. *No, that's not true; love is everything. Love is forever.*

Chapter 34

Sunday evening, Carol hurried into Hamburger Heaven. She paused, then spotted Lakeysha and Kenny in the back booth. They were eating burgers and fries. "What's happening, guys?" she asked.

"Sit down. I ordered a burger and a soda for you," Lakeysha said. "Kenny has something to tell us."

"Okay, what gives?" Carol asked as she slid into the booth beside Lakeysha.

"I have something very important to tell you," Kenny said as he leaned across the table and whispered quietly. "It must be kept completely confidential. And please don't talk about it anywhere someone might overhear you, or even mention it to me again," he said.

"For goodness sakes, what is it?" Lakeysha asked impatiently.

Carol nodded. "Get on with it."

"What I'm about to tell you would never hold up in a court of law because it's too clouded in hearsay, but I believe it's the truth, and that's why I'm telling you two."

He went on, "Cruiser told Jalen that he has only turned in two music assignments this semester, and he isn't doing any more. Mr. Bell has complained to Dr. Jennings, and according to Cruiser, Dr. Jennings has said he will fire Dr. Crane if she gives Cruiser a failing grade for midterm."

"You've got to be kidding," Carol said angrily. "Can Dr. Jennings do that?"

"He certainly can," Kenny said. "Any teacher who doesn't have tenure works on a one-year contract. He doesn't have to give a reason for not renewing her contract."

Lakeysha shook her head. "That is so unfair. Dr. Crane is such a good teacher."

"Now you know the worst," Kenny said. "I wanted to tell you because I know how much you like Dr. Crane. Whatever you do with this information is up to you."

He said thoughtfully, "I really should be reporting this to Coach, but I'm going to wait. Maybe Cruiser will have a change of heart and do his work. But if he has a failing grade, Coach won't let him play. If they did, and the NCAA found out, we would have to forfeit all our games, and that's just not fair. The team has worked too hard." He learned over and gave Lakeysha a quick kiss. "I have to go study for an economics test. I'll call you later," he said as he left.

The waitress brought Carol's burger and soda, but she sat stunned at the news. "Is there any chance that Dr. Crane would back down and give Cruiser a passing grade?" Lakeysha asked.

"I don't think so. She's adamant about everyone doing their own work," Carol said.

"There must be something we can do to save Dr. Crane's job," Lakeysha said.

Carol clenched her fist. "I can't believe this. Cruiser Bell is an indolent slob. It would be great if we could just get rid of him."

Lakeysha said, "I guess we could waylay him in a dark alley and break his arm."

"No," Carol said with a sardonic grin on her face. "He would just heal and still be around causing trouble." Her face brightened. "What does Cruiser want more than anything else in the world?" she asked as she picked up a fry and dipped it in ketchup.

"He wants to get a pro contract and make a million bucks."

"But does he have the talent to make it to the pros?"

"Kenny says he has really improved this year. If he were to show up big in the tournament, he just might get drafted."

"Then we have to make sure he gets to play in NCAA tournament so the pro scouts will see him," Carol said. "Do you think we could do three assignments and make them sound as dumb as Cruiser's would?"

"How would we know which ones to do?" Lakeysha said as she took a sip of her drink.

"You can bet Cruiser hasn't done any optional assignments. I think we could just do the first two. We have an assignment due a week from tomorrow. That's when midterm is up."

"We can type them on the word processors in the study room," Carol said, "and put his name on them. We'll leave them on his desk in the classroom before anyone else comes in."

"But will he turn them in?"

Carol said, "I guarantee that if Cruiser finds a folder of assignments with his name on them, he'll jump at the chance to turn them in."

Lakeysha said, "We would probably be thrown out of school if anyone knew, but it will be worth the risk to save Dr. Crane's job and get rid of Cruiser."

"Yes," Carol agreed as she smiled an evil smile. "And if Cruiser goes to the NBA, he will have to work harder than he has ever worked in his entire life or get booted out. That seems like justice to me."

"You're right about that," Lakeysha said. "Let's finish our food and get to work."

Chapter 35

Monday morning found Julia back in the classroom. She reminded her students that midterm grades would come out on Tuesday of the following week. That meant all assignments would be due next Monday. Some students groaned, but most seemed satisfied that they were doing well.

After class, Julia hurried back to her office. As she neared the door, she saw another white envelope in her box. She removed it and tore it open.

There was a single message: "If you weren't here, we wouldn't grieve. Why don't you go? You could just leave."

In this message, the meaning was clear. Someone wanted her gone, but who? The envelope was not in the box when she left her office at 9:00 a.m. It couldn't have been delivered by someone from the Music 102 class. They were all in class. And certainly it was not someone from Music 432, her opera class.

When symphony rehearsal was over at 4:00 p.m., she grabbed her coat and briefcase from her office and left the building. There, beside the door, with one foot propped up behind him, stood the man in the green hoodie. Once again, he was wearing the large yellow-rimmed sunglasses on a very cloudy day. He was also wearing navy jeans and brown gloves.

She went past and walked very fast down the street to the parking lot. He also walked very fast, maintaining a distance of about twenty feet behind. When she reached her car, she stopped and looked at him. He kept walking. "Who are you and why are you following me?" she said.

"You've got to be crazy, lady. I'm not following you," he retorted.

Can that possibly be true?

Tuesday, Julia got to school about 8:45 a.m. She had a violin student at 9:00 a.m. Her office was large enough to use as a teaching studio, so she positioned the stands so that she could see out the small window in the door. Her student came, and the lesson was underway, but no one came near the door. At 9:50, she dismissed her student and went to the restroom. When she returned, her 10:00 a.m. student was there. "Dr. Crane," she said, "you have a letter in your box."

"Who brought it?" she said.

"I didn't know him," the student said. "Some guy. A student, I guess."

"Was it Cruiser Bell?"

"Oh no," the student said. "I know Cruiser. It wasn't him."

Julia retrieved the envelope and tore it open.

She read the message: "It doesn't matter what you do. If you don't go, it's the end of you."

This message definitely seemed to be more threatening than the others. She stood holding the letter, trying to decide what it meant.

"Is everything okay, Dr. Crane?"

"Oh yes. Everything is okay," she said, trying to remain calm.

Wednesday, when she arrived at school, there was another message: "If you should go, we wouldn't care. You wouldn't be here. You wouldn't be there."

And on Wednesday, afternoon, at four o'clock, Mr. Hoodie was standing beside the door of the music building. Was there a connection between the messages and Mr. Hoodie, or was it just a weird coincidence? Once again, he made no threatening overtures but followed her down the street.

On Thursday morning, she had more violin students, but no message appeared. *Good*, she thought. Maybe the perpetrator was tired of his little game. After her string class, she went downtown to get her hair cut. When she came out of the salon, she saw Mr. Hoodie leaning against a streetlight. He smiled that strange, enigmatic smile. Julia began to feel uneasy. So far, there had always been others around, but what would happen if she was alone with him? She ran to her car, got in, and locked the door. He strode by her, laughing.

She really should tell David about the messages, but she knew he would become a vigilante and not rest until the culprit was found. In another day, she would be going to Nashville with David. She really needed to get away from this place.

Chapter 36

Friday morning, Julia stayed in her office until she felt sure all the students were there. There was no letter in her box. She walked into the classroom. Everyone was there except the girls on the basketball team. She taught her class, reminded the students that Monday was the last day for assignments to count on midterm grades, and dismissed the class.

As she turned the corner in the hall, she saw the white end of the letter visible above the top of the box. She ran to it, grabbed the letter, and ripped it open. As usual, it was a white sheet of paper. The message read: "I'll tell you a story, and it is true. If you don't leave, it's the end of you!"

She sat at her desk, thinking about the meaning of the message. *Does the phrase "end of you" mean I will be fired or something more sinister? Can Cruiser be behind these messages?* There seemed to be no indication that he was responsible. She remembered his actions in class. If he was, he was a very good actor. She wadded up the paper and threw it into the trash. In her mind, she felt that if she could get rid of the paper, the problem would go away. Perhaps she was being naïve, but she still couldn't see any real danger.

After lunch, Julia finished her work and rehearsed with the symphony for an hour. She had told Dr. Rubinsky that she wanted leave at three o'clock, and he said, "Sure, go ahead."

As she was headed to the front door, Dr. Jennings came in. "Well, Dr. Crane," he said, "it looks like you are leaving early today. I thought the symphony rehearsed until four o'clock."

She looked him in the eye and boldly said, "Yes, they do, but I am finished with my duties for today."

"Have you given any thought to our previous conversation?"

Had she given any thought? That's all she had thought about for the past week and a half. "Yes," she replied, "but I am still considering what I should do."

"You should know," he said sternly, "that I have come to discuss the matter with Dr. Salerno. Have a good weekend." *Is he kidding? How can I have a good weekend with so much on my mind?*

As she walked out the front door, Julia felt weak in the knees. Her mind was clouded with the implications of his statement. Surely Dr. Salerno would back her up. She looked around. There was Mr. Hoodie, standing against the wall beside the door of the music building. How did he know she was leaving at three today instead of four?

Who was he? He had to be one of Dr. Jennings's stooges. As she left, he followed her down the street. When she reached her car, she stopped. "Who are you?" she challenged. He looked at her, flashed that enigmatic smile, and continued on down the street.

David picked her up at three thirty in the Porsche, and they headed toward Nashville. David was in a happy mood. He turned on their oldies station and sang with the radio, "When I fall in love, it will be forever."

Julia was quiet. She had a lot on her mind. She should tell David or the police about Mr. Hoodie. But if she did, what would she say? A man wearing a green hoodie was walking down the street. She wasn't really worried about him. He had never made a threatening move toward her, but then there were always lots of people around.

Then there were the messages and Dr. Jennings's threat to fire her. Were they connected? "You're awfully quiet, babe," David said. "Are you feeling okay?"

"Yes, I was just thinking," she said. "I'm a little tired. I've had a busy week."

"I think it will do us both good to get away for a few days."

She could agree with that. "I saw your interview on Thursday." She paused. "David, do you really want a head coaching job?"

"Maybe sometime," he said. "There's no rush. There are certain things I want from a head coaching job, and I'm willing to wait until I find them."

"And what is that?"

He said, "I want to go to a college located in a nice little town where we would have a good environment in which to raise our children. I want a job where I would have full control of how I run my team, administrative support, and a good fan base." He paused. "This next thing should probably be at the top of the list. I want to go to a place where you can be happy, where you can teach as much or as little as you want, or stay with the children for a while if you want."

"Do you really think I could get a teaching job anywhere you went?"

"Absolutely! Babe, you've got good credentials. You could teach anywhere." He reached over, picked up her hand, and kissed it. "I waited until I found the perfect woman to share my life. I don't mind waiting until the perfect job comes along."

Julia had made a decision—not a decision to make a decision but a decision to postpone the final decision. In the words of that famous southern heroine, "I'll think about that tomorrow." She would enjoy the next few days with David and not think about her future. She would not worry about Dr. Jennings or Mr. Hoodie or the threatening messages. She felt safe being away with David.

Then, when the tournament was over, she would sit down with David and tell him the truth about everything. Maybe she wouldn't tell him about his uncle Ralph, but she had a feeling David would not be surprised to know everything Uncle Ralph had said. He knew his uncle Ralph.

"Still doing some hard thinking?" David asked.

"Not anymore," she said. "I'm going to enjoy the next few days. I really need a few days of rest."

"So do I," he said. "All those scrimmages last week really wore me out, but Rusty was insistent that we give the team a real tough defense." Then he added, "You know, this has been a tough year, but it will get easier. But I wouldn't trade it for anything. I love you so much."

"Yes, and I love you too." And she truly meant it.

Soon they were coming into Nashville. They saw townhouses and condos on the hill. David said, "They are building some new townhouses in Hoover, on the bluff overlooking the river. Would you like to live in one of those, or would you rather have a house?"

"A townhouse on the bluffs would have a wonderful view," she said. "I would like that very much."

They passed the football stadium, crossed the river, and soon were on lower Broadway in downtown. There were clubs, bars, and music-related shops on either side of the street amid tall buildings.

"We're staying in an old hotel downtown that's within walking distance of the arena. I wanted to be somewhere where we could park the Porsche and leave it."

They pulled into the portico of the hotel and unloaded their bags. The valet parking attendant came running up. David gave him the keys and a generous tip. "I will not be moving this car for a couple of days, so I want you to park it in a safe place," he said. "I definitely do not want to see a dent or a scratch when I pick it up."

"No, sir. Thank you, sir," the attendant said happily.

They went up to their room. It was a lovely suite with a beautiful extra-long bed. He said, "The game starts in about thirty minutes. Would you be okay if we eat concession stand food?"

"Sure," she said. "I would love to have a hot dog with everything on it. Let me change into my Chapman sweatshirt, and I will be ready to go."

"I have a present for you," he said as he handed her a bag.

"Pom-poms!" she said excitedly. "Green and gold pom-poms."

"When you feel a need to yell at the refs, just shake your pom-poms at them." They walked a few blocks to the beautiful basketball arena and found their places in the section behind the Chapman bench.

"Do you think they can win?" Julia asked.

"They should," he said. "Madge Carpenter, the coach, has done an excellent job. They won by twenty points last night."

The Chapman pep band began playing their fight song. Everyone cheered as the team ran onto the floor. Julia shook her pom-poms in time with the music.

The Chapman team played beautifully. Carol was unstoppable as she made layup after layup from the post position. Lakeysha made several three-point shots, and the Chapman defense was excellent. The Lady Cougars built up a huge lead.

"This is the kind of game I like," Julia said. "It's easier on the nerves."

After the game, David said, "Let's go back to the room. I'm really tired."

"So am I," she said.

When they got to the room, he took her in his arms and held her close. He kissed her fervently. "Are you feeling okay?"

"Yes," she said, "I'm doing fine. I'm going to get ready for bed." She pulled away. "I'll just be a minute." She had bought a sexy new nightgown. She went into the bathroom to put it on. After a quick shower and a splash of perfume, she was ready. When she came out of the bathroom, she saw that David had just pulled off his clothes and was lying on the bed. He was sound asleep.

She shook her head. "My poor, tired darling," she said as she covered him. "But it's okay. I'll be here tomorrow."

She knew that David would hold her, and comfort her, and tell her that everything would be okay, much as her father had done when she was a little girl, if only she would let him.

Chapter 37

David awoke feeling extra frisky. He threw his arm over Julia and pinned her to the bed. "Now, I have you, my pretty," he said in that evil voice he used when he wanted to be extra dramatic. "There's no escaping me now," he said.

She looked up into his mischievous brown eyes and said, "Sorry to spoil your fun, but who's trying to escape? Not me."

"Drat. Foiled again," he said, in his best villain voice. "You're just going to lie there and let me take you without a struggle?"

"Absolutely," she said with a giggle as she pulled off her nightgown.

It was such a pleasure to stretch out in that big bed with the man who loved her. She felt his loving arms around her and felt his kisses. His tender touch on her bare skin sent shivers of ecstasy through her whole being. How could she ever want for anything more?

After a while, he said, "You know what, babe? This has been great, but …"

"I know," she said, reading his mind. "Man cannot live on love alone. He needs biscuits and gravy."

"Right," he said. "I'm starving. Why don't you order breakfast while I take a shower."

"What do you want?"

"Surprise me."

She placed the order. When he came out of the shower, she said, "Breakfast will be here in about thirty minutes.

After breakfast, he said, "That was great. I loved the western omelet, and the biscuits and gravy were delicious. What would you like to do until the game?"

She said, "Why don't we go up to Church Street and look around. I heard there are specialty shops and quaint little boutiques."

They walked the short distance to Church Street. There seemed to be a large contingent of Cougar fans on the streets. Everywhere they went, they saw fans decked out in the green and gold. They met several who called to them, "Hi, Dr. Crane! Hi, Coach Cooper."

They waved and called, "Having a good time?"

"Sure. See you at the game."

David said, "I think a lot of students must drive down for the day. Since the game is at six o'clock, they have time to drive home after it's over."

When they came to a western apparel store, she said, "I want to get another cowboy hat. You know, I told you I used to play in a country and western band. I had a hat then, but I don't know what happened to it." She found a hat she liked and placed it on her head. "I think I'll just wear it," she said. "Now, all I need are some boots."

After a while, David said, "All this shopping is making me hungry." So they stopped at little pub on the corner and had roast beef sandwiches and a beer.

Julia said, "Now what?"

"Let's go back to the hotel and take a nap," David said. "The game will be over early, so I would like to go down to some of the clubs on lower Broadway and hear some country music."

The Lady Cougars were playing a local team, the Belmont Lady Bruins. Once again, the Chapman team played superbly. The first two quarters were rather close, but they pulled away in the third quarter and won by ten. David said, "I think the women will do well in the NCAA."

After the game, they walked down Broadway Street. It was clogged with regular Saturday-night patrons as well as fans coming from the basketball arena. They stopped on the street outside a bar. The music spilled out onto the sidewalk.

"I like the music coming from this place. Let's go in," Julia said. On one wall was a large, old-fashioned, beautifully carved bar. A bandstand was on an adjacent wall. Six band members, dressed in cowboy hats, western shirts, jeans, and boots, were playing. In front of the bandstand, there was a dance floor where several couples were dancing. Small tables filled the rest of the room.

The hostess showed them to a table. A waitress came by and took their order. "I'll have a Jack and Coke," David said. "And she'll have …"

"I would really like a strawberry daiquiri," Julia said. After the waitress left, Julia said, "I hate to order a daiquiri because I know how much a bartender hates to make them, especially when they're very busy. When I was playing at the club in Kentucky, sometimes I would help out at the bar."

David said, "You deserve a daiquiri if you want one."

A young girl in a leather-fringed outfit stepped to the mike and began singing in a smooth, sexy voice. "Come on," David said. "Let's dance." He led her to the dance floor, and they stepped out to the strong beat of the band. He held her close and sang into her ear.

After another dance, they returned to their table. Their drinks were there. The band announced that they were taking a break. David looked up and saw one of the band members walking toward them. Julia jumped up and ran to him and hugged him. He hugged her back and kissed her cheek. As she led the man to the table, she looked at David. She thought he had a bewildered look and maybe a touch of jealousy on his handsome face.

"David," she said, "I want you to meet Johnny Owens. He was a member of the band I played with in Kentucky. Johnny, this is my fiancé, David Cooper."

Johnny said, "Aren't you D. J. Cooper, the basketball player?"

David shook hands with Johnny and gave his stock answer, "I used to be. Now, I'm just plain David Cooper, assistant coach."

"David is a coach at Chapman State where I teach," Julia said. "Can you sit for a minute? What have you been up to? Are you still touring?"

Johnny replied, "No, I don't tour anymore. I basically do studio work; however, sometimes I come out on the weekends and play with the band."

"Whatever happened to Kathryn?" She turned to David. "She was our vocalist."

Johnny said solemnly, "The last I heard, she was happily married to some guy and had two children."

Julia said, "I'm so sorry. I know how you two loved each other. How long has it been since you've seen her?"

He laughed. "About four hours. We had an early dinner about five thirty before I came to work. We've been married for about four years."

"Still a comedian," she said as he punched him on the arm. "Did you two ever finish college?"

"She did," Johnny said. "She teaches second grade at a local elementary school. I didn't. I guess you could say I've been getting on-the-job training. I've been producing some albums and doing some songwriting."

Julia said, "I'm surprised it took you so long to be married. You were so much in love when we were in college."

"Yes," he said, "but it took us a while to realize that the dreams we were both chasing were not going to make us happy. Once we decided what was really important, we found a way to make it work."

"And what was that?" she asked.

"That we loved each other and wanted to be together for the rest of our lives."

Julia looked at David. He smiled and patted her arm. "You are fortunate you didn't do something stupid while you were finding out," David said.

"You're right," Johnny said. "Touring with a band is not good for a marriage, so we moved to Nashville where I could still be in the music business and not tour. Kathryn sings in the church choir and to her second graders. We're pleased with the direction our lives are taking."

"That's great. I'm happy for you," she said with a big smile.

Johnny stood. "It's so good to see you, but I've got to get back to the band." He gave her his business card. "Call us when you're back in town," he said.

David said, "Do you take requests?"

"Sure," he said, and David told him what he wanted. "We can do that one."

They listened to several numbers while they finished their drinks. Julia said, "Some of these songs are so sad. They remind me of opera."

David said, "I'm sure that most of the songwriters get their ideas from real life. That's why people like them so much." Then he said, "Do you know how to two-step?"

"Sure," she said. "I didn't work in a country and western club all summer for nothing. Sometimes I would dance with the single guys. Do you?"

"Once, we played a three-game set with the Spurs. Our Saturday game was in the afternoon, so that night, a bunch of the guys went to this big club in San Antonio. I met this girl there who was a dancing fool. By the time we left, she had taught me to two-step like a pro."

Soon the band played a tune with the proper beat. "Want to try it?" He took her hand and twirled her under his arm. Julia felt she was a little rusty, but she soon remembered the familiar pattern. Dancing with David was so much fun. He had those smooth moves and that excellent sense of rhythm that all great dancers and basketball players have.

As they returned to their table, a group of people with Chapman State gear came by. "As I live and breathe, It's Coach Cooper and the lovely Dr. Crane," Phil Gardner said. "Does a certain uncle know that you two are barhopping on lower Broad in Nashville?"

"No," David said, "and I think he would be just as upset to learn that half of the coaching staff of Chapman State was also barhopping on lower Broad."

"So why don't we consider his blood pressure and not tell him."

"Exactly," David said. "We're not barhopping. We like the music of this band, so we're just here listening and dancing."

"Well, we're barhopping," Phil said. "We want to see and do all Nashville has to offer. We're off to the Wild Horse next. Great game, wasn't it?"

"It couldn't have been better. Makes Chapman look good."

"You kids have fun," Phil said as they left.

Then a handsome young man stepped up. The band began their intro, and the vocalist crooned into the mike, "Maybe I didn't love you quite as often as I should have." The girl singer and one of the guitar players sang backup.

"That's our song," David said. "We have to dance to this." He took her hand and led her to the dance floor. "I like this better than the two-step because I get to hold you close," David said. She laid her head on his chest and listened to David singing in her ear. It all felt so right. "Tell me that your sweet love hasn't died. You were always on my mind."

Johnny was right. The dream she was chasing wouldn't make her happy if she lost David. Could she ever tell David that her love for him had died? Not in a million years.

Chapter 38

On Sunday morning, they slept late. Julia got up, showered, and dressed in her new blue sweater and nice slacks. She saw that David was beginning to wake up. "Do you want to order breakfast?" Julia asked.

"No," he said. "Let's go down to the hotel restaurant. They're known for their fabulous Sunday brunch buffets."

"Okay," she said. "I'll pack while you shower."

As the hostess took them to their seats, they saw that there were quite a few Cougar fans in the restaurant. A waitress took their drink order, and they headed to the buffet table. Julia had never seen such a spread. In addition to the regular breakfast fare, there were all kinds of specialty stations: crepes, omelets, Belgian waffles, and all kinds of fruits and pastries. "Be sure to try the shrimp and grits," Julia told David. Then she added, "I am having trouble making up my mind what I want. There is such a variety."

"I'm going to stick with stuff I know," David said, "like country ham, eggs, and biscuits and gravy."

They were nearly finished eating when Phil Gardner came by. "Did you guys have fun last night? And that game. Wasn't it great?"

"Yes," David agreed. "Madge really has it all together this year."

Phil said, "I've great news. I just got the word that the Cougars will play the first round of the NCAA on Thursday in Louisville."

"Good," David said. "Louisville is just about two hours away. That means we should have a good contingent of fans. Do you know who we'll play?"

"Not yet. The real announcement will come this afternoon. The committee was just giving the ADs a heads-up so we can start making arrangements." He added, "There's something else I need to talk to you about. Some of the guys told me that Cruiser Bell says he hasn't turned in all his music assignments and will not have a passing grade at midterm, but your uncle Ralph is going to fix it so that he can play anyway."

"What?" David said. "He told me he had turned in all his work."

Phil went on, "You remember, one of your jobs is to keep the team academically eligible. It looks like you dropped the ball this time."

David looked at Julia. "Is this true?"

"Well, I'm not sure," she said. "I still have some papers to grade. I got a little behind when I had the flu. Papers turned in tomorrow will still count. I have until 5:00 p.m. on Monday to report the grades."

"Well, look into it," Phil said as he left the table.

"I can't believe you didn't tell me he was behind," David said sternly.

"I'm so sorry," she said. "I knew he was a couple of assignments behind, but he's been coming up with them."

"That's because I've been after him all the time. Let's go," he said.

When they returned to their room, she said, "David, I'm so sorry I didn't tell you about Cruiser. I'm sorry I made you look bad to Phil."

He took her in his arms. "Don't worry about it. Phil is a great AD, but he can be a real jerk at times."

"Are you upset with me?" she asked in a quivering voice.

"No, babe, I could never be upset with you. I'm upset with Cruiser for lying to me and at myself for believing him. I should never have trusted Cruiser Bell."

"Yes," she said, "Cruiser has a way of bending the truth to suit his own needs, but maybe he's planning to turn in the assignments."

David called for the Porsche, and they were on their way home.

"Thank you for taking me to Nashville. I really did need to get away," she said. "I really did need the rest."

"Thank you for going." He reached down and squeezed her hand, "Oh, babe, I don't know what I would do if I didn't have you. You have become such an important part of my life."

Again, she thought about what Johnny had said. Sometimes you didn't have to chase your dream. It was right there for the taking.

Chapter 39

Monday, Carol and Lakeysha walked up the stairs to their classroom in the music building. Lakeysha said to Carol, "I'll wait here and distract Cruiser if he comes in before you can leave the assignments."

"Okay," Carol said. "I'll hurry. We don't want him to know who did them."

Before long, Cruiser came sauntering up the stairs. "Hi, Cruiser," Lakeysha said. "Who was that cute girl I saw you with at the movies last Sunday night?"

Cruiser stopped and walked toward Lakeysha. "Some freshman in my English class. I'm trying to convince her that I could make all her dreams come true."

Lakeysha edged around so that Cruiser's back was to the classroom door. "You're a lecherous creep, Cruiser."

"Don't I know it," he said with a happy grin. "I saw you and my man Kenny sitting there making out in the back row."

"We weren't making out," she said. "We were enjoying the movie like civilized people."

"Well, you ought to give old Kenny a go. He's probably almost as good as I am."

"Or maybe even better," she said.

He laughed. "You oughta stick with old Kenny. He'll probably be rich someday when he goes to the pros. He could probably already make it now if he would declare for the draft."

"Unlike you, he wants to graduate," she said. "He's going to law school. He wants to be a sports attorney and help you dumb jocks get good contracts."

"Not me. I'm not gonna stick around long enough to graduate. I'm going for the big bucks as soon as I can, but I would hire him," he said. "Old Kenny is one smart dude."

Carol slipped out of the classroom and moved around as if she were just coming up the stairs. "Hi, Carol," Lakeysha said. "A few more minutes, and you would have been late."

"Hello, sweet cheeks. I've been waiting for you," Cruiser said. "Want to go down to the river with me tonight and watch the moon rise?"

"Forget it, Cruiser," Carol said curtly. "I'm not that desperate."

"One good thing about Cruiser," Lakeysha whispered as they entered the classroom. "He doesn't seem to mind when you insult him, or perhaps he's too egotistical or too dumb to recognize an insult."

"Good morning, Dr. Crane," Lakeysha said as Julia came in.

"Good morning, Miss Thomas, Miss Hanson," Julia said. Lakeysha watched as Julia went to the front of the room, turned on the computer, and stood watching as the students put their writing assignment into her basket.

Lakeysha got up and walked to the front of the room as Cruiser came in and moved to his customary seat. She saw him sit, pick up the folder Carol had left, and begin leafing through the papers. She wanted to continue watching but didn't dare for fear of him seeing her and becoming suspicious. She put her assignment in the basket, turned quickly, and sat down.

"Good morning, class," Julia said. "I want to congratulate members of the women's team, who just won the Midwestern Conference women's tournament. Great job, ladies!" The class clapped.

"Did you see any of our games, Dr. Crane?" Lakeysha asked.

"Yes, I saw the games on Friday and Saturday. You all did great! And I wish both teams well in the NCAA tournament. I know you'll be missing some classes the next two weeks, so I haven't made any assignments due during that time." Then she began class.

After class, Julia said, "Your midterm grades will be posted outside my office door tomorrow morning." Then she dismissed class.

Lakeysha looked at Carol and shrugged her shoulders, as if to say, "It looks like we failed."

As Cruiser walked up to the front, he stopped and said, "Sorry, Dr. Crane. I forgot to turn these in. Here's three assignments."

"Three assignments. Cruiser, Coach Cooper will be so proud of you," Julia said.

"He oughta be. I worked hard on these."

Lakeysha saw Carol stand and clench her fist. Lakeysha put her hand on Carol's arm. "Steady, girl," she whispered. "We don't want to blow it now." *At least Dr. Crane's job is safe for a while,* she thought as she hustled Carol out of the room.

At noon, David received a text from Julia: "Cruiser turned in all his assignments. Should have a passing grade at midterm. Love. J."

David caught up with Cruiser at basketball practice. "Cruiser, did you lie to me when I asked you if you had all your assignments done?"

"Naw, Coach, I didn't lie, honest. You said, 'How's music going?' and I said, 'I got it, Coach.' I meant that I was working on my assignments. I just hadn't turned them all in yet."

"And what about Dr. Jennings? Did he say he would fix it so you could play even if you got a failing grade?"

"Well, he told my dad that maybe I could get an incomplete since it wasn't the final grade. I swear, Coach, I didn't lie."

"You better not," David said. "You'll be off this team in a heartbeat if you do." David still felt sure that Cruiser had lied about something; he just wasn't sure about what. What could he do? There was nothing he could prove at the moment. "Okay, Cruiser, let's work on those foul shots. They may be the difference in our winning or losing."

Chapter 40

Tuesday, Julia felt like a new person. She was happy beyond measure. Perhaps her life was turning around. She finally knew what she was going to do about David. Cruiser had done his work. There were no messages and no sighting of Mr. Hoodie on Monday. The sun was, indeed, shining brightly for her.

She arrived at her office at 8:45 a.m. She was shocked to see a white envelope in her box. The message inside read: "Think about it! It's no mystery. If you don't go, then you'll be history!"

Now she was really confused. Since Cruiser did his work and would be academically eligible, she didn't have to worry about being fired. Then why was she still being threatened? She felt there was no doubt now. Dr. Jennings had to be behind all this. But why was a respected university president resorting to such sleazy tricks? He must still be trying to get rid of her because of her relationship with David. If Dr. Jennings was responsible, then maybe there was not as much threat as she imagined.

David picked up Julia after practice and took her out to dinner. "How was your day?" he asked.

"Not bad. My violin students had all practiced. My string classes went well." But what she didn't say was, "No more Mr. Hoodie." Should she tell David about the messages? No, she couldn't bother him now.

After they returned to her apartment, he said, "The team is leaving at noon tomorrow. If we win, we will play again on Saturday and won't be back until Saturday night or Sunday."

"I'll miss you every minute you're gone."

"Why don't you go too? You could go as a chaperone for the band. I'm sure Dr. Salerno would okay it."

"It's tempting," she said, "but I hate to miss any more Thursday violin lessons. I'm still doing makeups for when I had the flu. I'm learning how to survive when you're gone."

"Good training for a coach's wife," he said and then kissed her. "I'm proud of you."

On Wednesday, Julia hurried to her office a little before nine. She was relieved that Cruiser had turned in all his work. At least that problem had been solved, and there were no visits from Mr. Hoodie yesterday.

She went to her classroom and welcomed her class. "Did everyone see your grades that were posted outside my office door? I am so pleased to announce that everyone in the class has a passing grade at midterm. I hope in the next half of the semester, everyone will keep up with their assignments as we begin our study of instrumental music of the Romantic period."

Before she dismissed class, she said, "Please read chapter 8 in your textbook. I know the basketball team will miss Friday, but hopefully you can find time to do your reading before next Monday. And good luck in Louisville."

As the class was leaving, she said to Cruiser, "Cruiser, did you notice that you have a B- at midterm? It just shows what you can do if you put in a little work."

"Yeah, I guess so," he said with a happy grin.

When Julia went to her office, she saw another white envelope in her box. She snatched it up and ripped it open.

It read, "What do you think? What do you know? It's time for you to go, go, go!"

Julia wanted to cry. She was hoping that this reign of terror was over. But maybe she was overreacting. It had to be a practical joke someone was playing on her. But who?

She left the building at noon to run some errands, and there was Mr. Hoodie standing with one foot up on the wall beside the door. Once again, he followed her down the sidewalk to her car.

At symphony rehearsal, she asked Molly if she had noticed a man in a green hoodie outside the music building. Molly said she had seen several students wearing green hoodies. The Chapman State hoodies were popular early spring wear.

After rehearsal, Julia left the building to go home, and there was Mr. Hoodie again. He followed her down the sidewalk. She sat in her car for a moment to see where he went. She noticed his car, a beat-up, old wreck.

She backed out and headed for home. When she looked in the rearview mirror, she saw the old car following her. What should she do? Maybe she shouldn't go home. She didn't want him to know where she lived, but he probably already knew. It would be no problem to find out. She decided to head downtown to the police station.

When she went in, she approached the desk sergeant. "I'm Sergeant Jefferson," he said. "How may I help you, ma'am?" he asked politely. She told him about the man who was following her. He took her name and address. She gave a description of the man and related everything that had happened. The sergeant wrote furiously on a pad of paper. Then Sergeant Jefferson said, "Now, let me get this straight. This man that you keep seeing has spoken to you only when you asked a question, has never made a threatening gesture toward you, and has only walked behind you for a short distance on the way to his own car."

"Yes, that's right," she said.

"And the only thing he has done is appear where you are."

She had to admit that this too was accurate.

"Yes," she said. "But his actions have just unnerved me. He always seemed to be waiting for me when I came out of places." Then she remembered the messages. She had saved the last two of them and pulled them out of her purse to give to the sergeant.

"Well, this is something concrete," he said. "May I keep these? We'll check them for fingerprints." Sergeant Jefferson pulled out a business card. "Here is the number of the station. If you ever see this man again, call us immediately. We'll send a car to pick him up for questioning." He added, "We'll send a squad car to drive past the music building every afternoon around four fifteen. If we see anyone who answers this description, we'll bring him in. That's about all we can do, ma'am," he said.

Julia got back into her car and drove home. She ran into the house and locked the front door. She checked the back door and looked out a front window. She wanted to talk to David, to tell him everything. He could be here in less than two hours. All she had to do was call.

"Don't panic," she told herself. No, she wouldn't bother David. He would be busy getting the team settled for the evening. They always had a team meeting on the evening before a game. She didn't want to be responsible for him not doing his job. She didn't want him to think she was some weak sister who couldn't take care of her own life. But as soon as David came home, she would tell him everything. She fixed some dinner, but she was too upset to eat much.

She checked her lesson plans for the next two weeks. She would wait until the basketball team came back to return the writing assignments. She put the plans and assignments in her briefcase and got ready for bed.

When her phone rang, she pounced on it. "Oh, David," she said in a trembling voice. "I'm so glad you called."

"What's wrong, babe?" he said. "Are you okay?"

"Oh yes," she lied. "I just wanted to hear your voice. David, I love you so much. I can't wait for you to ask me to marry you."

"I'm glad you're okay. I love you too. You know how precious you are to me. We'll take care of the asking just as soon as I get home. I have to warn you. I may not have a ring yet, but I'll get it soon."

"I don't need a ring," she said. "I just need to know that you still want me. Good luck in the game tomorrow."

Chapter 41

When Julia got to her office at nine o'clock on Thursday, there was a white envelope in her box. She opened it. It read, "I'll tell you a story, and it is true. If you stick around, it's the end of you."

It looked like this nonsense was going to continue. As soon as David returned home, he would put a stop to it. She was sure. After her 11:00 a.m. violin student, Julia went by Molly's office. "I'm going to the bank downtown. Go with me, and we'll have a Greek salad for lunch."

"I would love to," Molly said. "But I have a makeup violin lesson. Sorry. I'll see you at two o'clock at string class."

There didn't seem to be a parking place in front of the bank, so she went several blocks down the street before she found one. Her business in the bank didn't take long, but when she came out, there was Mr. Green Hoodie leaning against the wall beside the door. She looked at him, and he gave her that smirky, knowing smile.

Julia started down the street. She didn't look around, but she felt sure he was following her. As she came to the Italian restaurant, she ducked in the door. She would sit down and call the police. Before she could call, the waitress came, so she ordered a Greek salad.

When the desk sergeant answered, he said, "I'm sorry, Miss Crane, but there has been an accident out on the interstate. A lumber truck took a curve too fast and overturned. We've got two-by-fours scattered over all three lanes. Traffic is backed up for five miles in both directions. Every unit we have is out there directing traffic and assisting with the cleanup."

"I'm in the Italian restaurant on Main Street," Julia said. "I'm going to stay in here and have some lunch."

"Good," the sergeant said. "I'll try to get a unit down there as soon as I can. Maybe he will stay put for a while."

She picked at her salad, barely tasting it. All she could think about was Dr. Jennings. She felt sure he was the one behind the messages and Mr. Hoodie. It had to be a ploy to get her to leave. But why? Surely it couldn't be all that bad for David's career. She knew that he loved her, and she loved him. *Why can't people marry the one they love without others interfering?*

David had warned her. He said they would be all right if the world didn't get in their way. Well, the world was getting in their way—Dr. Jennings, her mother, and who knew who else. She would love David even if he were the penniless coach her mother believed him to be. She had made a decision. She wasn't going to quietly leave. Even if she never taught in a university again, she would marry David and have his children. She would have plenty of time to become a foremost authority on violin pedagogy and a full professor, sometime in the future.

Julia looked at her watch. She really needed to get back to the campus. She paid her bill and went out the door. There was Mr. Green Hoodie leaning against the wall. She started down the street toward her car. It was only about five blocks. If she could reach her car, she would be safe.

She started walking very fast. She looked around. He was following about twenty feet behind. She started walking very slowly. He walked slowly, maintaining his distance. She passed several streets. Her heart was racing. People were coming in and out of shops along the street. She slipped in between them and continued to walk fast. Pangs of fear were turning into feelings of terror.

Her heart was racing. Her car was on the next block. A city bus ground to a halt at the corner. She looked up and saw that the light was about to change. She looked back; he was still coming. She started running. If she could beat the light and cross the street, she could reach her car. She heard the bus start up. She saw it turning the corner just as she dashed into the street. She heard brakes squealing fiercely. She felt an awful pain in her lower leg and realized she was flying through the air. She came down with a thud and felt a terrific pain in her head, and blackness descended upon her.

David and the members of the Chapman State Cougars stood in the tunnel that led from the dressing rooms at the Louisville basketball arena. They were playing the second game of the morning session of the NCAA tournament. "There's a minute, thirty-two to go, and Georgia Central is up by three," someone in front said.

David looked across the court to Georgia Central's bench. Their coach, a well-dressed black man, was waving his arms and giving hand signals to his team. David liked to see coaches wear a suit and tie. *It gives the impression that they think their job is important.* Suddenly, the game was over, and Georgia Central had hung on to win. Members of the crowd erupted on the court. David saw a nice-looking white lady bound up to the coach and kiss him as no one but a wife should. At her side were two light-skinned brown children with black, curly hair. The coach leaned down and hugged the children and turned to congratulate his team and the opponents.

"Wait until they clear the court," Coach McDaniel said. Soon the other teams were gone. The Cougars and their opponents ran onto the floor. They began to run through their pregame warm-up drills while the Chapman State pep band played their fight song. Their supporters stood and clapped in time with the music.

Tyler ran up to David. "Coach Coop, have you seen Kevin?" Tyler said. "I need my asthma inhaler. I left it in my bag beside the locker."

"I'm not sure," David said as he looked for the student manager. "I guess Kevin is helping the trainer. I'll go get it. It's still twelve minutes until tip-off."

As David was going down the tunnel to the dressing room, the Georgia Central coach came out of their dressing room. "Congratulations, Coach," David said. "Your team really hung in there at the end." He extended his hand. "I'm D. J. Cooper."

The other coach shook his hand. "I'm Allen Parker," he said. "I thought I recognized you. Are you coaching now?"

"Yes, I'm an assistant at Chapman. Allen, may I ask you a personal question?"

"Well, sure, I guess."

"Is your wife white?'

"Yes, but what's it to you?" he asked sharply.

"My fiancée is white too, and my uncle, who is the president of Chapman, insists that if I marry her, it will be bad for my coaching career. Have you ever had any problems in that area?"

"Not really," he replied, "but if an AD or search committee has an issue of that nature, they won't tell you. They'll say you're not a fit for their program or you're too old or too young, that sort of nonsense.

"Second," he said, "if they're concerned with the color of your wife's skin, they'll be doing you a favor by not hiring you, because it would be a job that you wouldn't want anyway."

He went on, "I guess if I had several losing seasons, I might wake up to find a moving van parked in my front yard." He laughed. "But I think the white guys have that problem too. My advice to you is this: if you love the girl, marry her, no matter what color her skin or what anyone says."

"Thank you," David said. "I plan to. Good luck in the tournament."

David retrieved the inhaler and went back to the bench. He gave it to Kevin. "Please keep this for Tyler," he said.

"Sure. What's with you, Coach?" Kevin said as he looked up into David's smiling face. "You look like you just won the lottery."

"Maybe I have, Kevin. Maybe I have."

Chapter 42

The game was over. The Cougars fought back from a two-point deficit at halftime to win by eight points. Cruiser Bell made it down the court in record time, and the guards, Jalen Wilson and Teddy Baker, rained down threes in the second half.

David was elated. His first thought was to call Julia and tell her, but there was no answer when he called. He left a message. "Hey, babe," he said. "Call me as soon as you get this message."

David met with the team and the coaching staff and made plans for the next game on Saturday. He decided to call again. This time, a male voice answered, "Hoover County Police."

"Hello," David said. "Who is this?"

"Hoover County Police, Sergeant Jefferson. Who is this?"

"I'm D. J. Cooper," David said. "I'm trying to call my fiancée, Julia Crane. Do you have her phone?"

"You say Julia Crane is your fiancée?"

"Yes, that's right. Where is she?"

"Sir," Sergeant Jefferson said, "you need to talk to my chief."

David waited.

"Mr. Cooper," a voice said, "this is Chief Thompson of the Hoover County Police. I have Julia Crane's cell phone because she was involved in an accident this afternoon in downtown Hoover. She was hit by a bus and taken to University Hospital."

"How is she? What are her injuries?"

"We are not at liberty to say." Then he added, "Mr. Cooper, we really don't know anything. We're trying to reach her next of kin. According to an ID we found in her purse, her next of kin is a

Cynthia Crane who lives in Florida. We left messages, but she hasn't returned our calls."

"Cynthia Crane is Julia's mother," David said, "but she's on a five-week tour of Europe, and I don't know how to reach her. Her father is deceased. Julia is an only child and has no other next of kin."

"Mr. Cooper," Chief Thompson said, "I would suggest you go to University Hospital as soon as possible."

David punched in Molly's number. "Oh, David," she said. "Thank goodness you called. I guess you know about Julia."

"Do you know anything about her condition?"

"No," she said. "The police called Dr. Salerno's office after they saw her Chapman ID. I went to the hospital, but they wouldn't let me see her until her next of kin has been notified."

"We'll see about that," he said. "I'm leaving Louisville as soon as I can rent a car. I should be in Hoover in two hours. I'll go straight to the hospital."

"Drive safely, David," she said. "Please let me know what's happening."

David made the distance from Louisville to Hoover in less than two hours. At the hospital, he learned what he had feared. He couldn't see Julia or learn about her condition because he was not her next of kin.

"You will have to speak to the hospital administrator," the floor nurse said. "He should still be here. It's not five o'clock yet." The nurse gave him directions to the office.

The administrator's secretary said, "Can this wait until tomorrow? Mr. Richards is about to leave for the day."

David said, "Absolutely not!"

"All right," she said. "Go right in."

A short, balding man wearing wire-rim glasses was sitting at his desk. "Yes," he said. "How can I help you?"

David told him about Julia. "Her mother, Cynthia Crane, is her only next of kin. She's on a tour of European cities and will be gone about four more weeks. I don't know how to reach her."

"Yes," he said. "A Julia Crane was brought into the hospital this afternoon. I'm sorry, sir. There's nothing we can do until we get in touch with her next of kin. We're not allowed to go beyond minimum measures to keep the patient alive."

"And why not?"

"It's a matter of financial responsibility."

David said, "She's my fiancée. What if I assume financial responsibility? I'll sign anything you want as long as Julia can get the treatment she needs."

Mr. Richards was looking at him a little suspiciously. Although he was dressed in a suit, he had removed his tie. He knew his shirt was rumpled, and he probably needed a shave. "I'm sure that the financial burden will be quite extensive before she completely recovers," Mr. Richards said. "We would have to be sure you could meet the entire amount."

David said, "Sir, do you know who I am?" David hated it when people played the "Do you know who I am?" card, but this was different. Julia's life could be in jeopardy.

Mr. Richards looked at David again and blinked in recognition. "Well, yes," he said. "I believe you are D. J. Cooper."

"Then you should know that I have been a professional basketball player for the past eight years. I could buy this hospital if I wanted to, and I would too, if that's what it took."

Mr. Richards said, "Oh no, that's not necessary. But here's what you need to do. Call your attorney. Get him to set up a hearing to have you appointed as Julia Crane's legal guardian. That way, you can see her and participate in decisions regarding her treatment."

"Thank you," David said. "But can I see her? I just need to know that she's alive."

"Come with me," Mr. Richards said. "I think we can make an exception in your case."

He led David to an elevator. They went up two floors and down the hall to a large room filled with cubicles with beds and banks of instruments with flashing lights and digital readouts. "This is the intensive care unit," Mr. Richards said. He indicated for David to follow. He saw a man in a white coat bending over Julia.

David was aghast to see Julia lying quietly in the bed with all kinds of tubes emerging from under the sheets. She looked like a wax doll, so still and pale. Her beautiful dark hair was gone, and her head was swathed in bandages.

The doctor motioned to them, and they followed him into the hall. Mr. Richards said, "Dr. Freeman, this is Miss Crane's fiancé, D. J. Cooper. Mr. Cooper, this is Dr. Paul Freeman. He is the neurologist who will be treating your Miss Crane."

"Mr. Cooper," Dr. Freeman began, "Miss Crane has suffered a blow to the head that has resulted in a severe head trauma. Although she in now in a coma, she may awake at any time. I think we should continue the coma with medication until her brain has a chance to heal. If she were to awake now, she would be in great pain, and she might regress to a state where she would never wake up." Then he added, "We really need to begin this treatment immediately."

Dr. Freeman looked at Mr. Richards. "Go ahead with the treatment," he said. "Mr. Cooper is in the process of being declared Miss Crane's legal guardian. We need to get her records ready to fax to the judge, but I feel sure there will be no problem. We've had cases like this before."

"What will you do?" David asked the doctor.

"We need to administer antibiotics and glucose immediately. If her brain should begin to swell, we might need to do surgery to relieve the pressure, but that's not indicated at this time. After she's stable, we will do a CAT scan and electroencephalography to measure activity within the brain. She also has a broken leg, but we'll take care of that as soon as she's stable."

"Does she need round-the-clock nursing? I can take care of that," David said.

"No, not at this time," Dr. Freeman said. "She will be in intensive care, and there will be someone with her at all times. Mr. Cooper, I need to ask you one more question. Please don't be offended, but as her doctor, I need to know. Is there a chance your fiancée could be pregnant? It would be a great strain on the mother and the fetus if she is, and also, we will be giving her some very strong drugs and taking x-rays. We need to know everything we can about her medical history."

"No, Doctor," David said. "I don't believe so. We have been very careful. We know the complications it would make in our lives if we were to have a child now. However, we do want children in the future very badly. Will this endanger her ability to have children?"

"I don't think so," he said. "She should be able to lead a normal life, if she recovers. We just have to be patient. She may be in this coma for two or three weeks."

"Thank you," David said. "Is it okay if I stay a few minutes?"

"Yes," the doctor said, "but she won't know you, and she can't hear you, so don't be upset. We will do everything possible to save her."

As soon as the doctor left, David went in to see Julia. He picked up her hand and kissed it. It felt cold and lifeless to his touch. David broke down. He stood against the wall and sobbed copiously. It wasn't fair. Julia didn't deserve this. Finally, he regained his composure and remembered the things he needed to do.

As he came out of the room, David almost ran into an older man. Noticing his dark suit and white collar, he said, "I'm sorry, Father. I was disturbed. I didn't see you."

"Yes, I can see that you are distressed. Can I be of help, my son?" the priest asked.

David told him about Julia.

"Yes," he said, "I was on my way to see Julia. She is a member of my congregation. As I was making my rounds, I saw that she had been admitted. I'm Father Joseph."

"Please pray for her, Father, but no last rites. Not yet anyway," David said. "I have to have some hope that she will recover."

"Of course, my son," Father Joseph said.

Chapter 43

When David left the hospital, he punched in his attorney's private number. Charles McKinney had been a teammate when they played for the Indiana Hoosiers. David knew he needed excellent advice, and Chuck was the one person he would trust with Julia's life at stake.

"David, I just saw part of your game on TV. Congratulations. It looks like you have a winner. What are you up to?"

David told Chuck about Julia, and immediately, his tone turned serious. "David, you need someone local to handle this, because sometimes laws are slightly different from state to state."

David listened carefully. "Who can I get?" he asked.

Chuck went on, "I'm going to call a former law school colleague. His name is Bob Randall, and he's with the law firm of Pittman, Perkins, and Randall right there in Hoover. Don't do anything until Bob calls you. And don't worry, Bob is one of the best."

While David waited for Bob's call, he dropped off his rental car and had the rental people take him to pick up his truck. Then he stopped at the police station. He was surprised to find that Sergeant Jefferson was still there.

The sergeant told David where and how the accident had happened. "We're still investigating," the sergeant said, "but it's doubtful we'll ever know exactly what happened until Miss Crane regains consciousness. We've interviewed several people, and everyone agrees that she was running down the street, but no one noticed anyone chasing her. We still have her purse. We looked through it for any clues, but there doesn't seem to be any, and there doesn't seem to be any evidence of foul play. Would you like to take it?"

The sergeant related to David that Julia had filed a complaint the day before, but no one seemed to remember anyone who fit the description of the man she had reported following her. Everyone agreed that she ran into the street of her own accord.

David took the purse and drove through downtown Hoover. He spotted Julia's car a block away from where the accident took place. Then his phone rang. He pulled over to the curb and answered it.

A voice said, "This is Bob Randall."

"David Cooper."

"David," Bob said, "I have spoken to Chuck, and I'm familiar with your situation. I have everything set up. There will be a hearing at eight o'clock tomorrow morning with Judge Arthur Thomas Harrison in his chambers in room 112 of the Federal Building. Now here's what I need you to do. You need to bring three reliable witnesses to the hearing, people who know you or Julia well and are upstanding members of the community. You also need to fax a copy of Julia's hospital record to the judge's office."

"I'll don't know how to thank you," David said.

"I'm glad I can be of help," Bob said.

David called Molly and told her about Julia's condition and the hearing. "I'll be there," she said. "I think you should ask Dr. Salerno. After all, he's her boss."

"Yes," he said, "and who else? All my friends in the Athletic Department are in Louisville."

"Ask your uncle Ralph," she said.

"I'm not sure that's such a good idea," he said.

"Trust me," she said. "Ask Uncle Ralph."

David made the call, then decided to go by Julia's apartment, just to check on things. He took her key ring from her purse and opened the front door. Everything was impeccably neat, as he knew it would be. He checked the windows and the back door to see that everything was locked. As he passed the refrigerator in the kitchen, he opened the door to see if there was food that would need to be thrown out. There was not, but he noticed the beer, his favorite kind. Julia didn't drink beer, but she kept it for him.

He saw a plastic container filled with sandwich meat and cheese and remembered how hungry he was. He found a loaf of homemade bread and sliced off a couple of pieces to make a sandwich. He took a handful of chips from a bag he found in the pantry and went into the living room. Several first-round NCAA games were on.

He couldn't believe how comforting it was just to spend time in her space. Evidence of her love for him was all around—the homemade bread he loved, his favorite spicy mustard for his ham and cheese sandwiches, right down to his favorite beer in the fridge.

As he ate and watched a game, he began to relax. He stretched out on the couch and was soon asleep. Sometime in the night, he awoke, undressed, and moved to Julia's bed. He set the alarm for 6:30 a.m. He had to be on time tomorrow.

Once he awoke, it was hard to go back to sleep. He kept playing the accident over and over in his mind. Did she know what had happened to her? Was she scared? What if she never woke up? How could he live without her? Why hadn't he insisted that she go to Louisville with them? But the doctor had said he thought she had every chance to make a full recovery. He had to hold on to that. Finally, he fell into a fitful sleep.

Friday morning, David got up when the alarm went off and made coffee. He showered and shaved and dressed in a neat sports coat. He wanted to present a more affluent and responsible picture to the judge than he had to the hospital administrator yesterday.

He made eggs, bacon, and toast for breakfast. Somehow, he felt more comfortable in Julia's apartment than in his dorm room, even if he did have to cook. After breakfast, he put the dishes in the dishwasher, cleaned up the kitchen, and left for the Federal Building.

David met his uncle Ralph in the corridor outside the judge's chambers a few minutes before eight o'clock. "Uncle Ralph," he said. "I know you don't like Julia, but please don't say anything that would keep me from being named her legal guardian. It's very important that I be able to see her and have a say in her treatment."

"Of course it is, my boy," he said. "I know how much you love Julia. And how is Julia today?"

"I called the hospital earlier. There's no change."

Uncle Ralph had a sheepish look on his face. "My boy," he began hesitantly. "I am a little embarrassed to tell you that I have had a change of attitude about your relationship with Julia. I am convinced that you are capable of making decisions about your life without my help." David couldn't believe what he was hearing. Ralph went on, "I know that you and Julia will manage to work out whatever problems you may have."

"Thank you," David said. "Thank you very much. I really appreciate your change of heart." *We're making progress. At least he's calling her by her name instead of "that girl."*

A young man in his early thirties, impeccably dressed in a dark blue business suit, came up to David. "Mr. Cooper? I'm Bob Randall." He extended his hand.

"David Cooper," David said. "And this is Dr. Ralph Jennings, the president of Chapman State."

"Yes," Bob said, "I know Dr. Jennings. How are you, sir?"

David introduced Molly and Dr. Salerno, who were just arriving. Molly hugged David and said, "She's going to be okay. I just know it." They all went into the judge's chambers.

As they went in, Judge Harrison came over to Ralph. "Well, Ralph," he said, shaking hands. "It's good to see you. How are you, and how is Ophelia?"

"We're well, Arthur," he said. "This is David Cooper. He's Caroline's boy. We're very distressed because David's fiancée is in critical condition."

"Yes," the judge said, "I have been reading her hospital records. We'll see if I can help." He announced to the group, "Let's all sit down, folks. Mr. Randall, will you please present your case?" Everyone found chairs.

Bob began, "I am representing David J. Cooper, who is petitioning the court to be named legal guardian of Dr. Julia Crane, who has been critically injured and is now in a coma. Dr. Crane's only next of kin, her mother, is now touring somewhere in Europe, and we do not know how to get in touch with her. Someone needs to make decisions regarding her treatment as well as to assume financial responsibility."

"And are you willing to accept these responsibilities?" the judge said to David.

"Yes, I am, Your Honor," David said. "I love Julia Crane very much. We are planning to be married."

"And are you financially able to meet these responsibilities?"

"Yes, I am, Your Honor," David said.

"Where are you employed?"

"I am an assistant basketball coach at Chapman."

Ralph spoke up. "The boy has been in the NBA for the past eight years, Arthur. You know how they pay those boys. He can definitely pay her hospital bills."

"Why, yes," the judge said as he peered at David over his glasses. "You're D. J. Cooper. Sorry I didn't recognize you. I knew Ralph's nephew played for the Pacers, but I didn't know you were the one."

Bob Randall said, "I would like to hear from Mrs. Corbin. Would you state your name and occupation?"

Molly said, "I am Molly Corbin. I have been a professor of music at Chapman State for the past ten years."

"How long have you known Dr. Crane?"

"I have known Julia Crane ever since she was hired as an instructor of violin almost two years ago. We have become very close. I believe I am probably her best friend," Molly said.

Bob said, "Knowing Dr. Crane as you do, would you say that she would want David Cooper to be given the position as her legal guardian?"

"Oh yes, she loves David very much. I believe there is no else she would want in that position."

"Do you have anything to add, Dr. Salerno?" Bob Randall asked.

"I don't know much about Dr. Crane and Mr. Cooper's private lives, but I do know that she and Mrs. Corbin are very close, and I would trust, implicitly, anything Mrs. Corbin said about their relationship."

"Very well," Judge Harrison said, "I believe I have heard enough. I hereby grant the petitioner, David J. Cooper, the legal guardianship of Dr. Julia Crane for as long as she is incapacitated."

"Thank you, Judge," Bob Randall said. "Would you please fax a copy of your ruling to University Hospital as soon as possible?"

"So ordered," the judge said as he pounded his gavel.

David shook hands with Bob. "Thank you so much for your help."

"It was a pleasure. Sorry about the circumstances, but please call me again if there is anything else I can do."

The judge shook hands with everyone. When he came to David, he said, "I wish Dr. Crane a speedy recovery." And to Ralph, he said, "As soon as it warms up a little, let's go out and work on your golf game."

"Sure," Ralph said. "Since your game is beyond hope."

As they left, David whispered to Molly, "I didn't know they were friends."

"I did," she said. "They were together at the Valentine dance."

David said, "Molly, do you have time to drive Julia's car back to her apartment?"

"Sure," she said, "I don't have a class until ten."

After they picked up Julia's car, David took Molly to the music building. Before she got out of the car, Molly said, "David, after you have taken care of your business here, you need to go back to Louisville for Saturday's game. There's nothing you can do here."

"But I need to be here in case she wakes up."

"David," Molly said emphatically, "she's not going to wake up for a week or so. They're not going to let her wake up until her brain heals. Put me on the visitor's list, and I'll spend time with her every day. I'll call you after every visit."

David took Julia's insurance card to the business office and signed the necessary paperwork. Then he went up to intensive care. A young man with a name tag that read "Chris Reynolds, Neuro Technician," was attaching a band to Julia's head. David stepped forward. "I'm David Cooper, Dr. Crane's fiancé. What are you doing?"

The young man put out his hand. "I'm Chris Reynolds. I am doing an electroencephalograph, or an EEG, as we call it. It's really a brain activity test. We'll do one every day to monitor her brain activity." He indicated a machine with dials and displays.

"What are all these other things?" David asked, indicating the bank of machines with gauges and displays.

"We monitor her oxygen level, heart rate, and blood pressure every hour. We're really interested in her oxygen level. If it drops to a certain level, we'll put her on a ventilator to help her breathe. Right now, this is not indicated, as she seems to be breathing on her own with no trouble."

Dr. Freeman came in. "What's the news, Chris?" he asked. Chris tore off a strip of paper that the machine spit out. The doctor looked at it and said, "Mr. Cooper, everything looks very good. Her brain function is still minimal, but that's to be expected, and all her vital signs are normal for someone in her condition."

"Is there anything, I can do?" David asked.

"Not one thing now," the doctor said. "I want her to rest and let her brain heal. She can't hear you and would not even know you are here. We have to be patient," he said as he patted David on the shoulder. "In a few days, we'll start giving her some stimulation. Then you can talk to her, read to her, or play music."

David said, "You know, I'm an assistant basketball coach at Chapman. The team is in the NCAA tournament in Louisville. Would it be okay if I joined the team for their game tomorrow? Would you call me if there's any change?"

"Of course," Dr. Freeman said. "She's resting comfortably, and there's nothing more you can do here."

David left the hospital, got a fast-food burger, and went back to Julia's apartment. He got a beer from the fridge and sat on the couch, trying to decide what to do. He called Rusty, who told him the game would be at 6:00 p.m. on Saturday.

David said, "I'm going to stay here tonight, but I'll leave early tomorrow morning. I should be there before the morning shootaround." He told him about Julia's condition and the prognosis for her recovery.

Rusty said, "Okay, do what you think is best." David changed into jeans and a sweatshirt. He took his beer and burger and watched an NCAA game on TV. He had slept little the night before, so he stretched out on the long couch, and before long, he was asleep.

After an hour or so, David awoke. He felt thought he should go back to his room at the dorm. He knew everyone at the dorm would be watching the NCAA games on TV in the living room, but he didn't want to face the questions and noise that would be prevalent in the dorm. Julia wouldn't mind if he stayed. If was just that he kept expecting to see her coming out of another room or hear her playing her violin.

He put on his jacket and got into his truck. There was something he needed to do. He drove to the hospital and went up to the third floor in the elevator. At the nurses' station, a pretty, blond-haired lady was writing on an iPad. Her name tag read, "Judy Kelly, Intensive Care Supervisor." She looked up. "May I help you?" she said.

"Yes," he said, "I'm David Cooper, Julia Crane's fiancé. Would it be okay if I just sat by her for a while?"

"Of course," she said. "She's resting comfortably, but she probably won't know you're there."

"That's okay," he said. "I just want to be with her for a little while."

Another nurse came up. "Coach Cooper, I'm Helen Brandon. My husband and I watched the replay of yesterday's game last night. The Cougars were so good. You've done a great job."

"Thank you," he said. "They're playing great. I'm going back to Louisville tomorrow morning. Would it be okay if I called you later in the day to see how she's doing?"

Nurse Kelly said, "Of course. Call anytime you want. Here's the direct number of this nursing station."

Nurse Brandon said, "Can you believe it? If we win one more game, the Cougars will be going to the second round of the NCAA. I don't think any Cougar team has ever made it to the second round."

David went to Julia's bed. Once again, he was disturbed by how fragile and still she looked. As he kissed her cheek, he looked at some of the digital displays. There didn't seem to be any change in the numbers. He told her about the game yesterday and what he was going to do tomorrow, but there was no change in her at all. Not that he expected any, but he felt confident that one day there would be.

Chapter 44

Sunday, David got up early and had breakfast with Rusty. Then he got in in his truck and made his way back to Hoover. He called the hospital, and there was no change in Julia, but he still wanted to hurry back.

Most of the team was still sleeping. They had had a late night of celebrating after their crushing defeat of Georgia Central the night before. They were off to the next round of the NCAA tournament, the first Chapman State team to ever make it to the second round. Rusty was going to let them hang out at the hotel this morning. The bus would leave at 1:00 p.m., so there was no reason for him to stay.

Traffic was light this morning, so his mind wandered to thoughts of last night's game. He couldn't believe how well they all had played. Jalen Wilson was no longer the scared, skinny kid he had been the first day David saw him. Regular sessions in the weight room had added muscles and bulk to his upper body. The confidence he was showing on the basketball court was spilling over into his academic life, all As and Bs on the midterm grade report. He was becoming a competent point guard, bringing the ball down the court skillfully and distributing it to the shooters. He was also getting to be a defensive specialist with several steals per game.

Kenny Williams and Tyler Maxwell were exhibiting the calm leadership he would expect from upperclassmen. Even Cruiser had improved. He was racing down the court like a gazelle with a lion on his tail. He set up in his defensive position before the offense even made it down the court. Every day, David saw the results of his coaching. He was so proud of the entire team. It made him feel as if he had made the right decision to go into coaching.

David thought of the things he needed to do when he returned to Hoover. He had made a decision to continue to stay at Julia's apartment, at least until he heard from Cynthia. He felt sure she would want to come to Hoover as soon as she returned to the States.

It had been great staying at the athletic dorm in the beginning; it gave him a chance to get to know the guys on the team. But now he was enjoying the privacy and quietness of the apartment. In fact, he was thinking of finding his own place. He might call a Realtor tomorrow to show him some places. Maybe he would even look at the new townhouses. He knew Julia would love one of them.

When he arrived in Hoover, David went straight to the hospital. As he suspected, there was no change in Julia's condition. He took her free hand and kissed it. "You're looking great today, babe," he said. He knew she couldn't hear him, but it made him feel better to pretend she could. He told her about the game the night before and how well the team had done. Julia lay there pale and still.

After about thirty minutes, the nurses came in and said it was time to change Julia's position in bed. This was something that had to be done every two hours to keep her from developing skin abrasions, so David left to do his errands.

David went to his room in the athletic dorm and picked up a few things. He didn't want to take too much since he would have to move back when Cynthia came. Then he went by the grocery store and picked up a few things he could cook, mostly breakfast and sandwich stuff.

When he got back to the apartment, he put away the groceries and left a message for Cynthia, asking her to call him as soon she returned. He made himself a sandwich and moved to the living room to catch some of the Sunday-afternoon games.

He was watching Ohio State play Alabama. Ohio State pulled away in the second half. The announcer said, "It looks like the Buckeyes will play that surprising underdog, the Chapman State

Cougars, next Thursday in Indianapolis." So next Thursday would probably be the end of the road, but the season was already a success, no matter what they did on Thursday. After a while, he fell asleep on the couch.

When he awoke, he knew what he wanted to do. He was at the stage of his life that he saw no reason not to do what he wanted to do, if at all possible, and this was possible. So he headed to the hospital and sat with Julia for a while. It made him feel better just to sit and watch her. He kissed her hand and told her of his plans to look at the new townhouses.

As he was getting ready to leave, Nurse Kelly came in. "Mr. Cooper," she said, "Dr. Freeman would like to meet with you tomorrow sometime to discuss Miss Crane's treatment. He could see you at 10:00 a.m. If this time is not okay, please call his administrative assistant."

"That will be fine," David said. "Is this good news or bad news?"

"I can only tell you what I see on the charts," she said. "Her brain wave function is still minimal, but her vital signs are good. I know it's hard, but we have to be patient."

Just then, Nurse Brandon came in. "Oh, Coach Cooper, the Cougars were so good last night. Just two more games, and we'll be in the final four. Do we have a chance to win it all?"

"You never know," he said. He wasn't about to tell a loyal fan that there was not a chance their team would get to the final four. They were just too inexperienced this year, but maybe in a few years.

Monday, David was eating breakfast a little after eight o'clock when Molly called. "David, do you have Julia's briefcase?"

"Sure," he said, "I found it in her car."

"Would you see if she has her lesson plans in it? Dr. Salerno has hired Mrs. Crawford to finish the last eight weeks of school for Julia. She taught this class before she retired, so it will be no problem if you don't have them. It will just let Mrs. Crawford know what they've covered so far."

"Sure, I'll bring them by." David finished his breakfast and opened the briefcase. He found the lesson plans and a folder of graded assignments. He was curious, so he looked through the folder. He pulled out the neatly typed assignments that Cruiser had turned in.

Cruiser had received a grade of 8.5 and two eights on the three assignments. After David read the first assignment, his first thought was, *Cruiser didn't write this.* He looked again. *Well maybe, with a little help.* He saw an assignment that Carol Hanson had turned in. The phraseology was similar. Cruiser's paper has some sentence structure errors and some capitalization errors, but the wording was similar.

He found and read one of Lakeysha's assignments. Again, the wording was similar to one of Cruiser's assignments without the obvious errors. Had those girls done his assignments? But why?

He knew that Cruiser was at the bottom of their list of favorite people, and the team really would not have suffered that much if Cruiser had not played, so there had to be a reason they would take such a risk. Did Cruiser threaten them or did he know something damaging against them? David had no proof of any wrongdoing. He only suspected, so he decided to keep quiet. He dropped off the items at the music office and hurried to the hospital to meet Dr. Freeman.

When he reached the nurses' station in intensive care, he asked, "Any changes today?"

The nurse said, "No, but her vitals are still good. Mr. Cooper, Dr. Freeman would like for you to meet him in his office. That's 117 on the first floor. When you get off the elevator, turn to the left."

When he reached Dr. Freeman's office, his assistant said, "Please go right in. Dr. Freeman is waiting for you."

Dr. Freeman met David at the door with a handshake. "Thank you for meeting me," he said. "I want to give you an update on Miss Crane's condition and some recommendations for the future."

"Thank you for keeping me informed," David said.

"If her vital signs continue as they have, I would like to start bringing her out of the coma in another week. Also, a more vigorous campaign of stimulation is indicated. I know you have been talking to her and holding her hand, but I would like for us to do more. We have some private rooms on the third floor near the intensive care unit. I would like to move Miss Crane to one of those. We could have two private-duty nurses cover her care in two eight-hour shifts from 6:00 a.m. to 10:00 p.m. The third shift could be covered by the floor nurses."

"Will she still get the care she needs?" David asked.

"Oh yes," the doctor said. "She will probably get more care than in the ICU because she will have one-on-one care for sixteen hours a day. The private room will allow us to play music without disturbing the rest of the unit."

"Are these nurses available?"

"We have a registry of private-duty nurses available. Several have experience working with trauma patients. If this meets with your approval, I would like to move her as soon as we can set up the schedule with the nurses."

"Certainly. Can I assume she is getting better?" David asked.

"Let's just say she's holding her own. In one week, when we start decreasing the medication that's keeping her in the coma, we'll know."

David went back up to the third floor. Everywhere he went, both patients and staff commented on the great game the Cougars played on Saturday night. An elderly gentleman on crutches stopped David in the hall. "Coach Cooper," he said, "we're all rooting for the Cougars to beat Ohio State. Do you think we have a chance?"

"Thanks for your support," David said. "We hope to give them a good game." David went back upstairs and sat with Julia for a while. Then he hurried off to run some errands. He stopped at the

Realtor's office, picked up information about the townhouses, and got a recommendation for a cleaning service. He called them and set up a schedule for them to clean the apartment once a week. He wanted everything to be spotless when Julia came home.

Chapter 45

It seemed as if the entire world, or at least the northern part of Kentucky, was engulfed in the throes of Cougar mania. Everywhere David went, people were talking about the success of the team. They all wanted to know: Could the Cougars beat Ohio State? Could they go to the final four?

Even ESPN was touting the Cougars as this year's Cinderella, a lower-ranked team who excelled in the tournament. Some sports media claimed that Rusty McDaniel's basketball genius was almost as great as that of the Kentucky legend Adolph Rupp. They had no superstar player, but Rusty had taken a group of mediocre players and molded them into an efficient basketball machine.

Others credited the success of the team to the improved play of the Cougar big men, Tyler Maxwell and Cruiser Bell. Under the tutorage of former pro star D. J. Cooper, they were vastly improved. Some said Cruiser Bell had the talent to become another Larry Bird, that former Indiana State star.

David was still skeptical. He was certainly proud of the team for the way they were performing, but he felt they were playing far above their talent and experience level. He certainly wasn't going to say that though. On any given date, any team can beat any other team, and this just might be the Cougars' time.

David was not annoyed with all the excitement and questions while he was so concerned about Julia. He knew he would do nothing but worry if he did not have the game to think about.

When David reached the hospital, he found that Julia had already been moved to a private room. The familiar instruments were flashing and humming with a constant rhythm, and the familiar tubes were still coming from under the sheet. A tall lady with graying blond hair had uncovered Julia's good leg and was slowly massaging it.

"Good morning," David said. "I'm David Cooper. I'm Julia's fiancé."

"I'm Mildred Evans," she said. "I will be staying with Miss Crane from 6:00 a.m. to 2:00 p.m. I'm so happy to meet you. My husband is a big Cougar fan."

David said, "I can only stay about thirty minutes, but can you take a break while I'm here? Have you had breakfast?"

"Yes, thank you," she said. "A break would be nice. I have just recorded her vitals, and we won't reposition for another hour."

She left the room, and David sat beside Julia and told her about the team. He saw how much nicer it was to be in a private room. He thought Julia had more color in her cheeks, but it could just be the lighting. He made a mental note to bring a CD player and some CDs of some of her favorite music.

Soon Mrs. Evans returned. "The floor nurses will cover for me when I need a break," she said. She added, with a smile, "If there is any change in her condition, all hell will break loose with all the bells and buzzers that will go off." She laughed. "Julia is well monitored at all times."

Then she added, "Mrs. Walker will be coming at 2:00 p.m. We have worked together many times. Your fiancée is in good hands. We will have her awake in no time. We just have to be patient."

"Thank you," David said as he shook her hand. He was so tired of hearing "be patient," but he felt better knowing she was in good hands.

David hurried to the office. As he was coming into the Marshall Building, he saw Carol and Lakeysha coming out. "How is Dr. Crane?" they both said at once.

"She's resting comfortably. There's not much change now, but soon we'll start playing music and doing other things to help her wake up."

"I have a CD I know Dr. Crane would like," Carol said. "It's called *Famous Arias of Italian Opera*. It has some of the beautiful arias that she played in class for us."

"Thanks. Bring it by sometime."

Lakeysha said, "Did you hear, Coach? They're taking three chartered buses of students to the game in Indianapolis on Thursday. We're so excited. We probably won't get home until midnight, but at least we'll get to go."

"That's great," David said. "How did the women's team do in the NCAA? I have been so busy, I haven't had a chance to ask anyone."

Lakeysha said, "We did really well in the first game, but in the second game, we faced a team that had some great three-point shooters."

Carol said, "Yes, they made five three-pointers in the first quarter. We just never recovered."

"Too bad," David said. "But you had a good year."

"Yes, but we wanted to win it all," Carol said.

David smiled. "Maybe next year," he said.

He hurried to Phil Gardner's office, where he was meeting with Phil and Rusty. They discussed the travel schedule and team accommodations in Indianapolis.

Phil said to David, "Do you know a good place to eat in Indianapolis where we can have a late supper after the game?

"Sure," David said. "Charlie's. It's where the Pacers ate after their games. It's a small place. They probably can't take more than twenty-five or thirty at the most. Will that be okay?"

"Sure," Phil said. "Set it up for twenty-five. I think we should be there around nine o'clock on Thursday night."

David said, "If it's okay, I would like to drive myself to Indianapolis. I need to stop off in Rockwell and see my parents. I haven't had time to really talk to them about Julia. They are worried sick. I'll be there before bedtime on Wednesday night."

"Fine with me," Rusty said. "The team bus will leave on Wednesday at 1:00 p.m. I want the guys to all go to class on Wednesday morning." Then he added, "How is Julia doing?"

"Not much change," David said. "But they don't expect any until next week when they will try to bring her out of the coma."

"Did they ever find out why the bus hit her?" Phil said.

"All they know is that she ran into the street. Maybe when Julia wakes up, she'll tell us."

"Well, we're praying that will be soon," Phil said. "I'll see you in Indianapolis."

David went to the gym and got ready for basketball practice. There would just be a light workout today. He wanted them to practice some of their defensive alignments. He also thought it would be beneficial to practice disguising defenses. He had certain players move in and out of position so the offense would not know what they were really doing. When playing a more experienced team, a good defense could be the key to winning.

After practice, David went back to the apartment and started packing. He felt sure they would only be in Indianapolis for one day, but they might win, so he had better pack for three days. He didn't want to leave Julia for three days, but he had no choice. At least it would take his mind off his concern for Julia.

He found Julia's CD player and a stack of CDs. He found a well-thumbed book of poetry in her office and a book of inspirational readings in the bedside table. Dr. Freeman had said to bring some familiar things to read to her. He said the idea was to encourage her to remember all the things that had been a part of her life in the past. He loaded everything in a tote bag and headed for the hospital.

He stopped at Hamburger Heaven for a burger and fries. The joint was really buzzing with excitement for the game. Several students came up and asked about Julia. Others were asking what was on everyone's mind. Could the Cougars really beat Ohio State?

He gave his stock answer. "You never know, but we'll give them a good game." He was confident about that.

When he got to the hospital, he went straight to Julia's room. A plump, gray-haired black lady was writing on the iPad. She smiled at him and continued writing. He waited until she was finished. Finally, she finished writing, laid down the iPad and came to meet him with her hand extended. "Hello," she said. "You must be Miss Crane's fiancé. I'm Evelyn Walker. I will be here from 2:00 to 10:00 p.m. every day."

"How is she today?"

"I have just done her 6:00 p.m. vitals. Her blood pressure and oxygen level are good, and her pulse is strong. She's really doing very well."

David looked at Julia. She didn't look well to him. She seemed to be so very fragile, and suddenly, all the stress of the day came flooding over him. He burst into tears. Mrs. Walker came over and hugged him as his mother would. In fact, she looked like his mother. Maybe that's what set him off. That and the fact that he wouldn't see Julia for three days. All this waiting was wearing on his nerves.

"Now, honey," Mrs. Walker said soothingly. "I know you don't believe it now, but she *is* going to be all right. I've cared for hundreds of trauma patients, and most of them have made a full recovery."

"I'm trying to be positive," he said, sobbing, "but it's so hard seeing her like this day after day, so still and pale."

"I know, I know," she said, patting his shoulder. "It's tough to be macho when your heart is breaking. Now, here's what I want you to do. I want you to sit down here beside her. I want you to tell her how much you love her and what you are going to do *when* she wakes up. I want you to remind her about all the happy times you've had together. She has to have a reason to come back to us."

David sat down and took Julia's hand. Mrs. Walker said, "Now, she's not going to hear you, but she'll feel all the love you have for her, and she'll know you're here. I'm going to go down to the cafeteria and have a cup of coffee. I'll be back in fifteen minutes."

"Take your time. Have you had dinner?" he said. "I'll be here about an hour." He talked to Julia for a while. The he put a CD in the player. It was a Mozart symphony, one of her favorites, but there was no hint of recognition.

When she came back, Mrs. Walker patted him on the shoulder. "Feeling better, honey?"

"Yes, thank you," he said.

"That's our job, care for the grieving while we heal the sick." She looked at David. "Are you Caroline Jennings's boy?"

"Why, yes," he said. "How did you know?"

"Caroline was one of my best friends in grade school when we lived in Rockwell. Then we moved to Nashville when I was in the seventh grade, but we wrote to each other for years. I knew her son was a basketball player, but I didn't know it was you until someone in the cafeteria said you were a coach of the Cougars."

"Yes, I'll see my mother tomorrow. I'm going to stop in Rockwell on my way to Indianapolis."

"Well, you tell her that Evelyn Brown is caring for her future daughter-in-law."

"Mrs. Walker, would you give me your cell phone number so I could call you occasionally while I'm gone? If the team wins Thursday, I won't be back until Saturday night. I can't stand to go that long without knowing what's happening here." He said thoughtfully, "You know I wouldn't go if there was anything I could do here."

"Of course, honey," she said. "Now, you go on to Indianapolis and do the best for your team. When you get back, it will be that much closer to the time for her to wake up."

Chapter 46

Wednesday, David got up, put on jeans and a sweatshirt, and cooked his breakfast. After he ate, he cleaned up the kitchen, put all the dishes in the dishwasher, and started it. He checked the refrigerator to see if there was any food that would spoil in three days. He showered, dressed, and finished packing. He took a long look around the apartment. Everything was as neat as if he had never been there.

He went by the athletic office. He was sure Phil had taken care of all the necessary paperwork. Everyone on the team was academically eligible, but he wanted to make sure that there were no slipups, so he took additional copies of the academic dean's report.

He swung by a bakery and picked up two dozen blueberry muffins and took them up to the third-floor nurses' station. "Here's something for your break room," he said as he set the bag on the counter. The nurse took one whiff of the fragrant muffins and said, "Thank you so much, Coach Cooper. Miss Crane is doing great today. Good luck in Indianapolis."

He went in and sat by Julia for a while. He told Mrs. Evans about the muffins, and she went to have a cup of coffee. He took Julia's hand and kissed it. He told her that he might be gone for as long as three days, but he would be back soon.

When Mrs. Evans returned, David kissed Julia's cheek and left. Several people called, "Good luck, Coach Cooper. We'll be watching on television."

He left the hospital, got into his truck, and headed north toward Rockwell and Indianapolis. As he drove, he noticed that spring was just around the corner. Farmers were plowing fields, getting ready for spring planting, and trees beside the highway were showing hints of green. He would be glad when spring arrived. The winter was depressing.

When he arrived in Rockwell, his mom and dad were eager for news of Julia. The sat in the family room, and he related everything he knew about the accident and her condition. "My, my," Caroline said, "and they don't have any idea why she ran into the street?"

"Not yet," David said. "Maybe when Julia wakes up, she can tell us." He added, reassuringly, "The doctors are certain that she will wake up and be okay."

"Well, we hope so," Albert said. "Have you spoken to Uncle Ralph lately?"

David told them about the hearing. "Uncle Ralph really helped. It seems that he plays golf with the judge. I was surprised to learn that he has changed his attitude toward our relationship."

"Is that what he told you?" Albert said with a chuckle. He dark eyes sparkled with mischief. "It was more like his attitude was changed *for him*."

"What happened?"

"Ask your mom," Albert said.

"That man made me so mad," Caroline said with a triumphant gleam in her eye. "I was not about to let my conniving brother spoil my chances of finally getting you married. You know how much we love Julia. Ophelia and Ralph came by a week or so ago. They were on their way to Kristin's. I think Ophelia had convinced him that he should come by and apologize to me for the awful way he acted at Christmas."

David listened intently, with a grin on his face. Caroline said, "What he didn't know was that Ophelia and I had planned it all. We hit him with every argument we could think of." Caroline smiled. "I think he'll stay out of your business from now on—that is, if he wants peace in the family."

David put his arm around his mother's shoulder. "You know, Dad, those two ladies can be quite formidable once they set their minds on something."

"You've got that right. I almost felt a little sorry for Ralph," Albert said. "But not too much."

After dinner, David hugged his mom and dad. "I need to be going on to Indianapolis," he said.

"Okay, honey," Caroline said. "Be sure and let us know how Julia is doing. You know how concerned we are."

"Sure, Mom," he said, "and thanks for your help with Uncle Ralph."

When David reached the hotel in Indianapolis, he found that Rusty had called a team meeting for 8:00 p.m. in one of the hotel's meeting rooms. "Well, guys," Rusty said, "we've come a long way this year, and we're not finished yet. Thank you for your hard work and cooperation. Now, Coach Cooper will tell you about your schedule for tomorrow."

David checked his information sheets. He told the team when and where they would have their meals and what time the bus would leave to take them to the arena for shootaround in the morning and the game in the evening. He concluded with, "Be back in the hotel by ten thirty tonight with lights out at eleven. Coach McDaniels and I will be checking. We have a full day tomorrow, so we want you to get your sleep. Any questions?"

Kenny raised his hand and stood up. "Coach Cooper," he began, "the team would like to thank you for being here with us. We know you would rather be back in Hoover with Dr. Crane. We're sorry about her accident, Coach." He stammered, "W-we're just praying that she will soon get well."

"Thank you, Kenny," he said. "We need all the prayers we can get. Dr. Crane is doing well. We're just waiting for her brain to heal, so there's nothing I can do there at this time. Now, let's all go show the world that Chapman State deserves to be in the second round of the NCAA tournament." The team cheered.

When David returned to his room, he called Mrs. Walker. She said there was no change in Julia's condition. As he thanked her and pressed the "end call" button, he suddenly remembered something she had said last night. She had said *most* of her trauma patients had recovered. Did that mean some had not recovered? Did they die or were they just mentally incapacitated?

He thought about how smart and talented and alive Julia was before the accident. What would he do if she was severely mentally impaired? Well, whatever happened, he knew he would take care of her to the best of his ability for as long as she lived, even if he had to spend every penny he had.

Chapter 47

He was in the big hotel bed with Julia. She had taken off her nightgown with a sexy giggle. He wanted to hold her close and kiss her ardently. He wanted to feel her soft body against his and make mad, passionate love to her. He reached for her, but she was not there. He woke with a start. Despair flooded him when he thought about Julia.

Julia was not here. She was in a hospital room back in Hoover, and there was nothing he could do but miss her terribly. Then his head cleared. He needed to take charge of his emotions and focus on the job at hand.

David dressed and went down to meet Rusty for the hotel breakfast buffet. They reviewed their strategy for today's game. The breakfast crowd was dwindling, but he noticed that several Cougars were there. It was nearly nine o'clock. He made a mental note to knock on some doors as he went back to his room.

When he returned to his room, he punched in Mrs. Evans's number. "Good morning, Coach Cooper," she said. When he asked the usual question, she said, "Her vital signs are good, but there's not much change; however, Chris was in this morning to do an EEG. He thinks her brain wave activity is up ever so slightly."

"That's good news," he said. "Thank you so much, Mrs. Evans. May I call you tomorrow?"

"Certainly. Good luck with the game." It wasn't much, but he was thankful for every small improvement.

The team looked great at the shootaround. Teddy and Jalen hit their threes effortlessly. The rest of the team seemed relaxed and enthusiastic about the game. David ran some defensive drills with

Jalen and Teddy. He was amazed at Jalen's basketball instincts. He seemed to always know when to enact the double-team and when to maintain his position, and best of all, he was signaling Teddy when he should double-team. David said to the team, "No one expects us to win, so let's just play our best and have fun. We're under no pressure to win. Our season is already a huge success."

"No, Coach," Kenny said. "We *are* going to win."

"Great. I expect you to."

Soon it was time for the biggest game Chapman State had ever played. The Bankers' Life Field House was filled with Cougar fans. It looked as if half the crowd was wearing the green and gold. They cheered and clapped as the band played their fight song. The team ran on to the court and began their warm-up drills.

The toss went up. Cruiser anticipated it beautifully and tipped the ball to Tyler, who hit Kenny, who immediately put up a three-point shot, and the Cougars were up by three points. Jalen couldn't miss with his jump shots, and Cruiser was able to beat his opponent to the rim several times for layups. All through the first half, the Cougars seemed to be one step ahead of their opponents on defense. By the end of the half, the Cougars were up 33–18. As they headed to the dressing room, Rusty said, "David, will you do the TV interview? I want to get on back with the team."

"Sure."

The TV announcer said, "We're talking to Chapman assistant coach D. J. Cooper. Coach, it looks like no one told your team that they're ten-point underdogs. Your defense has certainly kept Ohio State off-balance the whole first half. To what do you attribute your success?"

"Thank you, Joe," David said. "Coach McDaniel and I are both committed to excellent defensive play. When your shots aren't falling, you can keep your team in the game with good defense. The defensive play of our guards, Teddy Baker and Jalen Wilson, in executing our zone trap, has been the key for us."

"Yes, it has. Those young men are certainly playing above their years. Thank you for your time, Coach," the announcer said. "Good luck in the second half."

In the second half, the Cougar offense played exceptionally well. The defense continued their excellent play. Ohio State made a late surge in the second half, but the Cougars held on to win by eight points.

The crowd went wild. They spilled out of the stands onto the court. The band played their fight song, and the cheerleaders performed a snappy routine in time to the music. The two teams lined up to congratulate one another on a well-played game. David hugged Rusty, and they went to congratulate the team.

In the dressing room, Coach McDaniel said, "Great game, guys. I know you're all hungry, so I'm going to do the postgame TV interviews alone, while Coach Cooper takes you to the restaurant."

Phil Gardner and his wife joined the team to go to the restaurant. As they were going down the steps to Charlie's, he said, "What kind of a hole-in-the-wall dump is this?"

"A hole-in-the-wall dump with great food," David said. He led the team through the restaurant to the back room. There were two long tables with chairs on either side. The walls were lined with pictures of Pacers, Colts, and Indiana U teams. David noticed that several members of the team were looking at the pictures. "Hey, Coach Cooper," Tyler said, "is this skinny guy you?"

"Yep, that was me in my rookie season," David said as he flexed his muscles. "These are the result of many hours in the weight room and a lot of good food at Charlie's. The Pacers eat here after every home game. I know you'll enjoy it."

As if on cue, Charlie and several waitresses brought out large trays of food and placed them on a buffet steam table. Charlie said, "Welcome to Charlie's." He ran through a list of the entrees. There was Peking duck, pork roast with roasted vegetables, lasagna, ravioli,

Kung Pao chicken, egg rolls, and numerous other items. The team lined up and began filling their plates.

As the team found their seats, the waitresses took drink orders. "I'll have a beer," Cruiser said.

"Sorry," the waitress said, "the athletes just get iced tea, lemonade, or soda." Cruiser looked a little chagrined but settled for a soda.

After a while, Phil Gardner stood and spoke. He praised the team and the coaching staff and wished them well in the next game. "How about this food?" he commented. "Is everyone getting enough to eat?"

The team all cheered. "Can we eat here again?" they asked.

David was next. He told them about their schedule for tomorrow and Saturday. There was no curfew tonight, but they were to be in the hotel by ten thirty with lights out at eleven tomorrow night.

"Aw, Coach, can't we have any fun?" Cruiser moaned.

"Sure," David said. "Have all the fun you want. Just have it before ten thirty. The game is at one o'clock on Saturday afternoon, so the bus will leave the hotel at ten thirty. Be packed and ready to go by ten fifteen. We won't be coming back to the hotel."

David paused. "Every year, on the day of a big game, ESPN's lead story is 'Blank players from blank university were dismissed today for violation of team rules.' You fill in the blanks. I hope it's not going to be Chapman State. In other words, you violate team rules, and you will be off the team. You might even lose your scholarship for next year. If a teammate thinks about doing something stupid, you might remind him of the consequences. Thanks for all your hard work this year. Glad you're enjoying the food."

Just then, the waitresses wheeled in a table with desserts. There was chocolate layer cake and peach cobbler. There also were big cans of ice cream with all kinds of topping. "This is a Charlie's specialty, an ice-cream sundae bar. Enjoy," David said.

"This food is first rate," Phil said. "Do you think we could eat here on Saturday after the game?"

David said, "Where else can you find comfort food from three different cuisines? I'll check with Charlie. He may have another team coming in." In a while, David returned. "It's all set. Dinner is here after the game on Saturday, but only if you win," he said. Then he added, "Just kidding, guys."

The waitresses brought out big trays of fortune cookies. David couldn't wait to hear some of Charlie's fortunes. Someone read, "It's not whether you win or lose; it's how you play the game." Another read, "The only difference between a good shot and a bad shot is if it goes in."

The players read their fortunes and laughed at some of the funny sayings. David was so glad to see the team so relaxed and happy. They had worked hard this year. They deserved it. Cruiser came by with a plate of chocolate cake, topped with several scoops of ice cream and chocolate sauce. "Are you going to eat all that?" David asked.

"Yeah, Coach, this is great."

Soon it was time to leave. "Don't forget, guys," David said. "Meet in front of the hotel at ten fifteen Saturday morning."

Chapter 48

Saturday morning, David lay in bed reviewing the events of the previous day. At nine o'clock, he had met with his financial manager, Dan Jordan. David showed him the information about the new townhouses in Hoover. Dan reviewed the specs and said he thought it would be a good investment. Even if Julia didn't want to live there, it was still a good use of his money. He felt sure he could sell it for a profit when the time came.

He told Dan about some expenditures he planned to make and asked him to make the cash available. Next, he had visited a jewelry store to pick up a purchase he had ordered in January. He felt good about his decisions.

He was going forward with his life as if Julia was going to be okay.

Most importantly, all members of the team had made it back to the hotel by ten thirty last night. He wasn't sure what the team had done all day, but as long as they were in the hotel by ten thirty and he hadn't had to bail anyone out of jail, he was okay with it.

He had called Mrs. Evans, but she was not at the hospital. It was her day off. He didn't have the other lady's number, so he called Mrs. Walker in the afternoon. She was excited to hear from him and gave him a good report on Julia.

He thought about the game today. They were playing mighty Duke University. There wasn't a chance of them winning. He just hoped they played well.

David got up, showered, dressed, and headed for breakfast. He filled his plate from the breakfast buffet and sat at a table beside

Rusty. "Well, Coach," Rusty said, "what do you think about the game today?"

David said, "We're playing a team that's bigger, faster, and more experienced than we are. They've been to twelve finals fours and won five championships in the past few years. They have a crafty coach who makes a seven-figure salary. If we hold our loss to less than twenty points, I'll consider it a success."

"That bad, huh?" Rusty said.

"But you have to remember," David said. "Win or lose, everything our young kids learn from this game will carry over into future seasons. We have no idea what they will gain from having played in this game."

"You're right," Rusty said. "We need to coach as hard as we can every minute of this game. We can't let them get discouraged and give up."

"If it's okay with you, I would like to leave immediately after the game. I'd like to get home as soon as possible," David said.

"Sure. I know how much you've missed being with Julia," Rusty said. "Go on as soon as the game is over."

After breakfast, David packed and called Mrs. Evans. She said, "Mr. Cooper, you need to call Dr. Freeman as soon as possible. Miss Crane is doing so well. Chris says there is even more brain wave activity today."

David placed a call to Dr. Freeman. After several minutes, he came to the telephone. "Mr. Cooper," he said, "thank you for calling. Miss Crane's vital signs are excellent. Also, we have been noticing an increase in the brain wave activity the past few days."

"What does that mean?" David said.

"It means that she's trying to wake up by herself, so we're going to help her by slowly decreasing the medication that's keeping her in the coma."

"How long will it take her to wake up? Do I need to come home immediately?"

"Oh no," he said. "It will still be several days, maybe even a week. Are you in agreement with this method of treatment?"

"Certainly," David said. "Please do whatever you think necessary."

David was elated. This was the news he had been waiting for.

They loaded on the bus at ten fifteen. "Did you check your rooms to make sure you got all your stuff?" David asked.

Everyone said, "Yes."

"Okay, let's roll," Rusty said.

The team went out to stretch and warm up in sweats, then came back to the dressing room to dress in their game uniforms. Once again, the stands were filled with excited fans who were wearing the green and gold.

The game was underway. David was thrilled with how well the team was playing. Jalen and Teddy harried the Duke guards and made several steals. The Cougars fought valiantly, but Duke pulled away. To David's surprise, they were only trailing by five points at the half.

In the second half, Kenny hit several jump shots, and the guards hit several threes, but Duke consistently did a little better. The Cougars refused to give up and held on to the end, but the Duke lead swelled to eight points, which was the final difference.

David was thrilled out of his mind. "Can you believe it?" he said to Rusty, pounding him on the back. "We lost to the number two team in the nation by only eight points. Look out for us next year."

In the dressing room, some of the players were dejected and down, but David told them how proud he was because they had fought to the end. "We didn't let them put us away," he said. "We were always in the game. Think of it this way. We weren't supposed to win the second game, and we won two more. We've had a great year. I want to thank you for all your hard work. I'm headed for home. I need to check on Dr. Crane. You go have fun at Charlie's, and I'll see you back home in Hoover."

Rusty said, "Don't get there too quickly. Drive safely."

David got his bag off the bus and walked the several blocks to the parking garage. He threw his bag into the back seat of his truck and headed to Hoover.

About thirty minutes later, he stopped at a fast-food place and got a steak sandwich and called his mom. He told her about Julia and apologized for not stopping. "That's okay, honey," she said. "You need to get on home and see about Julia. Keep us informed. I love you."

"I love you too, Mom." He ate his sandwich quickly and headed on down the road. As he passed the exit where he and Julia had stopped at Christmas, he felt a pang of longing. He remembered the three happy nights he and Julia had spent in the hotel there. It reminded him of how that beautiful lady had made his life complete. He had known her less than six months, but it seemed as if he had known her forever.

He thought about the very first time he saw her, sitting there holding her violin at the dedication dinner. She was beautiful, even if she was wearing that horrible black dress. He laughed when he remembered that surprised expression she made when she realized she had parked in his space. Her eyes became bigger and bluer, and her mouth was drawn up in an O. When they played "I Could Have Danced All Night," he had wanted to rush over, grab her up, and waltz around the banquet room. The only thing that kept him from doing it was that she would be so embarrassed she would never speak to him again, and Uncle Ralph would probably have had a heart attack. He smiled at the thought.

The next time he saw her was at her apartment. She had opened the door with no makeup on and her beautiful, long hair in a ponytail. Her willowy body was encased in tight jeans and a sweatshirt. He had loved her then. She had been rude and hateful, but he didn't care. He had a plan to win her over. He was surprised he had shown the restraint to wait two weeks before he kissed her. He was prepared for a slap in his face when he kissed her, but when she settled against him and let him kiss her again, he knew he was hooked. And the better he got to know her, the more he loved her, but he was afraid to tell her. He had the feeling she wasn't interested in a romantic relationship, so he planned to woo her slowly. And fortunately, it had worked.

David turned on the radio. A crooner sang, "When I fall in love, it will be forever." He *had* fallen in love, and it *would* be forever. He sang along with the radio, and soon he was in Hoover.

He went immediately to the hospital. When he saw Mrs. Walker, she grabbed him and hugged him. She said, "It's so good to have you back. I think Miss Crane has known you were gone. She's seemed a little restless. I'm going to take a little break. Now, you sit down here and talk to her."

David sat beside the bed. He took Julia's hand and kissed it. He held her hand and told her how much he loved her. He told her about the games in Indianapolis and how much he wished she had been with him.

He told her about the townhouse he was going to see tomorrow. Perhaps it would be their home. He looked at Julia, and he thought her mouth moved ever so slightly. Did she hear what he was saying? Was she trying to smile?

When Mrs. Walker returned, she said, "Honey, we're sure that comatose patients can hear, but we're not sure what they can understand. More likely, it was just a reflex action." Whatever it was, it was the first movement from her that he had seen, and he was encouraged.

Chapter 49

David slept late on Sunday morning. He was exhausted from the events of the past three days. He made coffee and turned on the TV. ESPN was reporting on the NCAA championship games from Saturday. The announcer praised the Chapman State Cougars for giving Duke such a tough game. The announcer said to his partner, "It looks like the Cougars may be here next year. They only lose two to graduation, and it's reported they have a great freshman class coming in."

"Yes, Joe," his partner said, "but don't be surprised if assistant coach D. J. Cooper isn't there. I'm sure he'll be selected for one of the head coaching jobs that are available."

Joe said, "Yes, D. J. Cooper would make a fine head coach, and he could probably name his own salary." David switched off the television. That was something he wasn't going to even consider until Julia was okay. He was much more interested in the job than the salary. He went to cook his breakfast.

After breakfast, David checked on Julia's mail. He looked to see if anything needed immediate attention and put the rest in a stack on her desk. There were two letters that he set aside. He felt that since he was Julia's legal guardian, he had every right to open her mail.

The first letter was a statement from the company that administered the student loans. He was appalled at the interest charges. "No more of that nonsense," he said. He got out his checkbook and wrote a check for the entire balance.

The other letter was from her credit card company. Everything seemed reasonable until he came to a charge on February 10 to The Boutique. He couldn't believe that his frugal Julia had made such a purchase. Then he remembered how ravishingly beautiful she had been in the blue ball gown. He remembered how the wide skirt had billowed around them as they waltzed around the ballroom.

During a slow number, she had molded her body next to his, put her head on his chest, and snuggled closely as he held her tightly. He could still feel her body through the thin fabric of the gown. She had said, "I would gladly spend the rest of my life dancing with you." He smiled at the thought and knew that she had bought the beautiful gown to please him. It was only right that he pay for it, so he wrote another check.

He closed his eyes and saw Julia in the wonderful dress. "It was worth every penny," he said as he put the check in an envelope. "Worth every penny!" He had every hope that someday she would wear the beautiful gown again as they danced.

David unpacked his bag. He put his dirty clothes in the washer and gathered up some of his things to take back to his room at the athletic dorm. He felt sure Cynthia would be coming before long.

He checked his mail at the athletic dorm and went by his office in the Marshall Building. There was mail and a CD in his mailbox, *Famous Arias from Italian Opera*. It must be the CD Carol was telling him about. Then he headed to the hospital.

When he entered Julia' room, Mrs. Evans was wiping Julia's face, hands, and arms with a damp washcloth. "I thought this would make her feel a little more refreshed," she said. "Would you help me reposition her?"

"Sure," David said. "Just tell me what to do."

"Just hold the sheet, and I'll turn her on her side so she'll face you while you're sitting." David held the sheet, while Mrs. Evans skillfully moved Julia to a more comfortable position.

"That's a nice fragrance you're wearing," David said.

"Thank you," she said. "They don't like for us to wear strong perfume because of allergies, but this is such a light lilac fragrance it masks the hospital smell. I think it makes the patients feel more comfortable."

David sat while Mrs. Evans recorded her vital signs. "Will you be here long enough for me to have lunch?" she said.

"Sure," he said. "I plan to be here for about an hour."

David sat beside the bed. He kissed Julia's hand and held it. He looked at her face. He wondered what she was thinking or if she was even capable of thought. "You're looking well today, my darling," he said. "I'm so sorry I have been gone so long. You would have been so proud of our team." He began to tell her about the basketball games. He watched carefully but saw no hint of recognition.

Julia didn't know where she was or even who she was, but she had a feeling of well-being. She was not in pain, but she could not see or hear. Neither could she could smell or feel a touch. It was as though she was floating in a sensory-free environment.

She thought she must be asleep because images passed through her mind that she thought must be dreams, but at other times, she just lay there with her mind blank. She tried very hard to wake up, but she couldn't. Her eyes just wouldn't open, no matter how hard she tried.

Then, slowly, she began to notice smells. First, she noticed a light, airy smell. It reminded her of the flowers that grew on the bushes in her grandmother's garden. That smell was very pleasant. Then she began to feel touches to her hands and face. She associated the flower smell with light, moist touches on her hands and face.

Next was a heavier smell, not just one smell but a mixture of smells—pine, citrus, and spice. It was familiar, and she associated it with happy times. It reminded her of the woods and camping with her dad when she was a little girl, and somehow, it reminded her of dancing. This smell appeared frequently, and sometimes there was a light, moist touch on her hand. She felt a certain presence near when this smell occurred, but she heard nothing.

It had been a long time since the woods smell had been there. She longed for the comfort and contentment it brought. Then it was back. She felt the moist touch on her hand and felt the familiar presence. Sometimes, she felt a touch on her cheek. She wanted to smile to show her pleasure, but it just wouldn't come.

She knew someone was speaking, but she couldn't understand the words. She felt the loving presence, the soft touch, and the comforting words. It must have a name. She racked her brain. She could not come up with anything, but it would come. She knew it would come. Every day, she was becoming more aware of her surroundings, but her eyes still would not open.

David continued to hold Julia's hand and speak to her. He thought he saw her mouth twitch and wondered if it could be an attempt at a smile. He put a CD in the player. It was Mozart's Symphony no. 40 in G Minor. It was one Julia's favorites.

Julia heard the music, very faintly at first, as if it were a long way off. Then it came closer. She recognized the piece. It was one of her favorite symphonies. She had played it many times. The fingers of her left hand attempted to form the notes of the first violin part on an imaginary fingerboard, but her fingers wouldn't move.

Mrs. Evans came back from lunch. David kissed Julia on the cheek and said, "I'll be back later today." He was meeting the Realtor at 1:00 p.m. He just had time for a quick lunch.

The townhouse was everything David had hoped it would be. There was a large living room in the front with a dining room on the left. A large master suite was to the left of the living room. On the right of the living room were two guest bedrooms with a Jack and Jill bath between. Two bonus rooms with a half bath were upstairs. But the selling point was the large kitchen and family room across the rear of the house. The room had large windows that offered a great view of the river and miles beyond. The Realtor said, "Mr. Cooper, if you act quickly, you can probably choose the paint color for the walls and some of the fixtures and floor coverings."

Heaven help me! This is a responsibility no man should undertake alone. But he thought he knew Julia well enough to know what she would like. "Okay," David said. "I would like to put a deposit on this unit. Can you convey my wishes to the builder? I would like more traditional hardware and fixtures throughout the house. I want the walls to be a soft gray and hardwood floors throughout the house. And one more thing: we must have top-of-the-line appliances in the kitchen. My fiancée is a gourmet cook, and I want her to have the best of everything."

"Very well, Mr. Cooper," the Realtor said. "I think you have made some good choices. These units are scheduled to be completed and ready to move into by May 1. I will notify you when we will set up a closing time." Then she added, "You must know that some of the things you have asked for will increase the price."

"Certainly," he said. "I want my wife to have the best, and if she doesn't like the color of the walls, they can easily be repainted." He took a deep breath. He was glad that was over. Perhaps, knowing about the townhouse would give Julia some incentive to wake up.

Chapter 50

"Good morning, my darling," David said as he entered Julia's room. He picked up her hand and kissed it. He began to talk to her as if she could hear every word. He was so excited. He told her about the beautiful townhouse he had visited. "I know you'll love it," he said. "As soon as we're married, we can move there." He was raving on about everything when a nurse came in.

"Good morning, Mr. Cooper," she said. "I'm Mrs. Stewart. Mrs. Evans has a dentist appointment today, but she will be back tomorrow." She checked the familiar instruments.

"Is everything okay?" David asked.

"Oh yes, her vitals are good." She turned to David. "It looks like you're really excited about your new home. I know Miss Crane will be too. I saw Chris down the hall. He'll be doing her EEG in a few minutes. Can you stay for that?"

"Sure," he said. "I have a few minutes before I have to be at the office."

Soon Chris came into the room. He was wheeling a machine with displays and dials. He put a padded band with metal pieces on the inside on Julia's head. It looked like a crown. Wires coming from it were hooked to the machine. He flipped a switch.

"Does it hurt? Can she feel it?" David asked anxiously.

"It doesn't hurt," he said. "It's just like a hat on her head." The machine buzzed quietly, then spit out a length of paper. Chris tore it off and looked at it. "This is great," he said. "Her brain is more active every day. I know Dr. Freeman will want you to keep up the stimulation. I think she'll be waking up very soon."

As Chris turned to go, he saw the CD David had put on the table. He picked it up and read, "*Famous Arias from Italian Operas.*" He looked at David, "You did say that Miss Crane is a music teacher, didn't you?"

"Yes," David said, "and a violinist."

"Does she teach opera?"

"Yes, she has an upper-division class for music majors, and she also teaches a unit for her music appreciation class. Are you familiar with Italian opera?"

"You might say that. My great-grandmother married my great-grandfather in Italy right after the war so he could bring her to America. Their daughter, my grandmother, trained as an opera singer. I used to stay with her a lot when I was little. I was listening to Puccini and Verdi when other kids my age were watching *Sesame Street* and *Barney.*"

He went on, "I would like to see if hearing some of these favorite arias have an influence on her brain waves. By studying brain responses to sounds, doctors can evaluate when or if a patient is likely to awake from a coma. Tomorrow, I would like to play some of these arias and see if there's any difference in her response. I have to go now, but I'll be back tomorrow."

"Thanks," David said. He kissed Julia. "I have to go to work, my love, but I'll be back this evening. Thank you, Mrs. Stewart."

David headed to work. When he got to the office, he called his financial manager and told him to expect several large checks. He also called the Realtor and asked her to recommend a good interior designer. He needed help choosing things for the townhouse.

He met with Phil and Rusty to discuss the new recruits who would be coming in the fall. "Do you think Cruiser Bell will be coming back next year?" Phil asked. "He looked really good in the second-round games."

"He surprised me too, but I knew he was capable," David said. "I think he'll be invited to the predraft workout camp, and if he does well there, there's a good chance he'll be drafted."

"It will be a couple of months before we know. I guess we'll have to hold his scholarship until then," Phil said.

David went back to his office and prepared a letter to be sent to the new freshmen. They needed to come into his office to plan their academic program for the next year. He told them he would not be in his office the last two weeks in May. He was taking a lot for granted, but he was planning to be married then. He finished the letter and took it to the secretary to be typed and printed.

Chapter 51

Julia was becoming more and more aware of her surroundings. She could hear people's footsteps when they came in. She knew when people were talking, but she couldn't make out what they were saying. She could hear music, and she knew when a piece was familiar, but she couldn't quite think of the name.

She wanted so much to think of the name of the person who came and sat beside her. She recognized his voice. In her mind's eye, she could see his handsome face, his wide smile, and his twinkling brown eyes. She racked her brain. Suddenly, it came to her. His name was David. Of course. Why couldn't she have remembered it before now? Then she knew it all. David was the one she loved, and David loved her.

Then another face came into view. He said she couldn't marry David. He said she would have to go away. Why couldn't she be with the person she loved? His face clouded her memory, but she couldn't remember his name.

David came into the room and kissed her cheek. He was surprised to see that they had taken all the bandages off her head. Her head had been shaved, but her hair had grown back from a quarter to half an inch in places. It gave her the appearance of a small child. "Hi, babe," he said. "You're looking great today."

Just then, Chris came in with his machine. "Okay," he said. "Let's play some Italian opera. Let's start with 'Un bel di' or 'One Fine Day' from *Madame Butterfly*. Chris put the band on Julia's head and started the CD. The sweeping melody played by the string section filled the room. Then the lovely soprano voice told the story.

She heard the familiar tune. It was so beautiful. In her mind's eye, she saw Cio-Cio-San, the lovely geisha girl who had married an American naval officer in a Japanese ceremony. He had returned to America but promised that one fine day he would return to get her. She stands and looks over the bay where his ship will come sailing in. One day, he does return, but he brings his American wife with him. Cio-Cio-San realizes her husband did not take his Japanese vows seriously. She knows that she cannot live with the shame of losing her husband, that she must die with honor in the Japanese tradition of ritual suicide, seppuku. Julia was overcome with sadness. Again, she thought, *Why can't I marry David?* She felt a tear trickling from her eye and running down her cheek.

The next aria came on. It was sung by a tenor portraying the Egyptian prince Radames, who was singing about his beloved, the Ethiopian slave girl Aida. He cannot be with her because of their races and stations in life. Radames has wrongly been convicted of treason and is sentenced to die by being sealed in a tomb. Aida knows that she will never be able to be with Radames in life, so she chooses to be with him in death. It reminded Julia of her own situation. She loved David, but she had been told that she couldn't marry him. The sadness returned. Would she have to die to be with David? It would be so easy. All she had to do was to let her mind go blank and not try to wake up any more. The tears turned into sobs. Then she was crying copious tears.

"Stop the music," Chris said. "Stop it now!"

"Why?" David asked as he stopped the CD. "It's some of her favorite music."

"It's not the music; it's the stories," Chris said. "It's making her sad. We don't want that."

"Sometimes she cries when she's happy," David said as he reached for his handkerchief to wipe her eyes.

"Don't," Chris said. He pulled on a rubber glove, tore open a package of sterile gauze, and wiped her eyes. "We don't want to introduce any germs into her system. She's not crying because she's happy. She's distressed." He looked at David. "You're about to enter into a biracial marriage with this girl. Has anyone ever given you any opposition to your marriage?"

David looked thoughtful. "Well, you might say that. My uncle is opposed to our marriage. He doesn't think I'll be able to get a coaching job in the South with a white wife."

"Has he ever said anything to Julia?"

"I'm not sure," David said. "I don't know; however, he has spoken to my mother about it. And Julia's mother is not too happy about it either. She thinks basketball coaches are penniless bums."

"I guess she's never heard about the Kentucky coach who just signed a multimillion-dollar contract," he said. "In these arias, people are prevented from being with the people they love because of the biases of others. I think Julia is identifying with these characters. But look at this," he said as he tore off the strip of paper that had come out of the machine. "It shows her brain wave activity is the highest it's ever been."

"Isn't that good?" David asked.

"Yes," Chris said, "but we need to make her happy again. Sometimes, when people are sad, they regress to the point that they never wake up. We have to show her that her life is worth returning to. Do you have some CDs with happy songs, or perhaps music that will remind her of happy times you had together?"

"Like songs we danced to?" David asked.

"Anything that reminds her of happy times," Chris said.

"I know what to do," David said. He kissed Julia and told her he would be back in the evening. He went to the apartment and to Julia's computer. He downloaded every song that they had listened to or danced to. Then he burned them on CDs. Julia would hear nothing but happy songs from now on.

When David went back the hospital, he told Mrs. Walker what had happened. "The poor dear," she said. "You need to assure her that you're going to marry her, no matter what."

David sat beside her and told her how much he loved her. Then he told her about the townhouse. He needed her to wake up and talk to him about it. Then he played three or four songs they had danced to.

Julia heard the music, and she heard David singing. Suddenly, the strong determination that had guided her life thus far came to the forefront of her subconscious. No, she would not die as Butterfly or Aida did. She would wake up and fight for her right to marry David. He loved her, and she loved him. It might take several days, but she was getting stronger. She *would* wake up.

David sang along with the songs, but he saw no reaction in Julia. After a while, he told Mrs. Walker that he was calling it a day, but he would be back tomorrow.

The next morning, he was back. He talked to her and played music until it was time to go to the office. There was not much going on in the Athletic Department as far as basketball was concerned. He met with Rusty a time or two, and they tried to make plans for next year, but it was hard to do until they knew exactly what the new recruits would bring to the team.

The next two days were similar. David came in the morning. He told her how much he loved her. He read to her, and he played music. He returned in the evening and did the same, but still Julia didn't wake up. David was beginning to become discouraged.

Chapter 52

Saturday, David awoke depressed and discouraged. Although Chris and Mrs. Evans continually expressed their confidence that Julia would soon awake, David was losing hope. He had been awake most of the night, trying to decide what he would do with his life if Julia never awoke. He made the decision to forego his morning trip to the hospital. It was just too painful to sit there, wondering if she even knew what he was saying.

Besides, he needed to meet with the interior designer sometime today. She was asking questions he could not answer about the townhouse. It would be good to talk things over with her and get her advice.

He cooked his breakfast. After he ate, he felt a little better. Maybe the food had revived his spirits. He decided to go to the hospital after all and call the designer to meet later in the day. He stopped by the bakery and picked up two dozen banana-nut muffins and took them to the hospital. The charge nurse was excited.

"Thank you very much, Coach Cooper," she said. "My husband is still talking about the great season the Cougars had," she said happily. "Miss Crane is looking better every day."

He went into Julia's room. Mrs. Evans said, "Good morning, Mr. Cooper. We have just had our bath and are ready for the day."

Why was everybody so upbeat? Perhaps it was because he was so gloomy. He didn't feel like talking, so he put a CD in the player. The gravelly voiced singer sang, "Maybe I didn't love you quite as often as I should have. But you were always on my mind."

Julia loved that song. She remembered when they danced to it. She remembered her beautiful dress that stood out when David whirled her around. And later, at the bar in Nashville, he held her close and told her much he loved her and how sorry he was that he had to leave her for his trips. Now David was singing, "You were always on my mind."

She wanted to say, "You were always on *my* mind, David," but the words wouldn't come.

He picked up her hand and kissed it, then held it to his cheek in a loving gesture. He laid his head on the bed beside her. He was so tired. Maybe he would go back to the apartment and take a nap. He sat up and looked at her. "Oh, babe," he said. "Please wake up. I love you so much. We could be *so* happy." He laid his head back on the bed.

"But, David," a small voice said. "We *were* happy. Don't you remember? We danced and danced."

He sat up and looked at her. Her eyelids were fluttering. Did he actually hear her? "What did you say?"

"I said we danced and danced, David, but your two-step needs some work."

Now her eyes were open. He stood up and kissed her cheek. "You're awake!"

"David, where am I?" she asked, turning her head from side to side.

"You're in University Hospital."

"Why am I here? What happened? My eyes don't want to work." She blinked repeatedly.

"You were in an accident."

Just then, Mrs. Evans came into the room. When she saw Julia's eyes open, she ran to her. "My dear, you're awake," she said as she leaned over and straightened Julia's pillow.

"Yes," Julia said, "I know you. You smell like flowers. Why won't my eyes work?"

"I'm Mrs. Evans. I have been taking care of you. Your eyes are getting used to working again. They'll be better soon."

"I'm so tired," Julia said, and closed her eyes again.

David was alarmed, "Is she okay?" he asked.

"I believe so. She'll be waking up slowly. All her vital signs are good," Mrs. Evans said as she looked at the instruments. "I'm going to see if the doctor is still here. He'll want to check her over as soon as possible."

David sat and watched. In a few minutes, Mrs. Evans came back into the room. Julia opened her eyes again. She said timidly, "I have to go to the bathroom."

"Just a minute," Mrs. Evans said. "I need to get some help. Don't let her try to get up. I'll be right back." In a few minutes, Mrs. Evans returned with two other nurses.

Mrs. Evans said, "Will you excuse us for a few minutes, Mr. Cooper?"

"Sure," David said. "I'll be right outside, babe."

David was ecstatic. He raced to the waiting room and called Molly. Then he called his mother and Julia's mother. There was no answer from Julia's mother, so he left a message.

He also called his aunt Ophelia. She was overjoyed. "David, I am so happy that Julia is awake. I hope she will continue to do well, and please don't worry about your uncle Ralph. He will not give you and Julia any more trouble."

"Thank you, Aunt Ophelia," David said with a smile.

She continued, "David, I want you to know that your uncle Ralph means well. It's just that sometimes he gets carried away with his own importance."

"Yes, I'm finding that out. Goodbye, Aunt Ophelia," David said.

Suddenly, he wondered if he was being a little premature in spreading the news about Julia. He really didn't know if she was okay, but she was awake, and she knew him. She even remembered his clumsy attempts at the two-step.

He hurried back to the door of Julia's room. Soon, Mrs. Evans came out. "We can't let her get out of bed because she has a broken leg with a very light cast," she cautioned. "She can't stand on it, and I'm sure she's too weak to stand anyway. You can go back in, Mr. Cooper."

When he went back into Julia's room, he saw that they had raised her head a little. "Look, no more tubes and wires," she said. "I'm on the road toward becoming a regular person again. But," she whispered to David, "I still have my diaper until I prove that I can control things." David looked a little embarrassed. "Would you hold me?" she said.

He sat on the side of the bed and took her in his arms. "Oh, my darling," he said. "I never thought this day would come. I have missed you so much."

"I have missed you too," she said weakly, but she managed to give him that sexy smile. "And if I ever get rid of this diaper, I will show you." David was so happy. At least she could remember things that were important to them.

Mrs. Evans came in with a huge glass of something that looked like a milkshake. "I thought you would be hungry, so the dietitian whipped up this drink for you. It's ice cream, bananas, and protein powder. Take a small sip," she said. "We need to check your swallowing reflex." Julia swallowed it down perfectly. "I'm not sure you can hold it. It may be a while before your hands will work."

Julia tried to reach for the glass. "My arms feel as if there are no bones in them," she said anxiously.

"Don't worry," Mrs. Evans said. "It may take a day or two."

"Thank you," Julia said. "I was starving, but what I really want is a hot dog with all the trimmings."

"Maybe in a few days," Mrs. Evans said. "Right now we want to you to work up to solid food gradually." She gave Julia another sip. "The orthopedic people will be coming in a little while. They'll put another cast on your broken leg so you can get out of bed as soon as you're strong enough to walk." Soon Julia had finished the entire milkshake.

"That was so good," Julia said. "Do you think I can go home soon?"

"When you're strong enough to walk," Mrs. Evans said. "The physiotherapy people will be coming in soon. They'll give you exercises to strengthen your muscles."

Just then, another nurse came in. "Mr. Cooper, Mr. Richards, the hospital administrator is here with a reporter from the newspaper. They want to take your picture."

"I don't think we're up for a picture, but I'll give you a statement." David went out into the hall and talked to the reporter. He gave him a small wallet-size photo of Julia.

When he came back into the room, he saw that the bed had been lowered. "David," she said weakly. "All this waking up has really tired me out. If nobody minds, I think I'll take a little nap. Don't worry. I promise to wake up again. Will you please bring me some pajamas, my robe, and slippers? And please bring my makeup. I must look a fright."

"No, my darling," David said and then kissed her. "You have never looked more beautiful."

Then he whispered to Mrs. Evans, "Is she really okay? Is this waking and sleeping normal?"

"Oh yes," she said. "She may do this for several days. Right now, all her vital signs are excellent. Mr. Cooper, you look as if you could do with some rest also. Why don't you go home and take a nap. She may sleep for several hours."

David went back to the apartment. He called the interior designer. He told her he wanted to wait a few days to meet with her since his fiancée was awake.

He fixed a sandwich, sat on the couch, and turned on the television. Duke was playing Virginia in a semifinal game of the NCAA tournament. Duke was playing magnificently and won by twenty-five points. David was elated. His team had lost by only eight. He felt more relaxed than he had in weeks, so he stretched out on the big sofa and fell asleep.

When he awoke, he went to find the things Julia had asked for. He found her pajamas, slippers, makeup, and her cell phone. He put it all in a small overnight bag. When he found her robe, it looked like something she had worn in high school. It was faded and threadbare. He checked the size. When he left to go to the hospital, he stopped by The Boutique and bought her a beautiful, dark blue, silk robe with pajamas to match.

When he got to Julia's room, he found Mrs. Walker holding another milkshake. "At least I can drink through a straw and swallow," Julia said. "I have never been so hungry."

Mrs. Walker gave her another sip. "This is the same formula we have been giving you every day with a feeding tube," she said. "For the next few days, you will be like a baby, just eating and sleeping. But you will get better quickly. Do you want to know a joke?" she said to David. "She called me Caroline. She thought I was your mother. That's the nicest compliment I've had in a while."

"Well, you remind *me* of my mother," he said as he hugged her. He put Julia's bag in the closet and showed her the robe. "Do you think it will fit?"

"I'm sure it will. Thank you so much. My old robe was getting rather ratty."

"Yes," he said. "Ratty, that's the term I was looking for. I have a surprise for you. It's something else I bought for you."

"If you're talking about the new townhouse, I know all about it."

"How did you know?" he said, surprised.

"I heard you talking to Mrs. Walker one night. I wasn't awake, but I heard, and I remembered. I was just waiting for you to tell me."

He said, "I hired an interior designer to help us make decisions about decorating. As soon as you're up to it, we can have her come by."

"How about tomorrow? I can't wait to see it."

"You're full of surprises," he said, "and I'm so happy you are."

Chapter 53

David stopped at the bakery to pick up some bran muffins for the nurses and saw a copy of Sunday's *Hoover Herald*. Julia's picture and her story were on the front page. The headlines read, "Music Teacher Awake after Fifteen Days in Coma."

David read the story.

> Dr. Julia Crane, instructor of violin at Chapman State, awoke yesterday after fifteen days in a coma. According to her fiancé, former pro basketball star D. J. Cooper, Crane was hit by a bus in downtown Hoover on March 5 and has been unconscious ever since. She suffered a severe head injury and a broken leg.
>
> Cooper reports that Crane's doctors feel sure that she will make a full recovery, although she will remain in the hospital for several days until she regains her strength. Cooper attributes the fast action of the Hoover County Police and the diligence of the doctors at University Hospital with saving Dr. Crane's life.

David thought it was a good article. *They put exactly what I said and didn't add their own speculation about what happened.*

When he got to the hospital, Julia was awake. She had on her new pajamas and was wearing makeup, but she was upset. "I don't have any hair," she moaned. "I look awful. I don't want anyone to see me until my hair grows out."

"I see you're wearing makeup," he said, "and your new pajamas look great."

"Yes," she said. "Mrs. Evans did it for me. My hands still don't want to work."

He went on, slyly. "I asked the interior designer to come this afternoon to talk to us about what we want in the townhouse, but if you're too upset to see anyone, we can always cancel the appointment. I told her to bring pictures of some similar units that she has done and a floor plan of ours."

By now, she was smiling. "I'm feeling better. Don't cancel the appointment."

"I thought you would be," he said smugly.

In a few minutes, Dr. Freeman came in. He came over to Julia and patted her on the shoulder. "Miss Crane, I'm Dr. Freeman. I've been taking care of you."

"Thank you, Doctor," she said.

The doctor pulled out a pen light and shined it into Julia's eyes. "Everything is looking good," he said. "Can you raise your arms?" She raised one arm slightly and then the other. "That's great! We're going to let you rest today, but tomorrow the physiotherapy people will be here to put you to work. I would say that you'll be able to go home in four or five days.

"Are you up to answering a few questions? I would like to check your memory just to see how much you've retained."

"Okay," Julia said.

"May we raise you up in the bed a little?" He motioned to Mrs. Evans, who raised Julia's head. "This would be a good time for a break, Mrs. Evans."

"Thank you, Doctor."

"Do I need to leave?" David asked.

"No, I may want you to ask her some questions too." Then he turned to Julia. "Are you comfortable and relaxed? I want you to answer to the best of your ability. If you don't remember, just say,

'I don't remember.' When you get tired, just say so. We can always stop. What is your full name?"

"Dr. Julia Ellen Crane."

"When is your birthday?"

"April 25, 1992."

"Looks like you will have a birthday soon. How old will you be?"

"Twenty-eight," she said. "When can I go home? David just bought me a new house, and I can't wait to see it."

"Oh, and where is that?"

"It's one of the new townhouses out on the bluffs. I haven't seen it yet, but I hear it's very nice."

"May I assume that you and Mr. Cooper are getting married very soon?" He looked at David. He nodded his agreement.

"Yes, just as soon as he asks me."

"He hasn't asked you yet?" he queried.

"No, he's waiting to see if I can stand living with a basketball coach. You see, I haven't known him very long, but I love David very much. I can't wait to be his wife."

"When was the very first time you ever saw David?"

Julia told him about the dedication gala and how she had parked in David's parking space. She told him everything about their life together right up to the Valentine's dance.

"You don't seem to have lost any long-term memory," the doctor said. "Now, what did you do after the Valentine's dance?"

She thought and thought, but nothing seemed to come to mind. "I don't know," she said slowly. "I do remember going to Nashville."

"And when was that?"

"I'm not sure," she said. The doctor looked at David.

"It was February 28," David said.

The doctor said, "May I assume that the Valentine's dance was on February 14, and the next thing you remember is February 28?" Julia looked confused. The doctor looked at David encouragingly.

David said, "Don't you remember having the flu? You were very sick."

"I had the flu?" she asked. "I don't remember it."

David said, "I went to St. Louis on February 17 to a conference meeting. When I came home on Wednesday, February 19, I went to your apartment. You were deathly sick with the flu. I nursed you for a day and a half. You missed two days of school."

"I don't remember that, but I remember going to Nashville."

"What did you do in Nashville?"

"We went to the basketball games, and we went shopping. And we went to a bar in Nashville, and we danced. That's when I decided that I would marry David." She frowned. "But I was really worried."

Dr. Richards said, "What were you worried about?"

"I'm not sure."

David interjected, "I thought she was a little down the entire weekend, as if something was weighing on her mind."

"Do you remember what happened after you returned home from Nashville?"

She thought and thought. "No, I don't remember," she said.

"Think, Julia," he said. "Why can't you remember?"

"I was frightened."

"You were frightened? What frightened you?"

"Something green," she said.

"Something green?"

She nodded.

"Was it in a park with green grass?"

She shook her head.

"Or maybe in a forest with green trees."

"No," she said. "It was a green man."

"A green man?"

"Yes," she said, "a green man with big yellow eyes!"

The doctor looked at David. He nodded.

"Where did you see this green man?"

"He was everywhere," she said. "He was everywhere. I don't want to talk about it anymore. I want to take a nap."

"That's enough for today," the doctor said as he lowered her head.

Julia said to David, "If I'm asleep when the interior designer comes, be sure to wake me."

The doctor motioned for David to come out in the hall. David related to the doctor what the police had told him about the man following Julia. "It looks like he may have been the reason she ran into the street. Buying the townhouse was a stroke of genius. You have certainly given her a reason to wake up."

"I had been thinking of getting myself a new place," David said. "You see, I have been living in the athletic dorm. When I saw the new townhouses being built, I decided to get a place where we could live after we're married."

Just then, Mrs. Evans returned. The doctor said, "Be sure and impress on her that she must not try to get up. Her limbs are so weak that she could easily fall and break another bone. But she's young and strong. She should bounce back quickly."

"Yes, Doctor," Mrs. Evans said.

"It appears that she's lost about two weeks out of her memory," the doctor said to David. "Do you know of anything else that she would want to block out of her memory?"

"Not really," David said.

"Perhaps it was a nightmare she had while she was so ill," the doctor said, "or perhaps something else happened to cause her distress. We may never know what happened during those two weeks or why she ran out in front of the bus. If she does remember, she may think it's a dream."

"Do you think she'll have any ill effects from this experience?"

"She may have some headaches or be moody at times, but that

should pass as she gets stronger. I think she'll make a full recovery, but I would like to talk to her some more later."

"Thank, you, Doctor," David said.

David decided to return to the apartment for a while. Julia needed to rest. On his way out, he ran into Chris. "I hear our girl is awake," he said. "I guess the Italian opera did the trick."

"You don't think it was too much?"

Chris said, "It reminded her that she had very strong feelings about you and your love for her. I think it stirred up her emotions and reminded her that she should wake up if she wants to be with you."

"I hope so, Chris. I sincerely hope so. Thank you for all your help."

Chapter 54

Carrera marble tile, granite countertops in the kitchen, a stacked stone fireplace in the family room. He knew Mrs. Perkins, the interior designer, had probably suggested a lot of these expensive things, but he didn't mind. He was so thrilled that Julia was awake. He would gladly spend whatever was necessary. She was turning those bare walls and plain floors into a home—their home.

David woke up in Julia's bed. He stretched and turned on his back as he remembered the events of yesterday. Julia woke up from her nap in time to meet with Mrs. Perkins. David had told her that whatever Julia wanted was okay with him. At least David didn't have to worry about the details of the townhouse. Mrs. Perkins would be his agent with the builder, and she would be working with Julia. It looked as if all he had to do now was pay the bill for the whole thing. A fair trade, indeed, he decided.

He looked at the bedside clock. It was half past seven. He had to get out of bed and get his day started. The cleaning service would be there at nine. He had to get all his stuff gathered up and moved back to the athletic dorm. Just as he stepped out of the shower, his telephone rang. It was Cynthia.

"David, I returned home very late last night. What happened to Julia?" she said frantically.

He told her all about Julia's accident. "But the best part is she is awake and doing well, but she'll have to stay in the hospital until she gets her strength back."

"Do I need to come immediately?"

"Not immediately, but she'll need you when she gets out of the hospital."

"When will that be?"

"Probably Thursday or Friday. Julia has her cell phone at the hospital. You can reach her there."

"Oh good. I'll give her a call," she said. "I'll try to come on Wednesday. I have some business here that I need to take care of. Yes, I think I can come on Wednesday. Can you meet me at the airport?"

"Sure, Cynthia, I will be glad to, and thanks for calling. Julia will need you."

"Goodbye, David."

David finished his morning chores and headed for the hospital. Julia was awake and looking perkier than ever. "Look," she said as she touched her thumb to each finger on each hand. "The therapy man taught me to do this, this morning. Soon, I'll be playing the violin. I tried to stand up, but my legs are still rather wobbly, but they're better. I couldn't do it today, but maybe tomorrow."

"Looks like you're doing well," he said as he sat on the bed beside her and kissed her.

"I'm working hard. I can't wait to go see my new house."

"So that's it," he said. "You only want to get well so you can see the new townhouse."

"Oh no, darling. I want to get well so we can go on with our life together." She added, "Mother called. She's coming Wednesday."

"I know," he said as he hugged her. "I have to get to the office, but I'll see you tonight."

The next two days went by uneventfully. Mrs. Perkins came by the hospital periodically with various samples of paint, wallpapers, and pictures of light fixtures. Julia would call David and ask his opinion, but generally, he told her to choose what she wanted. He knew she was having so much fun making decisions.

When he went by the hospital of Tuesday, Julia got out of bed and showed him how well she could walk with her crutches. "I'm ready to go home," she insisted.

Thursday, David awoke in the athletic dorm. It was hard to believe that Julia's accident had been exactly four weeks ago. Thank God, she had recovered. She was doing so well that he was taking her home from the hospital today. Cynthia came yesterday and had settled in at Julia's apartment. She was full of stories of her travels, and Julia was thrilled to see her.

He headed to the cafeteria for breakfast. He really missed not being in the apartment, but that was okay. He would be in his own home soon. The move-in day was scheduled for May 1.

He called the designer to see if they could stop by the townhouse. She said she would arrange it. He stopped by the apartment and picked up Cynthia. Then he swung by the rental place and got a wheelchair.

As they left the hospital, everyone wished them well. Julia said goodbye to all the nurses and thanked them for their care. As they left the hospital, Julia said, "David, is there a chance we could stop by the townhouse?

"Probably not," he said. "There will probably be too many workmen there."

"But couldn't we just stop and see?" she begged.

"Okay, we'll stop," he said as he winked at Cynthia.

When they pulled into the drive, they saw that the bricklayers were there. "Do you like the brick? We chose it because it's similar to the brick on your parents' house. The trim will be cream and a dark blue," Julia said.

"I like it very much," he said. "What do you think, Cynthia?"

He could tell that Cynthia was at a loss for words. "It's lovely," she said.

When he got out of the truck, he said to Julia, "Do you want the wheelchair or are you able to walk?"

"I am walking," she said firmly. "I have worked too hard not to.

"If you get tired, let me know, and I'll get the wheelchair."

As they walked through the house, Julia was amazed at how good the items she had chosen looked. The tile layers were in the master bathroom. They were laying the Carrara marble tile in a diagonal pattern. "Do you like that, David?" she asked. "And we decided to put a full bathroom upstairs."

"It's great, babe," he said. "Everything is great. You have good taste."

"Well, Mrs. Perkins made some suggestions. What do you think about the fireplace? We decided to put the fireplace in the family room. I wanted the room to be casual, so we chose a stacked stone." As they went through the house, Julia could see that David was really pleased with everything he saw, and that made her happy.

When they returned to her apartment, David helped Julia in. He kissed her goodbye. "I'm leaving early tomorrow to go to a conference meeting in Louisville," he said. "I won't be back until late on Saturday, but I'll call you when I get home."

After David left, Julia asked, "What do you think about the house, Mom?"

"It's very nice," Cynthia said. "Julia, I take it that you're going to marry David?"

"Yes, Mother. I love him very much. I know I'll be happy with him."

"Then it's okay with me," she said. "He's such a nice man. I like him very much." She paused. "Julia, tell me something. Does David have money or is his family wealthy?"

"No, Mother, he's the wealthy one. He was a professional basketball player, and he was paid very well."

"Oh, I know about professional athletes," Cynthia said. "Grandpa Harris's cousin was a baseball player. I think he got a hundred dollars per game for playing."

"Mother," Julia said calmly, "David made much more than that."

"Just how much more?" Cynthia asked.

"I have no idea," Julia said. "I do know that when he was twenty-two years old, he signed a rookie contract for forty-one million dollars for four years. He played for four more years after that. I don't know how much he made then. I fell in love with him before I knew he had money, so I try not to think about it. I love him for who he is, not what he has."

"Well, I knew someone must have money," she said. "That house is so beautiful and very expensive."

"But please don't tell him you know. He wants you to think he's a struggling basketball coach."

"Well, it's certainly a load off my mind. I won't worry about your future anymore," Cynthia said with a sigh.

Chapter 55

Sunday, Julia awoke very upset. She was even crying. In her nightmare, David had broken up with her. He'd come to her apartment and told her he wanted the Amati. He'd said he didn't love her anymore. Surely, that was not true. He had bought the townhouse for her, hadn't he? But a nagging voice said, "He has not asked you to marry him!"

She had been home from the hospital for two days now and was getting stronger all the time. She was beginning to eat solid food regularly and moving well with her crutches. She should be getting her cast off in a few more weeks.

She hadn't heard from David the day before, and she was worried. She felt in her heart that he might be getting ready to break up with her. She wasn't sure why she felt that way. Perhaps it was just her emotions running wild. The doctor had warned her it might happen.

It was great having her mother there. After breakfast, Cynthia said, "If you can manage a few hours alone, I think I'll go to church, and after that, I'll go by the grocery store."

"Sure, Mom, I'll be okay. You go ahead." Not long after Cynthia left, Julia's phone rang.

"Hi, babe," David said. "Sorry about yesterday. Did you get my text? My meeting ran over. I didn't get back until late. How are you today?"

Oh no, she thought. Her cell phone was in her purse, and she hadn't thought to check her text messages. "I'm feeling better every day," she said brightly.

"Would it be okay if I came over?"

"Sure," she said. "Mother's gone to church."

"Good," he said. "What I have to say is better said in private."

Her heart sank. Now there was no doubt. He was coming to break up with her. She had been so much trouble to him. No wonder he didn't want her anymore. If only she could remember why she ran in front of that bus. She went to get the Amati. She was sure he would want it back.

She dressed in a nice casual outfit and put on some makeup. She wanted him to see her looking her best. She ran a comb through her hair. She shrugged. There was not much she could do with it. Maybe she should get a wig to wear until her own grew back. Soon, she heard the doorbell. She hobbled to the door. When he came in, he wrapped his long arms around her and pulled her to him. "I've missed you so much," he said huskily and then kissed her gently.

"I suppose you've come for the Amati," she said sadly.

"Actually, I've come to make a trade," he said as he led her to the couch and sat beside her. He pulled a small box from his pocket. "I have two violins. I want to trade for the Amati."

"What if I don't want to trade?" she said. "I really like that fiddle."

"Wouldn't you like to see these violins before you decide?" he said as he opened the box. She stared at the box. Inside was the most beautiful ring she had ever seen. A sapphire sat in the center of a white-gold setting with two small diamonds on each side. A small violin worked in yellow gold was on either side of the diamonds. "It's a Baroque betrothal ring," he said. "I saw some in a museum in Paris when the Pacers were doing a European exhibition tour. I knew right then that I wanted one for my wife."

She sat quietly for a moment, taking in the significance of the ring. He continued, "I can see I need to sweeten the pot. If you take the ring, you also get the townhouse on the hill, and … you get me."

"Let me get this straight," she said. "If I choose the ring, I get the townhouse on the hill, and I get you."

"That's right."

"But, David," she said coyly, "it's so hard for me to make up my mind. You see, I want it all."

"You want it all?" he questioned as his heart soared, but he kept a straight face. "You drive a hard bargain, lady." He looked at her face and saw that sexy grin that promised everything he needed to make his dreams come true.

"Do you think you're ready to marry a basketball coach?"

"In a heartbeat," she said firmly. "I want the ring, the Amati, the townhouse on the hill, and most of all, I want you."

"Then you shall have it all, my love!" he said as he hugged her and kissed her soundly.

He jumped up from the couch, got down on one knee, and slipped the ring on her finger. "Julia Ellen Crane," he said, "will you do me the honor of becoming my wife? I will love you for the rest of my life with all my heart, forever and ever."

"I will," she said. "David Jennings Cooper, I will love *you* for the rest of my life with all my heart, forever and ever." She stood up, and he held her close.

"I never thought this day would come," he said and then kissed her savagely and ran his hand up and down her back.

He reached into his pocket and pulled out another box. In it were two white-gold rings with a semicircle of small diamonds on each ring. He removed her ring. "See how they fit around the betrothal ring. It's not everyone who gets two wedding rings." He slipped them onto her finger. "Some people say it's bad luck to try on your wedding ring before the ceremony, but I want to know if they fit." He added, "I think the wedding rings are a little big. We'll have to get them sized."

"Marrying you could never be bad luck," she said.

Just then, Cynthia came through the door with bags of groceries. "Well, it looks like you two are at it again," she said as she set the bags on the counter.

"David just proposed," Julia said. "Look what I have, Mother." She held up her hand.

"My goodness, David. I think Julia would have been happy with something a little less ostentatious. You'll be making payments on that ring for the rest of your life."

"I certainly hope so, Cynthia. I certainly hope so." He paused. "Would you two lovely ladies do me the honor of going to lunch with me? Can you make it okay?" he asked Julia.

"Sure," she said, "if someone will cut my meat for me."

Chapter 56

David felt as if his life was finally back on track, but things were moving at a frantic pace. It had been two weeks since he had proposed to Julia. The wedding plans were made, and the invitations were in the mail. Carol and Lakeysha and a couple of girls from the basketball team had come over and addressed wedding invitations for Julia.

The townhouse was almost finished. Julia and Mrs. Perkins were furniture shopping. School would be over in about three weeks. David was taking Julia to get her cast removed at two today. That would be the last reminder of her accident. He was sitting at his desk, doing an equipment order, when his phone rang.

"Hello, Coach Cooper, this is Marjorie Sanchez, Mr. Gardner's administrative assistant."

"Yes, Mrs. Sanchez," he said.

"Coach Cooper, Mr. Gardner would like to meet with you at your earliest convenience. He could see you at 11:00 a.m. or at 1:00 p.m. today or tomorrow at …" She paused.

"I can see him at eleven o'clock today," he broke in.

"Very good," she said. "We will see you at eleven o'clock today."

At five minutes to eleven, David went down to the first floor of the Marshall Building to Phil's office. "Come in, David," Phil said as he rose from his desk and shook David's hand. "Thanks for coming so promptly. I hear Julia is doing well."

"Yes, she's getting her cast off today."

"That's great," he said. "David, when you came on board with us, we gave you a one-year contract, at your request. Since the school year is nearly over, it's time to review your contract." He handed David several sheets of paper. "I've spoken to Rusty, and here is our evaluation of your work this year. Look it over and let me know if there's anything with which you don't agree."

David took the paper and looked over it. "This is very flattering, but I just tried to do my job as described to me by Rusty, to the best of my ability."

"I know," Phil said. "We're pleased with your work in recruiting and with the improved play of our big men. And your coaching in the game that Rusty was tossed during was terrific.

"But before we talk about your contract for next year, there's something I need to tell you. Because you're still under contract with us, another school cannot talk to you about a job without our permission. You should know that several Division I schools have asked if they can speak to you about a head coaching job."

"Yes, I heard rumors."

"Shall we give them permission?"

"Yes, I might speak to some of them, but I'll tell you up front I'm not looking for a head coaching job. I'm happy here. I just bought a new house in Hoover, and Julia is still recovering."

"I'm glad to hear it."

"I know Julia loves her job. Maybe in a few years we might want to move but not now."

"Good. That's settled. We'll be offering you a new contract soon. Now, what about our new recruits?"

"They've all confirmed that they'll be on campus in the next few weeks to plan their academic programs, and they're all aware that we expect them for three weeks in the summer for a preseason camp."

"Good. What do you know about Cruiser Bell? Is he declaring for the draft?"

"I believe he has," David said. "I know he signed up for the predraft workout. He looked really good in the tournament. I think he has a good chance of getting drafted. And he's sure to sign if anyone will take him." David added, "I don't think it will be a big loss if we lose him. We have some really good freshmen coming in."

"You're right about that," Phil said thoughtfully. "You know, Cruiser isn't a bad kid. He's just a lazy, spoiled brat. Brandon and Mary have given him everything he ever wanted, but he's not bad. Not like that brother of his."

"Yes, I've seen Cruiser's brother, Marvin, but I haven't met him."

"I thought he was still in the navy, but I could swear I saw him on campus several weeks ago. It was a very cloudy day, but he was walking down the street by the Music Department with a green Chapman hoodie pulled over his head and big yellow-rimmed sunglasses on."

David sat up, alert. "What was that you just said?"

"I said I saw Marvin Bell outside the Music Department, wearing a green Chapman hoodie and big yellow-rimmed sunglasses. You might let Cruiser know that he needs to inform us as soon as he hears anything. We can't hold his scholarship forever."

"Sure, I'll check with him today." So Cruiser Bell's brother was running around on campus. That might answer some questions.

"I guess that's about it," Phil said.

David stood up and headed for the door.

"David ..." He paused. "There's something else I've been meaning to tell you. I'm not sure, but I think it's something you need to know. The last night we were in Indianapolis, Brandon Bell and his wife went out to dinner with us. Brandon had had too much to drink, so I didn't think much about what he said."

"What did he say?"

"Well, he was thrilled with the way Cruiser played. Then he made this statement, and I quote, 'It's a good thing Cruiser did his music assignments, because Ralph told me he was going to fire Dr. Crane if she didn't give Cruiser a passing grade.'"

"Uncle Ralph said he was going to fire Julia if she didn't give Cruiser a passing grade?" David repeated, as if trying to wrap his mind around what he had heard.

"Yeah, that's what Brandon said. Of course, Ralph may have just said it to get Brandon off his back. I know he had been in to see Ralph about Julia. Do you know for a fact that Cruiser did his work?"

David said, "Julia texted me that morning after class when Cruiser turned his work in. I'm assuming she saw him turn the assignments in. I know she wouldn't have backed down and given him a passing grade if he hadn't done his work, so he must have done it."

"Okay, I just don't want something coming up later that will cause us to have to forfeit some games for playing an academically ineligible player."

"By the way, Phil," David said, "I would like to take vacation the last two weeks of May. I should be finished with all my advisee scheduling by then."

"Are we going anywhere special?"

"If the Clippers hang in there and make the playoffs, we would like to see some of the NBA finals games and maybe go to a concert by the Los Angeles Philharmonic."

"I assume you're taking the lovely Dr. Crane with you."

"Not this time, Phil, but I will be taking the lovely Mrs. Cooper with me."

Phil jumped up, ran around his desk, and pounded David on the back. "You sly old dog! So it's a honeymoon trip!"

"You should be getting your invitation to the wedding very soon."

"I'm so glad things worked out for you and Julia. She's a wonderful person and an asset to our university."

"I wish someone would tell my uncle Ralph," David said.

"I already have," Phil said. "Who cares if you're black and she's white. You love each other. End of discussion!"

"Thanks, Phil," David said. "I appreciate it."

"You know, David, your uncle Ralph is still living about thirty years in the past. Back then, things were probably as he said for a mixed-race couple. I'm sure he just wants the best for you."

"I guess you're right."

"Say," Phil said, "why don't you take an extra week? We'll say it's a bonus for those long recruiting trips you did. You'll be busy with summer camps when you return."

"Thank you, Phil."

David went back up to his office and sat at his desk. He felt he had almost solved the puzzle. He knew, beyond a shadow of a doubt, that Lakeysha and Carol had done Cruiser's assignments. The why was to save Julia's job. But how did they know?

Then he knew. Kenny. David knew that Cruiser was always bragging about something. Suppose he told someone on the team about Dr. Jennings, and Kenny heard about it. He would have told Lakeysha and Carol. They knew Julia would rather be fired than back down. He was guessing, but somehow, they left the assignments so that Cruiser could find them, and if Cruiser found three assignments with his name on them, he would surely have turned them in. He remembered the neatly typed assignments he had seen in Julia's briefcase.

Marvin had managed to scare Julia, and somehow she had been so upset over what Uncle Ralph had said that she blocked it all out of her memory. He wasn't sure what had caused her to run in front of the bus.

He wasn't sure of any of this, so he decided he should say nothing. There was too much at stake, and he couldn't prove anything anyway. Carol and Lakeysha could be in trouble if he let his suspicions be known, and the team would have to forfeit the last three games they had won.

David thought about his life. Julia had fully recovered, and he would soon be marrying her. She would make his life complete, and he would love her forever.

He had a fulfilling career. It was a job where he felt he could make a real contribution to the lives of young men. What more could he want from life? He was content with the decisions he had made. He refused to let his annoyance with Uncle Ralph spoil the happiness and contentment he was enjoying.

Chapter 57

David sat at his desk in his office in the Marshall Building. This was the last week of school. He was basically finished with his work for the year. He had completed all the reports, inventories, travel claims, and paperwork that he had to submit before the school year was over. His advisees were all set with schedules for the new school year. He had met with all the incoming freshmen and hopefully had solved all their problems. He had met with Rusty to plan their summer activities. He felt confident that nothing had been forgotten.

On the personal front, he would be moving into the townhouse this weekend. David had paid Carol and Lakeysha a small fee to help Julia. They had packed everything she could spare for the next two weeks—boxes of books, clothes, and dishes, which, other than her couch, computer, and television, were about all she owned. David had enlisted some of the guys on the basketball team to move boxes for him.

Julia seemed to be about back to normal. With the cast gone, she was moving around like her old self. She still wasn't up to speed as a violinist, but it would come with practice. Best of all, she would be able to walk down the aisle on Dr. Salerno's arm without the aid of a crutch.

The wedding would be a week from Saturday at 10:00 a.m. at St. Peter's Church. Everything was planned. Julia had said she wasn't getting married until her hair grew back; however, when she realized that hair only grew about a half inch per month, she changed her mind. Of course, she and Molly had gone shopping for her wedding dress. They also found a beautiful veil that disguised the fact that she didn't have much hair. They wouldn't let him see the dress, but he knew it would be beautiful.

David's mom and dad were coming next week and would stay at the townhouse until after the wedding. Cynthia would stay at Julia's apartment until Thursday. They would clear out the fridge and take everything to the townhouse. Then they would close the apartment and move to a hotel for two days.

The entire restaurant at Leonardo's had been reserved for 150 guests for a wedding lunch and reception. Their plane would leave at 4:00 p.m. to take them to California for a three-week vacation. David smiled at the thought. He and Julia both deserved a long, restful honeymoon.

David finished his work and went down the elevator to the first floor. As he was exiting the elevator, he saw Carol and Lakeysha coming from a study room. "Good afternoon, ladies," he said. "Do you have time to speak to me?"

"Sure."

"Let's go into a study room." They went in, and David shut the door. "I want to thank you for all the help you've been giving Julia," he said.

"We were glad to do it," Lakeysha said.

"Is there something else?" Carol asked.

"Not really," he said. "I have this suspicion about something I think you two did. I don't know for sure, but I suspect." They looked at him questioningly.

David said, "It's just a suspicion, and if I'm correct, please don't tell me because then I would have to act on it. I want to thank you for sticking your necks out like you did for Dr. Crane. And if I'm wrong and you didn't do what I think you did, just forget it. I have no proof at all, and your secret is safe with me."

Lakeysha looked at Carol.

"Since I have no proof, then I can't tell anyone, can I?" David said. "But I really appreciate what you did for Dr. Crane. I know she would appreciate it too, if she knew, but she will never know, because I will never tell her."

Carol looked at Lakeysha. They looked at David. "We have absolutely no idea what you're talking about, Coach Cooper," Carol said.

"Good," he said. "I hope you have a great summer."

"We hope to," Lakeysha said. "We're both going to summer school, and I'll be working a few hours a week at the Women's Clinic. I've decided to go into gynecology when I go to med school."

"We'll see you at the wedding," Carol said.

"There's one more thing," David said. "Did you hear that Cruiser Bell got drafted by a professional basketball team? It looks he won't be coming back to Chapman next year."

"Oh really? Cruiser Bell won't be here next year," Carol said as a crooked smile crossed her lips. "That's just too, too bad."